For Len,

(handwritten inscription)

FRACTURED COMPASS

ALLAN STEVEN

April 2nd 2022

Cover art by Martin Gorst

"Who goes to the Hills goes to his Mother."

Ancient Hindu saying

Dedicated to M, B, P, S & G

Prologue

'Snooty Ooty'. Like a girl's dress on a windy day; now you see it, now you don't. The Nilgiri Mountain Railway's serpent tracks teasing you with new and repeated vistas. I had boarded the blue steam train in Mettupalayam. The noise of the rack and pinion keeping time with the dislocated beat of my heart. At Coonoor we switched to diesel. Disappointed tourists. Ootacamund, Queen of the Hill stations. Cool summer residence for the British Raj, long lost. Loss, losing, lost...never had. Station sign, *'Udhagamandalam'*. Independent name. Independence. Gained, regained, established...mine.

Step down from the train. Courteous porters. Can carry my own rucksack, but provide work. He leads. We slither through the clamour of compressed humanity. Our serpentine path a human caravan replicating the train journey. Corrugated heart beating to the rise and fall of my footsteps. Eyes, admiring eyes clasped to my long and burnished legs. Want to laugh, and cry out. In England you would be arraigned before the 'Distaff Police' for ogling so brazenly.

"Here ve are miss. My Uncle Billy's auto-rickshaw. Best driver in Ooty."

"You still call it Ooty?"

Billy, "Oh yes, miss. We are the coming nation. No need for chip on shoulder."

Billy's brother loads my rucksack. Receives payment with dignified thanks. Sit in rickshaw. Scan the sights. The air, audible in its thanks and delight for the privilege of circulating beneath a serene blue heaven.

"Miss, miss. Oh my goodness, you were away with the fairies. Where to, miss?"

My laughter. So loud that it draws looks.

"Away with the fairies! Where on earth did you learn that? It's so English."

He sees my pleasure, and knows that there's no offence in the question. His smile is everlasting.

"I am pretty much old codger myself now. Something my *Dada* used to say when I was knee high to a grasshopper. We are Anglo-Indian. His *Baap* served with the Welsh Guards."

English expressions of yore come thick and fast. Pride riveted to them.

"Forgive me. *'Dada'* – father. What is *'Baap'*?"

"You are forgiven, young lady." Twinkling eyes lit by a laughing soul. "Ever so bloody confusing my language. Pardon my French. No, *Baap* is father, *Dada* is grandfather."

A cooling heart feels a tremor, and molten lava bubbles.

"Do you know a place called *'Uttar Aanand Kare Kee Pahaadiyon'*? Sorry for my terrible Hindi."

Billy throws his head back.

"Good try, miss, damn good try. Always give it a go I say. That's something else *Dada* taught me*.*"

The wisdom of grandfathers. A cliché?

"So you know it?"

"I should flipping well say so. Everyone knows *'Achchhe Pita'*."

Puzzled face. Cue more gurgling laughter from Billy.

"The *'Good Father'*. Everyone in Ooty calls him that. Bit of a long ride, miss…"

"My name is Anna, Billy. Call me Anna."

"Mrs. Anna," he roars. "I have seen *'The King and I'*. Bloody good film. Pardon my French."

Stern face. Mock serious. "Billy, you are forgiven."

Companionable laughter, and we hit the road.

*

"The long and winding road, that leads to your door..."

"It most certainly is, Mrs. Anna."

"What is?"

"You were humming a Beatles song. Damn good choice for this road."

We negotiate a hairpin bend at interesting speed.

"That bloody Maharishi, what a con artist." More chuckling.

Astonishment out of ignorance; wonder born of newness. Like cruising through English country lanes. Views to die for. Ascension from the town. Look back to the expansive lake. Sporting dots at play on the brilliantined water. Facing forwards. Ever climbing into woodlands obscuring the horizon. Then broken open. Pine tree branches, jagged and irregular, framing the mountains and valleys.

"You know *'The Good Father'*, Mrs. Anna?"

A non-committal grunt. "Why is he called that?"

"Because he is a bloody fine, top-notch, number one fellow."

I think about pressing the question. Instinct tells me I already know the answer. Somewhere. In a recess. Which one? Billy begins to caterwaul *'The Long and Winding Road'* to a tune marginally approximate to the original. Careening around another wild bend. Craning the head upwards for a change. The expansive bungalow breath-taking in its beauty on the stepped hillside. Billy chugs his way up the twisting drive.

"Thank you, Billy. I can manage the bag."

Displaying the palm of his hand, into which I have just placed money.

"Thank you, Mrs. Anna. I see the Good Mother has come to visit the Good Father; his equal in generosity."

I stand alone, looking to the distant hills. The reverie is broken. Rotating, trying to find signs of life. Overwhelmed with the beauty of the garden. So many English flowers. Flourishing in the temperate air of the hill station. A large property. At the far perimeter, to my left, I distinguish the figure of a man. His back presented to me, bent over. Tending the most succulent rose bed. A hand over brow. Peer, and glimpse the rich brown of arms and hands, feet in flip flops. The pale blue of his Indian 'pyjama' suit blending with the sky.

"May I be of assistance?"

Whirling. An Indian lady approaches. Thirty-something. Her sari yellow as the sun. Eye-blinking brightness. Her hair tidied away neatly to reveal a face of such beauty that it illuminates everything within ten metres.

She bows, "Good afternoon, miss. Are you lost?"

On the tip of my tongue to reply with a pseudo-philosophical witty remark.

"Good afternoon. I'm sorry to trouble you. Is this the home of Mr. Adam Sampson?"

The lady looks protective. "It is. May I enquire who is seeking after him?"

My trembling voice does not pass unnoticed.

"His granddaughter. I'm his granddaughter. Anna. Anna Wilbey."

The birdsong ceases. A slender arm reaches. Tapering fingers, their tips touching my face lightly. A hand withdrawn. A finger put to the owner's lips. Conspiracy with a smile. The lady walks away. I follow. An arm outstretched, palm displayed, 'wait there.' On to the rose garden. A hand on the gardener's shoulder. He stands upright, and she holds his arm as sweet-nothings are whispered. A butterfly kiss brushes his cheek. She bypasses me with a glorious smile of joy-shooting rays. Gone into the bungalow.

Still his back is a wall. The birds silent in anticipation. Feet shuffle and he faces me. Takes his broad-brimmed hat from his head, and I see cascading silver hair. The hat tumbles from his hands. Adam arms outstretched, and I run as if the finishing line will never come. In each other's arms amidst the blooming roses, whilst the birds sing.

*

"Mishka. Why is he called the 'Good Father'?"

Seated on a terrace. Mishka sticks a plaster on a wounded leg. The air lusty this high in the hills. Fragile building clinging to the hillside. Happy chatter and occasional peals of excited laughter burbling through the open windows.

"Reyansh, would you answer for me, please?"

The boy, no more than eight, presses the edges of the plaster. Shining eyes engage with Anna's.

"The Good Father gives us what no one else will give, Miss."

She cocks a quizzical head. "And what is that, Reyansh?"

"Love."

Anna overwhelmed. Wet eyes drenching the hills. Head averted.

"Leg fixed. Off you go, my little ray of light. Nearly time for lunch."

Reyansh kisses Mishka, and whoops a cheery goodbye to Anna.

"What a boy. I've stuck enough plasters to him to decorate a wall."

Anna, drawing in gulps of air. "He is a ray of light. All of the children are."

"That's what Reyansh means, Anna, *'ray of light'*." Mishka takes Anna's hand. Caresses it with infinite care.

"What did he mean, Mishka? That no one else will give them love?"

"India changes daily, Anna, but those of us who are born Dalit still remain on the outside. At best we are allowed in the doorway to see the world of possibilities." She pauses. "The children are orphans, and Adam is their father. When he settled in Ooty he was so angry. Angry with the world; angry at himself. He heard of our small and struggling work with the children, and volunteered to teach English and sport. It took over his heart and mind. Each day he comes. He tends the children with more care than he gives to his beloved roses, and they are prize-winning roses."

"A missionary, Mishka. Has he become a missionary?"

Mishka laughs. "Oh, he talks about Jesus sometimes. But he talks about lots of things to the children. About Ghandi, Rugby, Martin Luther King, and chocolate ice cream. Most of all he plays cricket with them; boys and girls together. His Father Christmas is a wonder to behold. Everyone knows it's Adam behind the beard, but the game is played with faces as straight as their bats, and joyous anticipation in their hearts. Is he a missionary, Anna? I suppose so, but not like the Victorian gentlemen. He does not oppress. Adam is a ray of light to those shunned and condemned to darkness."

Anna, half-laughing. "He doesn't think he is Jesus?"

Mishka solemn. "He would be mortified that anyone should think so. I have never known a man so inflicted with the knowledge of his own imperfections."

"And you and he..." Anna begins.

"Top hole bloody day!" Billy's cry resounds amongst the hills, as his autorickshaw gasps for breath.

Mishka, eyebrow raised. "Billy, your language is the limit. What on earth are you doing here at this time?"

"The gaffer said I was to collect the three of you. He has given himself a half day hol. This afternoon we shall, together, escort Mrs. Anna on a sight-seeing tour of Ooty. Aha!"

They turn to see Adam emerge. Clamouring children at the windows shouting their goodbyes.

He stops. Assumes the pose of batsman at the crease. Children drum on the walls. The pounding hooves of the fast bowler in his run-up. And then. The fearsome bouncer is elegantly hooked over the deep fine leg boundary.

"A six," they cry, "A sixer!" And applause, as polite as any to be heard on a Kentish field, accompanies Adam to his waiting family.

*

The summer season is not the best time to be in the Nilgiris. Monsoon showers are widespread. Good fortune has walked beside them through the afternoon and evening. Mishka's dinner was delightful. Anna felt that she was teetering on the edge, despite the relaxed and courteous hospitality. She reminisces through selective memory. To regale Mishka with a childhood spent in a bower of bliss. Adam does not correct or contradict her. Speaking sparingly, he addresses Mishka to explain certain anachronistic concepts of a once English upbringing.

Dry thunder ratchets across the hills during the darkest hours of the night. Lightning agitates Anna's febrile mind, producing flashbacks. Her limbs thrash and her back arches, as she tries to escape. Then her cries overwhelm the loudest thunder. Hands on her shoulders. A silken voice singing: *"Chanda re tu so jaa, Chandini tu so jaa…"* a lullaby of hope. She embraces Mishka so tightly that singing becomes difficult. Raising her head, she sees the silhouette of her grandfather. Momentarily he is gone. Only to materialise carrying a bedroll. She feels like a voyeur when Mishka and Adam wrap their arms about each other, and two became one. Mishka blows her a kiss and leaves. Adam lies on the bedroll, outstretched beside her *charpoy*. Anna chokes between tears and laughter when she reaches out in the dark to find his hand waiting for hers.

"That's a funny noise, dumpling."

"Oh Grandad. Nobody has called me that in twenty years. Even then it was only you."

The thunder is a dying sigh in the distance. No more an omen of despair.

"When did that podgy little girl vanish? You'd already become a beauty before I left."

Before he left. No, there would be time for that.

"Do you want to know why *I've* run away?" She asks the question as if affronted. Bold, embarrassed, but ready to speak in the now comforting dark.

"Now is always best time, Mrs. Anna."

A boulder shatters into stars, and she breathes easily.

"Good grief, you sound like Billy. Is everyone in Ooty obsessed with *'The King and I'*?"

He lies still, their fingertips entwined. She visualises herself. Once more that slightly rotund child who she thought she had long outgrown. School sports day, and lined up for the egg and spoon race. Anna always came in to the rear of the field, but she never cared. It was the taking part that mattered. Wasn't it? Good sportsmanship. Being a team player. Fair play.

"I hate it Grandad. I hate it with all of my heart."

"It has become that bad?" Silence prevails. Adam sits upright, and turns on the bedside lamp. "Say it Anna. Don't be afraid to say it."

Kneeling beside her bed. Holding both hands.

"I hate the people. I hate my country. I hate England!"

Lightning flashes and thunder reverberates, unannounced. The rains rake the bungalow with the force of machine guns scything an army, ill-led by its commanders.

Adam rises, and stretches his arms wide.

"I'm sorry Grandad. You should be resting peacefully in your bed at your age."

They stare at each. Then their joint laughter competes honourably with the downpour.

"I'm eighty next Friday. There'll be plenty of time to sleep in the not-too-distant. Now then. Nearly dawn. Let's go and sit comfortably, and you can say what you want to say. How about some tea, Vicar?"

*

"Where is your parish?"

"Buckinghamshire, Gramps, leafy Bucks."

"Loadsa money!" he exclaims, in imitation of an old comedy sketch.

Anna's shoulders sag. "That's half the problem, Gramps. Oh, they're pretty good people. They make and bake and give their time and money, but sit before me on a Sunday morning content to be affirmed in the righteousness of their existence. And the ritual is never so hollow than at Christmas. Decorative Christianity."

Adam inserts some mischief. "How are you getting on with the Oxbridge Mafia – or as they prefer to be known the hierarchy of the Church of England?"

She responds gleefully, "The Bishop is hearty, and gives a passable impression of being 'a man of the people'."

"And hirsute?"

"Positively the incarnation of the 'Old Bull and Bush'."

In their easy laughter they reach out and hold each other, before her tears return.

"Sorry Gramps, sorry."

"Nah!" He examines her with a forensic eye. *"A time to weep and a time to laugh."*

"Ecclesiastes 3. Popular at funerals," she grimaces in mock seriousness. Are you still a Christian, Gramps?"

"Oh yes. It's more tenable here than in England." He pours tea. "My morn time passion, Anna. Tea, tea and more tea."

"Does Mishka keep you well-supplied?" she asks archly.

The old Gramps laughter plays Squash off the walls of the bungalow. It is the familiar roar of uninhibited joy she heard throughout childhood.

"With EVERYTHING, Anna. Are you shocked your Reverence? Don't be. We're not *'living tally'*, as your great-grandmother would have said. Mishka and I are married. Do you know what 'Mishka' means? *'Gift of love'*. But what about you? No wedding ring. I assume you're pursued around the parish by eligible bachelors."

"More a case of dirty old men, when their wives aren't watching."

She becomes thoughtful and subdued.

"I did the wild bit at Uni. Rebelling, I suppose, against the dutiful and honourable child. Sex and drugs in abundance, but I drew the line at Rock n' Roll. Do you still like Haydn?"

"Adore him."

"Me too."

"Digression isn't always helpful."

Anna smiles at the man she adores most in the world.

"I would love to be married. Like Granny's parents. Forever and forever. She's well, Gramps."

"That's good, darling, but I'm truly over all that. Mishka is not a replacement – I hope this won't sound hurtful – she is something finer. What about eager young clergymen?"

Anna rolls her eyes heavenward. "Forgive my uncharitable words. They're all so bloody wet and insipid. They have the courage of everyone else's opinion – well, the Bishop's at least."

Adam speaks from the depths of his own disappointment.

"They used to be strong men. Their words were the Word of God; not a calculated response to the fashion of the day. You know who used to get on my wick? Another expression of your great-gran's. That former pop star-cum-vicar, all over the radio and T.V. What did the great and good think he was going to achieve? 'Oh look, a nice vicar on T.V, and he used to be in a pop band. I think I'll turn to Jesus!' Arrant nonsense."

Anna giggles, "That's my old Gramps. Feisty as ever."

"Hmmm? Only on high days and Holy days." He leans forward. "Anna, you haven't come half way around the world because you're pissed off with work, and haven't got a boyfriend at the moment. They're easy to get. You said you hated England."

She knows that he has channelled her.

"It's become such a mean-spirited country. Divided and selfish; barely an ounce of community left. Oh, they'll spare some change for Children in Need and slap each other on the back. When it comes to everyday courtesy and civility it's more a case of '...the second Commandment is this, fuck your neighbour!' Sorry Gramps."

"Always thought it a wonderfully illustrative word, in the right context."

"There's no sense of duty any more. Honour is mocked." A painful rage disfigures Anna's face. "Why did you and Granny, and Mum and Dad burden me with such a virtuous load? I was raped, Gramps, raped in my own home by two young men dripping in the unctuous slime of duty and honour!"

Adam closes his eyes for an instant. Then looks at his darling child. She isn't crying. Just slumped. Defeated. He waits.

Quietly. "There was a grand village party to celebrate another great English victory of yesteryear. God, do they ever stop? The father is 'The Lord of the Manor'. Well, in his opinion. His daddy was a knight of the realm once upon a time. Pukka school, and pukka accent – that's an Indian word isn't it, 'pukka'?"

Adam nods.

"His son turned up at the last moment, with his friend. Pater had a houseful, and asked me if I could put them up for the night. No room at the Inn," she says ruefully. "Middle of the night, drunk as skunks, they took me. You know what the joke is Gramps? These two seventeen-year-olds go to the very best of public schools. The sepulchres of all that is dutiful and honourable." Anna raises her head, daggers of disgust glinting in her eyes. "No, I didn't go to the police. I went to see 'His Lordship'. Thought I'd give them the chance to turn themselves in. The noble vicar. Everyone else first, me last. Know what he said? 'I will give it due consideration. Excuse me now Vicar, we have people to lunch'." The anger turns her eyes pitch black. "An hour later the telephone rang. Bishop Arthur. 'A grave error of judgement by two fine young men under the influence of drink'. Was going to call me anyway on Monday. A benefice in the North of the county where I would be elevated to Rector. He'd had me in mind for it for some time. Arch Deacon Ingrid was on her way with the balm of counselling, and lots of tea no doubt. I packed my rucksack, and fled to the airport."

Adam stands, and opens the shutters. He lifts his eyes to the hills.

"What did you say, Gramps?"

His voice trembles. "Whenever he spoke of his honour, we started counting the spoons."

She goes to him. Links his arm. Her head on his shoulder.

"Who said that?"

"Ralph Waldo Emerson, American writer. About a dinner guest. Probably a politician…. or a bishop."

"More tea Adam?" Mishka has padded into the room.

He and Anna look at each other, and guffaw until tears run down their faces. Anna strides over to Mishka and rains kisses down upon her.

"Yes please, my love. A large pot of tea for three on the veranda. You don't mind if Mishka joins us, do you Anna?"

*

Mishka speaks first. "What you have suffered is dreadful. I would not have believed it of English gentlemen."

Anna does not respond to the naivety.

"Mishka darling, the world is as it is, not as it was in the stories of old men when they told you tales of the honourable sahibs of yesteryear…"

Anna breaks in, "And that's why I asked you Gramps."

"Asked me what?"

"Why you and Granny, and my parents, forged virtues in me from a world long gone?"

For the first time Adam has to reflect. He expresses it simply.

"Because they are the values that were handed down, and despite my disappointment I still believe in them."

"Disappointment Gramps?"

"It's only fair I tell you why I ran away. No, that's untrue. I didn't run away. It was time to leave. I left England for much the same reason as you. It was a land I no longer recognised."

Anna interjects, "But why India? No disrespect, Mrs. Sampson."

Adam chuckles. "Why India? Because the Indians are more bloody English than the English!"

"*Pyaare*. Don't swear, you sound like Billy."

"What did you just call him, Mishka?"

"It means lovely. Adam is my *mere dil ka pyaar*; he is the love of my heart."

They hold hands, as Adam continues.

"Don't go all Disney, Anna. India and the Indians are far from perfect. But the civility and courtesy you were talking about; the community and good neighbourliness are still bedrock. Of course, there remain the human diseases of hypocrisy, greed and violence. As for the Wisdom of the East, if I may have recourse once more to your great-granny's treasure trove of phrases and sayings: '*That's all me eye and Betty Martin!*' But they have kept a wisdom which the West has abandoned. They adhere to their religions. Hindu, Muslim, Christian – it doesn't matter which – it gives them, at the very least, a civil and functioning society that can persevere and strive to improve itself. And a damn sight more pleasant to live in, for all its shortcomings. Here endeth the first lesson. More tea Vicar?"

"Dear Lord no! I'll start to believe I'm back in the village visiting the pensioners."

Adam cocks an eyebrow. "I am a pensioner!"

"I still don't understand fully, Gramps. Duty, honour, others first. You saw the world changing. Why not change with it?"

She has never known him so indecisive, and nor has Mishka. The women turn to each other in puzzlement. His chest fills with a great intake of air that startles.

"Because constancy in the face of wrong is all we can ever do if we are to play a part in the redemption of the world. You know Bonhoeffer?"

"*The Cost of Discipleship'*. Hanged in Flossenburg concentration camp, two weeks before the 2nd World War ended."

"Churchill put it another way. 'KBO', keep buggering on. That's what was passed on to me, and I'll go to my grave constant in that belief. I will not give in." His jaw sets, almost in parody of the great wartime leader.

Mishka leans forward, and plays with his fingertips. "Who passed it on to you Adam, your parents?"

Memory overcomes him, and he seems pale beneath his bronzed skin.

"Yes Mishka. To begin with my parents. Then women. So many women. Women saturated in duty; furnished with honour, and consummated in love."

His head droops, and his aged body wracks with sobs.

"…and I loved every one of them…and lost every one of them. England…the world…became darker and uglier. Then I ran, Anna. Yes, I ran away…"

Anna does not presume to take the place of a wife. She stands silently, as Mishka croons to her husband, leading him back to his abandoned seat.

"Who were they *pyaare*? Can you not tell us?"

The old man sweeps back his long hair.

"We would need days. The story of my life."

"I'm not going anywhere Gramps, and Mishka certainly isn't."

"You must both be hungry. I am."

The women are disconcerted.

"A deal, Anna, I'll make a deal. In return for my story you work with me at the orphanage, as Mishka does. Mishka. No deal for you my love. It's only right and proper that my wife should know."

Anna is eager. "With joy and with love, *Achchhe Pita*."

"Come Anna, we will prepare breakfast together."

"No you will not! We will all do it together. Tonight. Tonight after dinner I will begin to tell you a plain tale from the hills."

The women take his arms, and they argue about Kipling.

*

North

Annie Sampson clutched her left eye in pain. She sat bolt upright in bed. Her husband, Ted, was clattering pans downstairs. It was August first. Ted knew what was coming, and always rose that bit earlier at the commencement of each month. Tears meandered down Annie's face, as she sat motionless waiting for the pain to subside. Eight trials down and four to go before the cycle began again. Happy New Year. The wraith of her long-departed mother slipped into the ether; the memory did not. Standing before her, as a child, on the last day of every month. Shaking ever so slightly, and bracing herself.

"This is for what I *haven't* caught you doing!"

A hand flew forwards towards Annie's face, and its index finger poked her in the eye.

The shards of memory that cut Annie, a dozen times each year, were sharper and more penetrating than that lance-like finger. She felt wide-awake as a scalpel reopened the wound. A disappointment. She was a disappointment to her Edwardian mother. All she'd ever known was tough love.

Annie swung her little legs over the side of the bed, and popped on her housecoat. She bustled along the small landing, and entered her son's bedroom. Looking down at his sleeping form, she was stricken with love for him.

"Adam, Adam." She stroked his face into wakefulness.

His opened eyes peered at her, in that ever-watchful way he seemed to possess.

"Hiya Mum. What time is it?"

"Time to get your glad rags on, my lucky lad. Big day today. Come on, shift yourself."

"What's for breakfast, ma?"

Annie paused in the doorway. "The Lord High Executioner has sanctioned egg and bacon."

"Has Dad left for work yet?" Even at eleven years of age Adam recognised the Gilbert and Sullivan allusion.

"Not yet. He wants a word with you, before he leaves." She drew closer, and sat on the edge of the bed. "Eh Tom Tiddler, less of the 'Ma'."

Furiously, she began to tickle him, and the screams of their laughter reached Ted in the kitchen.

Ted's footsteps made the treads creak on the stairs.

"Morning son. Happy birthday. I'm off now, Annie. We've a big drop at Ridgate Park before the funeral cortege departs." He faced Adam. "It's a great honour you've all been given, son. To sing at the Colonel's funeral. Best foot forward, and best behaviour. I'll be seeing Tommy Greenwood tonight at the PCC."

Tommy was the choirmaster, and Ted's implication impressed itself on Adam.

"I should be home by four-thirty Annie. Cake and candles, eh son," he said with a smile, before his habitual busy stride took him out of the room.

Annie grumbled under her breath.

"Don't know why they need a delivery today of all days...and at this time of year."

"What are you chunnerin' on about Mum?"

She was sunshine itself. "Eh you, you cheeky divil. I'll give you chunnerin'. Breakfast in half an hour." Annie pulled back the curtains to reveal a

31

rather dismal and wet August day. "Ee," she murmured, "it's *persistin'* down. Happy birthday, lovey."

Adam threw back the eiderdown and wiggled his limbs in glee. Eleven today. The bonus of three-and-sixpence for singing at Colonel Vivian Lionel de Halsall's funeral. Last scion of the squirearchy that once ruled over the small Lancashire village of Ridgate. He scratched his balls as he visualised the Colonel's widow. Ellen Laurel de Halsall neé D'Anyers. He'd seen her around the village all summer. In and out of her sleek and sporty number. The lads said she was about forty-seven, and she was luscious. Red hair fell to her waist, set off by a dazzling mouth of perfect white teeth. When she moved there was a rustling. Ellen undulated like dunes shifting slowly over millennia in the Sahara Desert. Milkman Ernie Ogle put it best:

"By gum, with a swing like that she'll need a bigger garden!"

Adam had noticed Ellen's large and powerful hands. Ernie's son, Ronnie, who exceeded his father in lewdness, responded to his observation:

"Never go out with a woman with big hands – makes your cock look small."

Adam leant on the windowsill, chin in hands. Tommy Greenwood had prepared them for the big day. He felt great affection for the choirmaster. Always rushing into the church, straight from work in the local steel goods factory.

"Reet lads, we're under instruction. First hymn, 'Bread of Heaven', that's a nod to his Welsh cousins – they get about a bit…"

"Ay," Ernie Ogle interjected, "pray on their knees on Sunday, prey on the neighbours the rest of the week."

"…followed by dark satanic mills…"

Maurice Rothwell stuck his two pennorth in. "Jerusalem again!"

"Na then Maurice. That's where they made their brass. Mills that is, not Jerusalem. No *'four bys'* in the family tree. 'Love Divine' to round us off. Presumably, a tribute to his happily married life."

"Ah'd a thowt he'd have gone for *'Wi me little stick o' Blackpool rock.'* "

The young uns sat mystified at Ernie Ogle's suggestion, whilst the men chuckled. Tommy brought them to order.

"An extra shilling for puttin' him to rest in family crypt to Stainer's 'God so loved the World'. Reet, get yourselves in stalls, and let's mek a start."

*

St. Barnabas' Road. A steep climb. Mother and son leaning at forty-five degrees into the unseasonal wind and wet. Immaculate gardens drenched. Roses flouncing, playthings of the mischievous zephyr. The creations of good-hearted men mocked and tormented.

"Annie, Annie!"

"Is that you Josie? I can't stop; Adam's warbling at the funeral."

"I'll come with you. This'll be the last time we get to have a gawp at a big funeral. Here, get under my gamp. Adam, you get under Hazel's."

Hazel Macklin. Elfin class mate. Pretty and fragile. He sneaks a look. Oh yes.

Now an expedition. Forging a path through the elements as an act of duty. Passing the ponderous clumps of rhododendrons in the graveyard. They bow to the gravitational pull of the wind. Adam watches them intently. He knows that they are genuflecting to him, in homage to his honourable observance of the rites to come.

The choir is assembled outside the vestry door.

"Nah then, Delilah."

Ernie Ogle's familiar tease greeted Mrs. Sampson.

"It's Annie to you, Ernie Ogle. If I have any more of your cheek, it'll be Annie get your gun."

Adam studied Ernie Ogle, and his lips cracked a smile. Mum had bested him.

"Get yourselves in vestry, and get robed." Tommy Greenwood materialised from nowhere. Adam recalled the innuendo of Kenneth Williams on his favourite radio programme, *'Round the Horne'*:

"He manifested himself amongst the rhododendrons."

"What are you giggling about?"

"Nothing mum."

Annie clutched him tightly, determined that the wind would never carry him away. He was her universe.

"I'm as proud as can be, I am. Your Dad was right. A great honour. Do your best, lovey, always do your best. Give us a kiss for Christmas. Come on Josie, I want a good seat."

Vicar Robert Harris entered the vestry, as the last surplice went on. The ex-paratrooper evident in his muscular frame.

"The cortege has arrived. Tommy, when you see me at the West door Michael Bradbury will strike up the organ. Then it's best foot forwards. I'm sure that you will be at your brilliant best today."

Tommy wheeled about. "Give these boys a check, fellers. See that they're shipshape and Bristol fashion."

Amidst the detritus of a Church of England vestry, gnarled-handed men, reeking of cigarette and pipe smoke, straightened ruffs and smoothed out surplices.

"All in order?"

"Eee Tom, they look like prick at ball's wedding!"

Ernie Ogle had not yet mastered *sotto voce*. Hidden at the back, Adam peered at Ernie with intent. Despite his own laughter, he disapproved. Not priggish. Just wrong in this sanctuary. His pal, Colin Harvey, was spiralling into hysteria.

"Colin Harvey get a grip, or your father'll hear about it."

That chastening thought stilled the room. Men and boys alike knew of Mr. Harvey's penchant for wielding his leather belt.

The Colonel's obsequies were under way, and the choir entered the stalls like Red Indians weighted by their mournful travails along the *'Trail of Tears'*. Funeral director Norman Cussiter led the procession. He bore himself with the *savoir faire* of screen actor Adolphe Menjou; his son Fred brought up the rear, his scowling resemblance to a young Oliver Reed often remarked upon. Behind him was Ellen de Halsall. Every eye in the house was on her.

"She's no better than she ought to be."

Annie Sampson's pithy comment drew a raised eyebrow from her companion, Josie Macklin.

"I am the resurrection and the life..."

The minister's words slipped away, as Annie's mind turned to her husband. She saw his face in the open pages of her hymn book. Looking up, she visualised Ted and herself on the Chancel steps; her simple post-war wedding dress a delight. To love, honour and obey. Wanted, needed. The ache in her belly gone at last. She knew that she loved Ted with all her being in that marital moment. The hollow of parental disdain filled. Days passing. Months rolling by. Years turning. A mound of ash growing larger, as the fire shrivelled. Not in her, but in him. First of the month. Sex tonight. Annie had the insight to know that it had become an onerous duty for Ted. Yet she would cling to him. Fury, love and disappointment driving her. She emerged from her reflections.

"What's that you say, Annie?"

"Later Josie."

Annie's face an icy mask. Ellen de Halsall bowing to her late-husband. Annie willing a shard to splinter from her face, fly across the pews and pierce the widow's spine. Two hearts racing. Mother and son. Ellen upright. Her eyes lock with Adam's and soften. She turns. Momentarily, widow and wife stare at each other; one of them puzzled by the anger of the other.

"...whosever liveth and believeth in me shall never die."

The promise of life free from suffering.

Vicar Harris proceeded through the offices. Adam was gripped by Psalm 90. Did people really live to be eighty. Not a bad stretch. Yet what was the bit about their strength being labour and sorrow? He'd find illumination five decades ahead. A witness to mother and father. Silent. Alien-eyed. Struggling for breath.

"And did those feet in ancient times..."

The Cussiter boys had already sung *'Bread of Heaven'* in the style of Caruso and Gigli. Now they assailed *'Jerusalem'* in soaring operatic heights. The range of runs, trills and leaps added a bizarre coloratura to the well-known hymn. No surprise to choir boys versed in their competitive antics. The Lord Lieutenant of Lancashire experienced shell-shock, bemusement and disbelief at the light opera in three acts presented by Norman and Fred Cussiter.

Robert Harris addressed the congregation from the pulpit.

"Eh up, Annie," whispered Josie Macklin, "this is the bit we've come for."

Sitting in the choir stalls Adam, unknowingly, concurred. The Vicar spoke of a life of service. The Colonel had fought in both World Wars. Benevolent employer. Charitable giver. Loyalty to regiment and employees; duty to country and those less fortunate; integrity in all of his dealings. Virtues composite in honour. The rain beat a mournful tattoo on the church roof. Adam was with Noel Coward on the deck of his destroyer in the wartime epic *'In Which We Serve'*. He was flying beside Kenneth More portraying fighter ace Douglas Bader in *'Reach for the Sky'*. In the cold church he elevated them to glory. Wrapped warm in the character of Richard Hannay, the epitome of honour and the hero of the John Buchan novels he avidly devoured. Noble. Unselfish. He would become that man. Deserving of a beautiful wife. His marriage would be like the de Halsalls, and like his Mum and Dad's.

"That's all me eye and Betty Martin."

Josie stirred, "What's that, Annie?"

As her son sang his heart out to *'Love Divine all Loves Excelling'* his mother told it straight.

"He wasn't too keen about paying his bills on time. Ted was kept waiting for weeks on end."

"Aye," Josie ventured, "them as has it aren't quick to part with it."

Time for the final act. Norman Cussiter at the slow march. Michael Bradbury playing *'Jesu, joy of man's desiring'* exquisitely. Pall bearers passing. Funeral party processing. Adam behind Ellen de Halsall. 'Colonel of the Regiment' to the following choir. His gaze caressed by the sensuous rolling of her hips. A demonic face waggled on her buttocks. Local lad Ronnie Ogle. His words escape from Adam's ears and fill the Holy space.

"You don't look at the mantelpiece when you're poking the fire. If it's a nice arse...it's a nice arse!"

Rain gone. Graveyard steaming. The expected August sunshine shooing the clouds inland. Still a persistent Lancashire breeze transforming surplices into party balloons.

Adam caught his mother's eyes. He loved her dazzling smile. Unaffected and heartfelt. Her lips moving. It was all he could do not to guffaw. She was singing *"Happy birthday to you..."* under her breath. An army cadet concluded *'The Last Post'*.

He was thankful. The lad had covered up his mother's bad behaviour.

Vicar and Choirmaster. A discreet glance. Stainer's composition. Speaking for a world as yet still clothed; unassailed by the naked and unprincipled creed of individualism.

"God so loved the world, God so loved the world, that He gave His only begotten Son, that whoso believeth, believeth in Him should not perish..."

The Colonel's mortal remains descended into the family crypt. Adam sang, and looked into the chasm with curiosity. He looked at his mother. Good grief. She was still mouthing *'Happy birthday'*. Steadying himself. Head raised to scour the broad and expansive Lancashire sky. Unfurling in a shimmering haze towards the western coast. Life. Fantastic. Loved. Delightful. Head lowered. Puzzled. Out of the corner of his mouth.

"Where's she gone, Col?"

Colin Harvey. Fervent disciple of Ronnie Ogle.

"In the crypt. Arse like a split peach."

Ellen emerged. Customary words of consolation from the Vicar. She spoke to Tommy

Greenwood, and passed down the line. Shaking hands with men and boys alike. Adam. A pause. A smile worthy of Doris Day lit her face. A gloved hand brushed his cheek. Gone.

Annie aggrieved. "Did she say owt to you?"

"Nothing Mum, not a word."

A frown.

"Get your skates on love. The bus'll be here soon."

Racing to the vestry. Ernie Ogle, church treasurer. Fox in the chicken coop.

"Na then, two an' a tanner each weren't it?"

Paddy McAteer, Head Choirboy. Sixteen. Ginger. A face that wouldn't be out of place on Mount Rushmore.

"Bollocks Ernie. Three and six. Hurry up. I've to clock on in half an hour."

Dashing out of church. Skid to a halt. No rush. Annie and Josie locked in verbal combat. Speed-talking simultaneously. Hours of trivia. A friendly struggle for dominance. Adam proud. Mum the reigning champ. Ted not so approving. Years revolving, and he driven to the point of insanity. Annie rising at six. A stream of consciousness on permanent boil. Unabated until her head hit the pillow fifteen hours later. The respite of eight hours at work insufficient to sustain Ted. An older Adam would sometimes remark:

"Bloody hell mother, give it a rest."

"Huh, you think I'm bad. You should live with Josie Macklin, she never stops. Daft as a brush that family."

It filled him with glee to hear this. Kevin Macklin was decidedly odd. One day the gang saw him riding his bike without tyres. Ronnie Ogle opined.

"See that Sammo. That's what you end up like when half of you's dripped down your dad's leg."

Kevin's sister Hazel was an altogether different matter.

Watching his mother and Josie going at it thirteen to the dozen. Adam had no idea why they were the Victoria Falls of verbosity. He knew nothing of being unloved and unheard. Female submissiveness was not on his radar. In craving attention Annie Sampson drove people further away from her. The scent of desperate love is an odour that repels. Fearful humanity runs. Shuddering and embarrassed by the offer of unconditional love.

Ernie Ogle passed by, cronies in tow.

"…and vicar pointed to a lass on front pew and said, 'Ernie, int that Fanny Green?' Nay vicar, says I, it's a reflection from stain glass window!"

Hoary old joke. Bellowing laughter.

"Na then Mrs. Sampson, did you enjoy the service? Your lad sang well."

"Thank you Ernie, I'm as proud as punch of him. Ay, service went well. I could've done wi' less prancing around by widow woman."

Maurice Rothwell piped up.

"She's a handsome woman."

Josie Macklin stuck her two pennorth in.

"Handsome is, as 'andsome does."

Ernie Ogle was never one to resist mischief.

"Will your Ted still be mekin deliveries now the Colonel's gone? I hear he's filled her coal 'ole regular like over the years. She's particularly fond of a bit of nutty slack they say."

"You've too much to say for your sen, Ernie Ogle. You'd be more use keeping an eye on that new vicar of ours."

Silence. Sudden. Chastened men.

"Adam. Adam! Come on lovey. Did you get your money?"

An affirmative nod.

"All of it?"

That did for Ernie.

"Annie! If we shake a leg, we might just make the bus."

Bustling to the church gate. Josie and Hazel hand in hand. Adam grabs Annie's hand, and together they skip along. Her humour restored.

"Can we go upstairs Mum?"

Boy and girl going ahead.

"Annie, what were all that about the vicar? Has he been up to no good?"

"Hold your horses, Josie. Little folk have big ears."

Upstairs. Front seat empty.

"Hazel love, go and sit with Adam. Me and his mum have things to discuss."

Adam secretly delighted to have the pretty girl beside him. Of course, he wouldn't tell her, but she would be his Ellen for the day. Ding, ding. Wagons roll. Adam scanning the pristine blue sky. In the sun he sees Ellen's face smiling at him. He sings.

"Oh! The Deadwood stage is a rollin' on over the plains,

With curtains flappin' and the driver slappin' the reins.

Beautiful sky! A wonderful day!"

Hazel catches his eye. He thinks her smile just as good as Ellen's. The tag line comes from behind, as Annie and Josie sing through their tearful laughter.

"Chris Chattaway, Chris Chattaway, Chris Chattaway!"

*

"Do you think he is Annie?"

Annie Sampson took a slurp from her tea cup. Leaning across the café table she looked Josie foursquare in the eye.

"Not certain. I think he'd help out if the shop got busy."

They were engaged in a bit of character assassination. Josie spluttered into her tea cup at Annie's retort. A sharp bit of backslapping sorted her out. Annie continued, whilst the children were at the counter selecting a pastry.

"There's some as say his mother made him a homosexual."

Josie's riposte was lightning quick.

"If I give her some wool, do you think she'd mek one for me?"

The table was short of one person and a cauldron to stage a scene on the blasted heath.

"We've both chosen Eccles cakes, Mum."

Hazel's voice tinkled with the seduction of wind chimes.

"Not the only thing you've got in common, lovey," Josie suggested. "Off together to Field Lane in a few weeks. They say it's a smashing new school."

Annie stuck her oar in.

"Praps you can go together every day."

Adam was delighted by the thought, but knew that it wasn't practical. His mates would have a field day with him.

"Dad said I could go on my bike, and I've already agreed to meet up with Judda and Huddy halfway down Cock End Lane."

Annie's face was wreathed in lovable mischief.

"Well I'm sure Hazel has got a bike."

Josie greeted the wink with a hearty laugh.

"Aye, mebbe you could go tandem."

The two witches read each other's mind, and burst into song.

"Daisy, daisy, give me your answer do,

I'm half-crazy all for the love of you.

It won't be a stylish marriage,

I can't afford a carriage,

But you'll look sweet upon the seat

Of a bicycle made for two."

Josie laid a hand on top of Adam's.

"Don't look so worried, lovey. Hazel will be taking the bus."

"Ee, look at the time Josie. I'll have to get my skates on. If his tea isn't ready Happy Larry'll have a face like a wet weekend."

Adam knew that she was referring to his Dad. On the bus home he mused upon his mother's treasure trove of sayings. Annie Sampson talked through analogy, metaphor, pithy sayings, and an immense back library of song. Only in adulthood did he understand why. It was simple. Ted Sampson belittled his wife. He wanted a divorce. He also wanted his boy. The joint didn't fit, so they remained wedded. In his frustration he mocked his wife. His most frequent pronouncement.

"You talk bloody rubbish, Annie."

Annie continued to talk whilst burrowing into herself. Old sayings were recycled, ad infinitum. She was cocooned in the reassurance of past days, when life had, for a short while, been happier. Unfettered love flowed from simplicity of heart, but a dam of disregard staunched the flood. It never mingled with the sea of someone else's devotion.

"...happy birthday dear Adam. Happy birthday to you. Make a wish."

He knew precisely. Eyes screwed shut. Inside his head.

"Let every day be like this day."

Adam lay on the living room floor. Another Buchan novel. *'A Prince of the Captivity'*. Heroic Adam Melfort, married to a woman who cannot return his love for her. The kitchen. Clatter of dishes. Murmuring voices.

"Are you going to speak up Ted?"

"Someone has to. We can't let it go on."

"He should be ashamed of himself. God knows what his poor wife must think. As for her…she's no better than she ought to be."

"Well, that's as maybe…" Evasion in Ted's tone. "I'll make a move."

Church Hall laid out for the Parochial Church Council meeting. Heads looked up, as Ted entered.

Ernie Ogle broke the silence.

"This is a bad business Ted."

"What do you suggest Ernie?"

Maurice Rothwell.

"Someone's got to speak up."

Everyone looked this way and that. Best not to catch an eye, and be mistaken for a volunteer.

"I'll do it." Ted spat it out, like a bad taste. "It can come under any other business."

"We're right behind you Ted."

The chorus of approving support metamorphosed into 'Good evening', as Vicar Harris appeared.

Finances, grass-cutting, and faculties required from the Diocese to effect changes. The Temazepam of PCC meetings. Robert Harris apologised for the lengthy meeting. Enquiry around the table for AOB.

"There is something Vicar..."

"Go on Ted."

"There's been talk..."

"What about?"

Ted inhaled deeply.

"People in the village are concerned about your relationship with your secretary."

Robert. A tone of regret. Beloved of public school headmasters.

"I'm sorry that you listen to gossip Ted. Would your wife be part of the cabal blackening my character? Not to mention the calumny heaped upon Eunice."

Eunice Bickerton. Young, slinky and sexy. Her husband. Gormless. Face like a well-smacked arse.

Ted bristled.

"Annie has nothing to do with it. I'd be obliged if you'd avoid blackening her character."

Harris. Officer and gentleman. Magisterial disdain.

"May I enquire if Ted's sentiments are shared?"

Big men of Lancashire. Unflinching from blows at work, or on the football field. Seeking solace. In teacups. Critiquing the reproduction of *'Christ before Pilate'* hanging high on a wall.

Whipped cur. Ernie Ogle.

"Not Christian like, is it. A bit of a misunderstanding…"

Sound. Chair scraping. Ted gone.

Adam in bed. Reading.

"What went on Ted? Did you say owt?"

Irritated.

"Anything Annie, anything. Not owt. How do you expect Adam to speak properly if you don't?"

"What's made you see your arse?"

"Don't be so bloody crude. You're not with your father now."

Fatuous remark to restore peace. "Did it not go down well?"

"They said they'd back me up. Not one of them had the guts. You can keep taking Adam on Sundays, but I'm finished with that place."

A down-to-earth woman, who knows what's what.

"Well, what did you expect? Ernie Ogle'd set fire to his grandmother to save his own skin. They've all got two faces under one hat. I suppose the Vicar denied it, and stood up for that madam Eunice Bickerton."

Ted's voice raised.

"Give it a bloody rest Annie. You go on like a bloody toothache."

Unwise afterthought.

"Leave Eunice out of it. He's the one who's supposed to know better."

Dog with a bone.

"You would stick up for her."

Silence.

"I've seen the way you make up to her when you think I'm not looking."

 Book discarded.

"You talk bloody rubbish."

"Mebbe I do, but Robert Harris isn't the only one who gets talked about in Ridgate. Ernie Ogle had a few things to say about you and the widow Halsall."

Screeching.

"If you think you're mekkin a fool o' me, Ted Sampson, you've another think comin'."

Miss the fourth step down. It creaks. Living room door. Peer through crack. Father. Face of stone. Immobile. Mother. Ever shifting. A boxer on the move. A tirade pouring from her. The 'banshee'. Annie wailing. A war dance on the carpet. Face screwed in temper. Hands clenched. Little legs stamping up and down with terrifying rapidity. All the time the pitiable cry of loss retched from her. A tantrum. Justified?

Two steps at a time. No thought for creaking treads. Nearly safe. Adam halted on the landing. The guillotine of silence. He looked into his bedroom mirror. Where did his summer tan go? His eye caught by the open book on his pillow. Picks it up. *'A Prince of the Captivity'*. With studied care he read the 'Dedication'.

"As when a Prince

Of dispers'd Israel, chosen in the shade,

Rules by no canon save his inward light.

And knows no pageant save the pipes and shawms

Of his proud spirit."

Thus said Jesus, upon whom be peace.

The World is a bridge; pass over it, but build no house upon it.

Pulls the cover from its stapled moorings. Sets the book adrift under the bed. With deliberation he tore the cover into four pieces.

"Morning Adam."

"Aunty Christine. What…"

Ted interrupted.

"Your Aunt will be staying with us for a week."

"Where's Mum?"

"Mum needs peace and quiet for a while. Doctor Jackson drove her up to Ridgate Hospital. She'll be there for the week."

"Can I visit her Dad?"

Uneasy glance between brother and sister.

"Write her a nice letter, son. I'll take it to her." Tone. A forced change. "Fish and chips tonight."

"Can I have mushy peas, please?"

An affirmative nod.

"...and Mum will be back in a week?"

"A week today."

Ted's bold stride took him out of the house. Adam knelt on the sofa in the bay window. Saw his Father emerge from the side entry. A stagger. A hand on the low brick wall. Head hung mournfully. Attention. Upright. A monumental inhalation of breath, and he was gone.

Seven days disappeared in a bath of summer sunshine. Saturday morning. Ted tending his garden. Annie put the tray of fairy cakes in the oven, whilst Adam scraped the bowl. Bliss. A cackle and a giggle, and Annie grabbed hold of him.

"Monday morning we'll be off into Liverpool to pick up the rest of your school uniform. Think you could manage a visit to the sweet stalls in St. John's Market? Josie and Hazel will be coming along. You like Hazel, don't you?"

Without waiting for a reply, she began to sing.

"Hi ho! Hi ho, it's off to work we go, with a shovel and a pick and a walking stick, hi ho, hi ho, hi ho…"

Hands held. Round and round like a carousel, but Adam did not sing. Walt Disney. What a liar.

Shadows

" Damaged. Great-granny was very damaged."

Anna links Adam's arm, as they stroll towards the exit. After the distressing event earlier they sought respite and relaxation in the *Udhagai* Rose Garden. Two thousand varieties of rose; colours creating a palette to satisfy the most exacting of artists.

"Let's get some tea, and *payasam*. I can't resist it. Can never decide on my favourite. It's between mango or pineapple."

Anna doesn't demur from the deflected conversation. She senses that it is only temporary.

Pointing to the open range.

"That's a heck of a hill, Gramps."

"*Doddabetta*! More a mountain than a hill. 8,650 feet with road access, and a telescope observatory on top. We can go there one day, if you like?"

She nods assent.

"We'll head for the Upper Bazaar. There's a little place I know."

He falls silent. Unbroken on the arm of his granddaughter.

"Wow! That's really quite something."

"Adam's Fountain. Built around 1886."

They pause to admire the multiple tiers of the fountain, with its gilded accents and cherubs. The sun paying an extended visit between the rains.

"Here we are, darling. Oh my aching bones. Ready for a sit down."

"Are you alright, Gramps?"

He eases himself into a chair, and grins.

"Absolutely top notch, bloody fine, top hole."

Anna recognises the patter of Billy, their driver.

"*Namaste*, Hem."

Indian café owner. Tall, portly and beaming.

"Adam, my friend, and who may I ask is your beautiful companion?"

"My granddaughter Anna."

Hem bows, palms together in greeting. When he comes upright he frowns. A man, white-suited, has sat at a nearby table.

"Hem...Hem!"

"My apologies. The usual?"

"For two please."

Hem gives a strained smile. He disappears through the door of his café, and shoots a look backwards. His frown deepens. Beyond 'white suit', he counts three. Strong young men, lounging against a wall in apparent nonchalance.

"I hope you don't mind me harping on about it, Gramps, but the girls; it was dreadful. Does this happen often?"

Earlier in the day they had gone to the railway station. They were seeking abandoned children. Outside the station they were joined by a police inspector, and two of his men. It did not take long before they spotted the girls, aged about ten and seven. They watched them from the shadows for a while. A train arrived, and the passengers disembarked. The children were alert and waiting. Anna noticed the elder whisper to her companion, and then the girls moved forwards. A white man, in early middle age, was conversing with a porter. He was overweight and sweating. Suddenly his eyes switched from the garrulous porter to the two girls swaying towards him, preening and pouting. The look on his face became lascivious. Anna's hand went to her mouth.

"Oh dear God! They're soliciting."

Bile rose in her throat, and there was an audible retch. Adam gripped her hand tightly, and offered her his handkerchief. He did not speak. The police inspector touched his arm. He had been scanning the crowds, and had lighted upon what he had been searching for. Adam followed the line of his gaze. A tall young man. The girls' minder. At the Inspector's silent command, the two constables approached him. The Inspector, with Adam and Anna, went toward the children. The tourist saw them first, straightened stiffly, and took a deep interest in the porter. A puzzled look was shared by the girls, and then the Inspector's hands fell on their shoulders. Immediately, they submitted. To their surprise, the Inspector whispered kindly in Hindi,

"Do not be afraid little ones. I will not punish you. See this man. This is *Achchhe Pita*. You have heard of *Achchhe Pita...*"

The children looked at Adam in awe.

"It is over. Your old life is over. You will go with *Achchhe Pita* to the Orphanage. Safe at last...and see the lady, that is *his* little girl who he cares for very much."

Anna held out her hands. There was a moment's doubt, and then the younger of the girls flung her arms around Anna's waist. Her sister reached out and took a hand. Adam drew the three of them to one side, as the Inspector spoke to the tourist.

"Good morning, sir. May I see your passport?"

The fat man wheeled about.

"Say, what is this? I'm an American citizen."

"Indeed sir, and you are visiting India for what purpose?"

Beads of sweat furrowed the man's brow, and he thought better of further protestation. He handed over his passport, and burbled,

"A tourist sir, just a tourist. Taking in the sights of your wonderful country. Educational sir, yes sir, here for new experiences…"

The Inspector did not look up from his notebook. Whilst he spoke he wrote down the man's name and passport number.

"…and perhaps some not quite new experiences?"

His notebook snapped shut with a crack, and his piercing eyes arrested the American's face.

"I…I don't know what you mean, sir."

"You are Mr. Neil Gross. How long will your stay in Ooty be, sir?"

There was a change of tone, and the Inspector spat out the word 'sir' with thinly-veiled contempt.

"Three days, sir, three days."

"Enjoy your stay Mr. Gross."

With that he turned smartly on his heels, and took two strides. He delivered a parting shot.

"Oh, Mr. Gross. If there is anything we can do to make your stay more pleasant don't be afraid to approach one of my men. They are everywhere. Everywhere."

The pale American trotted after his porter, unsteadily.

Anna was a mixture of irate and puzzled.

"You aren't going to arrest him?"

Adam and the Inspector exchanged shrugs.

"No crime has been committed Miss. My hands are tied. All I can do is give him a warning shot over the bows. I have his details. They will be passed along the chain of command. Eventually, they will reach the American Embassy in New Delhi. The best we can do. Okay Adam, I leave these young ladies in your care. The usual registration processes, please, in the next forty-eight hours. Excuse me, I have pressing business."

With a smart bow he headed off in the direction of his two constables, where they stood watch over the girls' former minder. Anna had one last glance, as they exited the station, heading for Billy's rickshaw service. She saw a swagger stick held under the chin of the young man. Swiftly, she looked away as the man gave a sideways turn and locked his eyes on hers.

"All the time, Anna. Every day, somewhere in India, it goes on. Not only in India."

Hem arrives with their refreshment. Whilst he lays it on the table he speaks quietly into Adam's ear.

"You said damaged, Anna. Quite so. Let's hope that by catching them young they are not damaged for life, like your great-grandmother was."

He becomes intense.

"Poor Mum. These days she would have a better chance. Think Anna, think. She was not sexually abused, as many of the children at the Orphanage have been. Or made to work as slave labour. But she did suffer as a child; punished and unloved..." he trailed off.

"So that's why you give your life to these children?"

He laughs gently.

"Not entirely..."

He stops laughing.

"There are many elements to it. Partly, making amends for..."

"Forgive my intrusion Miss, sir."

Anna is surprised. Adam is not.

"You are not, perhaps, tourists?"

Adam stretches in his chair.

"You know I am not, Mr….?"

"Khan, sir. Ilaiyaraja Khan."

He laughs loudly, almost to the point of tears.

"The name of a stranger amuses you?"

"Oh it does, it does. Your Christian name means *'superstar'*. Is that how you see yourself, Brother Khan?"

Khan is ice, in his offended soul.

"I am not a Christian. I take no offence…Mr. Sampson."

The gloves are off.

"Now there is a name to conjure with. Did not your Samson of the Bible go blind, and lose all of his strength?"

"You are an educated man, Mr. Khan. If not a Christian man, what?"

Khan's turn to laugh.

"Do you follow other gods?"

Khan is amused and reflective.

"I am a modern man, Adam. May I call you Adam. Truly, I do not subscribe to, what do you call it, 'tosh'. Perhaps there are moments when I feel an affinity with the spirit of Kali."

Anna interjects.

"What does that spirit stand for, Mr. Khan?"

Before he can speak, Adam rattles it off.

"Not to be confused with the Goddess Kaali. The spirit takes the form of a tall and muscular dark-skinned person dressed as a wealthy man. He is the 'god' of all vices. Am I not right to say, Mr. Khan, that the present age is called the *'Yuga of Kali'*? Righteousness and goodwill have been replaced with greed and fair weather friends." Adam luxuriates with a sip of his tea. "You are not a modern man; your type is as old as the hills."

Maintaining control. "My respect, sir, you are a fine student."

"And no disrespect to you, Brother Khan. Kali inhabits the Western world also. We call him the Antichrist."

"Adam, we must come to an arrangement. You are beginning to have a detrimental effect upon my business interests. A few children for your orphanage is neither here nor there, but you are persistent. How can I put this? You are depleting my stock at an alarming rate. The affair at the railway station this morning...well, it was not good. If you look over my left shoulder you will see someone familiar."

They see the young man 'interviewed' by the Inspector. His face bears bruises, and one eye is swollen.

"Do not be concerned for the state of his health. He is young, and he will heal. Your tame policeman could prove nothing. I have recompensed my man well for being faithful, and sticking to duty."

Adam leaning across the table. Hissing.

"Duty! You know nothing about duty. Our first duty is towards life; the life God gave us. But it is towards the goodness of life. Not the destruction of innocence..."

"Oh come now sir, you are naïve..."

"I said innocence, not naivety. You confuse the two. Naivety is avoidable idiocy, Brother. Self-created through a lack of observation. Innocence is trust in the goodness of people..."

"Then it is misplaced trust Adam..."

Anna jumps in.

"No it isn't. If we show trust in others we encourage them to fulfil all that is best in them. We know that people can be cruel and capricious, but if we hold fast to our innocence – even in the face of provocation – it is an act of integrity. Love."

Khan removes his hat, and flexes the brim with care. When he looks up he is polite, but glacial.

"I have enjoyed our philosophical reflections very much. Time presses. You have become a citizen of India, Mr. Sampson, but you are not Indian, and you will never understand the psyche of…" his hand sweeps up the masses, crowding the Upper Bazaar, in contempt, "…of these people. You, and your granddaughter could vanish in a flash, and no-one would care. This is the East, and we are apathetic towards death. This rag tag people you see about you. They might hear of your disappearance one minute, and relapse into their dumb passivity the next." Khan stands and raises his hat. "Good afternoon." He pauses. "I am curious. You persist in calling me 'Brother' when I am palpably not?"

Adam raises himself to his feet.

"All men are brothers, and sisters too. Brother Khan, do not hold humanity in contempt. Love it. Come out of the shadows."

He extends his hand. Khan raises his hat, and departs.

"Who is he, Gramps?"

"Shall we say, I am aware of him, as everyone is in this part of the world. A gangster. One thing we can be sure of; his name isn't Khan…"

"Indeed it is not." Hem has appeared silently. "No one knows his name for certain, not even the police. I am truly astonished, and deeply concerned for you, my friend. We have all heard of him, but he is rarely seen. You asked him to come out of the shadows. It would be best for you, and for all of us if he did not."

"We must agree to disagree, Hem. In the light he can either grow, or shrivel. Either is preferable to the malign shadow he now casts. Come my friend, how much do I owe you? Here is Billy, and on time."

"This one on the house, Adam, and may God go with you."

"Hello Billy. Having a profitable day?"

A distracted Billy responds to Anna's enquiry.

"Zero, zero, fuck all, blank!"

His hand goes to his mouth.

"Oh my goodness! It is not even my French you must excuse this time."

Before he can apologise. Anna and Adam break into fits of laughter. Anna links Billy's arm. They stride towards his rickshaw.

"Anglo-Saxon Billy, good old Anglo-Saxon. Oh for some light relief. You are an angel Billy, a shining angel."

"Where to gaffer, home?"

"To the Orphanage, please Billy. We'll look in, and collect Mishka."

Adam insists upon doing the washing up, whilst Mishka and Anna relax on the verandah.

"It has been a troubling day, Anna?"

She pauses before answering. Processing.

"An unusual day, outside my experience. Troubles for Aasmi and Talika, but hopefully over now that they're in the Orphanage. Bigger troubles for Gramps, I think, with that very dangerous man around. I thought you said he just helps out with the teaching?"

Mishka. Deciding.

"Your Grandfather is a humble man despite his temper, which is rarely seen. He is not like the hypocrites in the temple who broadcast their good deeds..."

"Matthew 6."

"Oh my goodness. I am teaching my grandmother to suck eggs."

Anna laughs.

"Not at all, Mishka. The Bible is not the personal property of ministers. So, how else does he contribute?"

"With his money, with his time, and with his wisdom and determination."

"Don't the local people resent him? The outsider. The Westerner coming down from the mountain."

"No, no, no. Not at all. You see, he has no official position, and he seeks none. He simply puts himself beside the people and works amongst them. I told you before, he is not a missionary. Except in the sense that he is a follower of our Lord, Jesus Christ."

"But surely people resent that? Trying to impose an alien religion upon them."

Mishka shakes her head vigorously.

"Not once have I seen him try to do that. Anna, he lives the life; he follows the narrow way. Everyone knows that he is a Christian, but they also know that he places no obligation upon them to be so."

Anna sits. Warmed by the beauty of her Gramps. Chilled by the uncertainty of her own belief.

"What did you make of the first instalment of his life?" Anna asks, with a whimsy she does not feel.

"What did you make of it?" a voice asks, redolent with curiosity.

Adam sits. Drawing on his long, cool drink.

The light fades. Outlining the hills in sepia. Should a photographer pass by he would see an eternal image. Family gathered at the end of the day. Only Anna's clothes betray the modern world.

"Has there never been any honour? Is that what you were telling us, Gramps?"

Another sip.

"Golden ages. They come along every time a child is born."

Quizzical looks. He grins.

"Most of us look back to childhood, and garnish it in glory." He sings. *"Fings aint wot they used to be."* A long draught from his glass. "What I was telling you, through my story, is that the notion of a society in perfect cohesion is ridiculous. Honour resides in each of us as individuals, or not."

Anna. Now troubled.

"Then what makes this age any worse than the ones that have gone before?"

"Cohesion wrought from civility. I mentioned it the other day. We three may want everyone to be committed followers of Christ, but we know that it is improbable in our lifetime. What we can do is persevere in proclaiming His Message. Religion must be kept alive, and encouraged to thrive. Whatever a person's doubts and hypocrisies they can at least imbibe the Good News, and set store by it. Then we have the chance, however slim, of holding mankind together in civilised cohesion. That is the difference between this age, and the world I was brought up in."

"Baby and bath water, Gramps?"

"That's one way of putting it."

Mishka.

"*Pyaare*, were you not brought up to believe that everyone was honourable?"

"The error was mine, Mishka, not my parents. I swallowed the nonsense of silly books and films. The pedlars of comforting illusion, making themselves fortunes. I walked around with my eyes and ears closed. The three wise monkeys are not wise, except for speaking no evil. Evil is always with us, and there is no point in stopping our ears to it, or screwing up our eyes to avoid seeing it. We must never compromise with it. Consign it to damnation – where it belongs."

A taciturn mood leaves them mute.

"Gramps. I asked you the reason why you help these children. You said that there is something you are making amends for."

Adam stares deeply into his nearly empty glass. Then he smiles.

"You want part two of this thrilling adventure do you? What a pair of idlers. The old man has done the washing up. The least one of you could do is pour me another drink."

*

North

Ronnie Ogle paused from rearranging his father's milk float.

"Oright Sammo, wot you doin' 'ere?"

"Didn't your dad tell you? I'm standing in for Col Harvey. He's gone to Butlin's for the week."

Ronnie's attention span was notoriously short, and he spotted Barry Wetherspoon entering the yard.

"Bit late Bazza. Had trouble getting' out of the wankin' chariot? 'ope you've washed your hands."

Ronnie was fourteen, big, and hard as nails. He was fond of giving a good kicking to those who offended his delicate sensibilities. He baptised this methodology, and made it known locally as, *'Sticking the Timpson's in'*. His speciality, however, was the head-butt. Ronnie's features were Cro Magnon, with the merest hint of Neanderthal. He scorned physical fear. Adam would, occasionally, wonder if Ronnie was scared of anything. He had a dim supposition, which he was unable to sculpt into intelligible form. Might Ronnie be afraid of love. Certainly, he spoke of girls and women in a conscious and unending stream of obscenity and gynaecological detail. Maybe his extreme physicality was a stone tower, within which he could defend his heart from the fear of rejection.

"Hello! Wot are you doin' 'ere, young Adam?"

Adam repeated himself to the forgetful Ernie.

"Reet then. Wagons roll."

Adam soon got the hang. He was grateful to Ronnie for assisting him with an aggressive Alsatian dog that barred his path. Ronnie strode up to it, and gave it a tremendous boot in the bollocks. Then he imparted words of wisdom which the Buddha would have been pleased to recite.

"If all else fails, stick the Timpson's in."

Bazza and Ronnie were smirking beside the milk float. Adam was wide-eyed in astonishment. Ernie Ogle had just disappeared into the house of Jean Rutherford. She was Ridgate's most notorious resident. The local prostitute, aka the Village Bike.

"Come 'ed lads. We can 'ave a break if we do the Close quick. The old feller'll be a while."

At Ronnie's urging, they whizzed around Green End Close. In no time at all they were flaked out on the grass verge. Ronnie lit a Woodbine.

"Gizza drag," Bazza pleaded.

The code of honour demanded that the request be met.

"Spect you're wonderin' what the old man's up to, Sammo?"

Adam had a fair idea.

"He pops in for a quick ten bobs' worth."

At Adam's blank stare, Ronnie enlightened him by sucking noisily on his middle digit.

"Hey Bazza, here a minute."

Barry shuffled on his knees towards Ronnie. Quick as a flash, he stuck said middle finger under Bazza's nose.

"Meet the girlfriend!"

Ronnie rocked back and forth in, what Prince Charles would call, spasms of mirth.

"Eh up," he said in surprise, "the old man's finished."

He thrust the nearly-smoked cigarette into Adam's hand.

"Nah then, me lucky lads, let's get crackin'. I'm ready for me bacon and eggs. Adam, get rid o' that ciggie. Nasty habit. Tha'll be sick, tha'll be, smookin'!"

By mid-day Saturday Adam's stint was over. Whilst Ernie popped indoors for his leather satchel, he mused upon the experience. Each day was much the same. Ronnie mined a sexual vein with unwavering, if varying, degrees of lewdness.

"Barry, me lad. Attention! One pound, for the use of. Adam, tenshun!"

Ernie played out the scenario every week, as self-appointed Pay Officer. A crumpled ten-shilling note was thrust into Adam's hand. He had been expecting a promised pound.

"I'm a bit short this week. Help yourselves to some orange juice off the wagon."

Adam's complaint, at being short-changed, received short shrift from his father.

"He's the boss. He can do what he likes."

Adam shrugged inwardly. Oh well, one more week of summer freedom before 'big' school. He would blow the lot. One consolation. That would be the last intimate occasion he would spend in the company of Ronnie Ogle.

Big Wood was the favoured haunt for local children. Deep inside Ridgate Park. A half mile beyond the lichen-covered stone gateway and lodge. There a supreme vista of England thrilled. The ground descending to a shimmering lake. Wild bushes and rough tussocks of grass beginning to parch in the Late-August summer heat. Mature trees standing as sentinels on the other side of the lake. Plunge beyond them, and you could hold your revels amidst the giant ferns. Tumble into fairy dells. Scale their slopes in homage to a *pot pourri* of famous British victories. Machine guns blazing. Grenades exploding. Hard as you might try, the beauty of the scene was irreducible. Simple explanations beyond the ken of man or boy, woman or girl. Their England. Their joy.

Adam had set out in the early morn, collecting Col Harvey on the way. Attendance at Church had dwindled to almost nothing since the fracas between his Dad and the Vicar. Annie's heart was no longer in it if Ted wasn't with them. Before long, Adam left the choir.

"I'm a dive bomber!"

"I'm an ack-ack gun. I got you, I got you. Bail out."

Col had shot him down. They flung themselves to earth in the depths of the hollow.

"Great shot Col."

"I'm starving."

"Sarnie time!"

They delved into the bags strapped on their backs, extracting the sandwiches and 'pop' their mums had stowed within. In the stillness of the Wood, munching jaws accompanied the sweet choral song of the birds.

"Last day, Col. School tomorrow. You looking forward to it?"

Colin made an indeterminate noise, and wrinkled his nose.

"Spose so."

"What's wrong?"

"Thing is, Sammo, you're clever than me. It'll be easy for you. My mum says she's surprised you didn't get into the Grammar."

"Glad I didn't. Imagine having to spend another five years with that little tit Derek Dewhurst. Eh, remember when Bazza poured that bottle of ink down his shorts? Turned his balls blue."

The lads rocked back and forth in glee at the memory.

"I reckon you're right, Sammo. AND, you'd just be with lads. We get to mix with the tarts. Just think. They get bigger and bigger."

Screaming laughter from dirty-minded little boys. *Plus, ca change.*

"You fancy that Hazel Macklin, don't you?"

Unconvincing protestation from Adam.

"Bollocks. She just hangs around with her mum all the time, and *she's* my mum's best mate."

Col Harvey jeered.

"Aaaah, come off it. I bet you're always havin' a w...."

"Dunno about him, but I do!"

Ronnie Ogle had approached with the stealth of a Commando.

"Nah then wankers, wot you up to? Playin' soggy biscuit?"

Ronnie had a knack for appearing out of nowhere. A ghastly wraith, wandering the Earth in search of fresh blood.

"Giz a bit of that pop, Col." He swept the bottle out of his hand.

"Actually, a bit must be solid. Liquid comes in drops."

"Yeh, well I cum in drops too. Wot the fuck are you on about?"

Ronnie was more belligerent than usual. Tread softly. He sat between them with a crash.

"Eh, that Hazel Macklin's oright i'nt she? Their Kev's a soft melt! I'd give her the old pork sausage."

Ronnie found nothing incongruous in speaking this way about an eleven-year-old. Adam stared at the ground. Furious and frightened. Col steered the conversation.

"How's your old feller? Still bangin' Jean Rutherford?"

"Nah, he can only get it up once a month. Jean prefers me." He leant forwards and beckoned them closer. "You know wot gets a tart excited?"

Mouths open. Expressions agog. Ronnie leapt to his feet, and dropped his trousers. Todger in hand. Skinned back. The glans penis exposed.

"That's the bit that thrills 'em! Shut your gob, Col, before I stick this in it."

Col looked to his Timex.

"Shit! It's quarter to one. The old man'll murder me if I'm not back in time for dinner."

Scarpering through the ferns. The Hounds of Hell in pursuit.

"Worra 'bout you Sammo? Fancy playin' a game?"

Adam worried away at it in the years ahead, but never understood entirely what possessed him to obey Ronnie. Before you could say 'Jack Robinson' he was standing in that glen with his underpants around his ankles. Ronnie remained in a similar state of *dishabille.* The instant Ronnie's flesh touched his he grasped his clothing and fled through the woods.

"You alright son, you look a bit bothered?"

He knew that he could not share this with his Dad.

"No, I mean yes Dad. Just been running fast. I'm hungry. Is dinner ready, Mum?"

They sat at the dining table in relative silence. Annie and Ted didn't chat much these days. Mum's cooking was as good as ever, and Adam fairly walloped it down. Surreptitiously, he eyed his parents. He knew that he loved them, as he always had, but something was lost. Since their flaming row, and his Mum's stay in hospital, a transition had occurred. Ironically, Ronnie Ogle's attempted buggery, barely an hour before, was the trigger. Adam's epiphany came over homemade apple pie and custard. People didn't keep to their word. They were false. You couldn't trust them. Ronnie sexual assault must be kept to himself. No-one was to be trusted.

*

Hazel Macklin had no idea there was someone else at Field Lane School who loved Adam Sampson. She had divined the depth of *her* feelings for him when she was ten. The revelation came as they sat beside one another on a pageant 'cart', the previous summer. The Rose Queen Parade. Annual village event. She in Mock-Elizabethan dress, and Adam arrayed in full Scottish regalia for his role as Page Boy. Throughout the junior years she had observed him. He was always amidst the rough and tumble of the playground, but she perceived a gentle spirit. Hazel loved his courtesy and good manners, but there was something else. When sparks flew between the boys she alone spied the momentary hurt in his eyes, at a cutting remark, before his temper boiled over. She was touched by his vulnerability. Hazel was wise beyond her years. Josie would muse upon it, with Annie as her sounding board. Josie could barely breathe.

"Joe and me don't mention it much, Annie."

During these heart storms Annie had the sense to remain silent, and give her friend time and space.

"We don't know how long she'll be with us."

"She's a credit to you both, Josie. Bright as a button. She says things that make you put your thinking cap on. You know what she said to me the other day?"

Josie shook her head.

"We were in the kitchen while you were having a *'Jimmy Riddle'*. 'Aunty Annie,' she says, 'your Adam's as gentle as a kitten.' Well, I can tell you, I could have shown me arse on the town hall steps! I haven't the foggiest where she got that from. Between you and me, he gets more like his bloody Father every day. Awkward. More than once, when he's been sharp with me, I've said to him, 'Aye, alright Ted'!"

Josie pondered.

"She seems to see things, Annie, that we don't. Her time is short. Maybe the Good Lord has given her second sight in compensation…?"

Josie sobbed in Annie's arms.

"Here lovey, have my hankie."

"You'll keep what I say to yourself, Annie? We don't want folk fussing over her."

Annie Sampson couldn't keep a secret to save her life, but she was faithful this time.

It was rare for her and Ted to share much in the way of intimate conversation, these days.

"Ee, Ted. Josie was beside herself again about their Hazel. God knows how she and Joe will cope when the day comes."

Ted would dwell soberly before replying. All he could bring himself to say was, "I'm afraid the child isn't long for this world, Annie." To his own surprise, he would mutter under his breath, "There, but for the Grace of God, go I." The thought that he might ever lose his boy was unbearable to him. It was the only time he ever experienced the religiosity he had lost. A silent prayer would be offered. Let the natural order of life be maintained. He was determined that his time would come before Adam's. In the recess of his soul, Ted knew the futility of such thinking, and it left a fracture in his heart.

"Let's get him a new bicycle for his birthday, Annie. I'm tired of mending the old one. He's worn it out these last three years, up and down Cock End Lane to school."

Their mood lightened. The rest of the evening was almost companionable, as it once had been.

The Christmas party at the end of term. Headmaster Nelson Horsley started the dancing off with his wife, Mary. The giant Maths and Rugby teacher, Andy Bailey, swept Rose Hanson onto the floor. It was an incongruous sight. He about twenty-five, and six-feet four inches tall, and she in her forties and as diminutive as a merry Robin.

Naturally, big Doris Burford stuck her oar in. Accompanied by Isabel Holmes they propelled Adam across the room. It was no use resisting. Doris alone could have given the Wigan pack a run for their money. She would grow into one of those no-nonsense Northern women. Heart of gold, but woe betide you if you cross them.

"Here you go, Haze'. Adam says he wants a dance." Beneath the noise of the music, she whispered to him, in her *basso profundo* voice, "Two dances, or I'll get you up against the bike sheds and snog yer 'til your keks drop off!"

A fate worse than death.

Gyrating on the dance floor. The era when you let it all hang out, Adam froze. A memory bubble, imprisoning Ronnie Ogle, floated by. Well, perhaps not hanging loose in that sense. Hazel and he melted into the crowd, where he hoped to find anonymity from his mates. No such luck. Judda, Huddy and Bazza were lurking at the edges, and they gave him the thumbs up. Then they were bent double in laughter. Adam realised it wasn't directed at him. Col Harvey was the recipient of their tender mercies. He was doing the Twist with Doreen Spencer. Doris Burford was big and muscular, Doreen was enormous. Known to the fraternity as 'Two lunch

Doreen'. A dare. Adam knew. It had to be a dare, and Col was up for it.

"Adam, Adam."

He faced Hazel, ready to rock and tremble. She took his hand. Voltage soared down his spine, to find the parts other beers can't reach.

"I like the old ways. See. Just copy Mr. Bailey and Miss Hanson."

It wasn't *'Come Dancing'*, but they made a passable show. Adam kept a good twelve inches between them; six would have been disastrous. The music ended, and he made to leave with a muttered, "Thanks." His half spin and immediate reversal were comical. Adam had noted Doris Burford. Steely-eyed and resolute; legs akimbo and arms folded.

"Shall we have another dance, Hazel?"

Both were thrilled. The dance was a 'slowie', and he ventured closer to her. Confidence rose gracefully, and he even managed a smile for Miss Hanson and Mr. Bailey as they glided by. He could have sworn he heard the big man say, "About time too. Three years. Not exactly a fast mover is he?"

As they fluttered away, he distinctly heard his English mistress add, "But a smooth one, by the look of it."

"Phew. I'm a bit out of breath Adam. Let's sit down."

"You wait there. I'll get some lemonade."

He was on a roll.

"Excuse me, excuse me."

Yes, yes, yes. At last. His dream come true. And he knew that he loved that fragile girl. In all of her loving kindness, and generosity of spirit. "Ellen," he almost murmured, "I've found my Ellen."

"There you go, Hazel..."

A hand tugged at his arm, and he spilled a little of his drink.

"Sammo, Sammo, quick! I've got something to tell you."

Adam transfixed in desperation between Hazel and Col Harvey. He so wanted to shout at Col to sod off.

"Won't be a sec' Hazel. What, what do you want?"

"Bin dancin' with Doreen Spencer..."

"So what's new…"

"When we did the 'slowie'…she let me put my hand on her arse. Come ed. We're all sneakin' outside to the bike sheds. Bazza's got a bottle of Whiskey. Some of the girls are comin' as well. Isabel Holmes is one of them. She fancies you. Got knockers like two ferrets fightin' in a sack. There's gonna be 'games'."

'Face', the Chinese call it. Saving Face. Adam knew he was on a loser.

"I…I…I've just got to nip to the bogs."

He could have snipped off his tongue at the crudity.

"Sorry…sorry. I'll try not to be too long. Will you wait here?"

She wasn't going to show disappointment.

"I'll be here for a while."

"Okay then…see you soon."

Col Harvey dragged him away.

Pupils in party finery. Random departures from all points of the compass. Cautious glances. Andy Bailey grasping the arm of Judda.

"Where are you off to?"

"Need the toilet, sir."

"You too, Huddy?"

"Yes sir, bursting."

"Off you go then."

Adam smiled, and spoke quietly to Nelson Horsley. They both laughed, and watched and waited.

Events outside didn't last long before the teachers materialised. Long enough for Isabel Holmes to press up against Adam in the dark recesses of the bike shed. Hazel was forgotten. It became difficult for Adam to distinguish the rigidity of his crossbar from his personal appendage. The old adage remained true:

"A stiff prick hath no conscience."

When they were shepherded back indoors, he looked for Hazel. She was gone.

*

"Eh Mum."

Christmas gone. Annie was taking down the decorations. Twelfth Night. She was a stickler for tradition, and the superstitions surrounding them.

"What can I do for you, Tom Tiddler."

He resisted the temptation to be grumpy. Adam would be fifteen soon, and he couldn't abide the baby name his mother still employed. Cool. Nonchalant.

"I saw Kev Macklin the other day."

"And?"

"He said his mum's been ill."

"That's right."

It was like drawing hen's teeth.

"What's wrong with her?"

"Flu. It's gone through the family like a dose of salts."

"Oh." With mild disinterest. "What, their Hazel too?"

Annie from behind. Shoulders shaking.

"Aye, Hazel too. 'Spect she'll be as right as rain for school on Monday. You'll get to see her then."

The lady doth protest too much. "I was only…"

"Aye, we've heard ducks fart before."

*

Lancashire winds howling through the lanes. Adam took the full force as he breasted the rise of the bridge. Playground empty. Twigs, torn from the Rowan tree, shot arrows at him. Corridors void. Godforsaken. A ghost ship, bereft of warmth.

Adam peered through the glass panel. Bewildered children. Girls embracing. Doris Burford hugging Isabel Holmes. Ruddy cheeks a maelstrom of tears. Crippling silence.

A manly-voice wrenched from a female frame.

"It's Haze, Adam…" Tremulous. "She's dead."

"Oh." Adam sat on the chair Judd had pulled from under the desk. Owlish classmates stared. "They know, they know."

"What happened?"

A dumb sepulchre. Bled of speech.

Doris steadfast. "She wasn't well, Adam…"

"I know. She'd had 'flu'…"

"For God's sake, Sammo. You must have known. Her mum and yours are old mates."

Adam brain-addled.

"She was never going to reach old age. Hazel had a hole in her heart. Nuffin they could do about it. It was too much for her…"

Tears turned to wailing. Tough lads, faces hidden.

Adam muttered. "What's a hole in the heart?"

Glyn Matlock. School bully. Braying. "Same as the one in her arse!"

Acres of blood drowned Adam's senses. Hands around Matlock's throat. A head beating time against the parquet. Powerful hands gripped Adam's collar. Andy Bailey. Matlock a whimpering mass.

"What's going on…?"

"That little get started it. Adam's not to blame."

"Language Doris!"

Rose Hanson in the doorway. A wounded expression.

"I'll see to the class Mr. Bailey."

Bailey's long legs. Double time to the Headmaster's office.

"Wait!"

Childish pipes and trebles resounded from the Assembly Hall. 'Guide me O Thou Great Redeemer. A one-time choirboy roared the Third verse in agony.

"When I tread the verge of Jordan,

bid my anxious fears subside:

death of death, and Hell's destruction,

land me safe on Canaan's side:

Songs of praises

I will ever give to Thee."

No-one. No-one is to be trusted.

Two strokes of the cane. Matlock dismissed.

Nelson Horsley stared through his picture window, examining the woods beyond the playing fields.

"A wild day, Adam." Shoulders heaved. A hiss of air. "January – a desolate month. Do you ever feel that? Sit down."

"Yes sir."

"Why?"

"Trees bare. The cold chewing your marrow. The Sun, trapped in the shadows."

"By gum, lad! You've a way with words. Do you see any promise in the world?"

Hesitant. Tentative.

"Well, the snowdrops are with us…"

Excited. "Yes, yes."

"…and the daffodils are starting to show."

Nelson, paced like a demented artist, as he spoke.

"The appearance of desolation everywhere, but the lodestar of promise. Spring adjacent. Blossom will be on the trees, and the days will be warm. Easter will leap before us. Christ will go down into the grave, but on that glorious Sunday He will rise again." Careworn hands. The softest touch on a child's unhappiness. "Do you see, Adam? Do you see?"

"Hazel won't rise again."

Pain in a caring man's eyes. He too he has lost a rare human being.

"She's beyond all suffering. Now, she's with her Father."

Back to his window.

"Hazel was filled with beauty and with light. Not mere external beauty – that's an accident of nature. She possessed inner beauty. Kindled in her unaffected grace and thought for others. It never asked for a reward. Love, Adam. That's what places us with the angels." Bent over his desk. "Love. Never be ashamed of it; never be afraid of it. Give, and you shall receive."

Coffin. An angel's feather on the shoulders of pall bearers. Hazel, pure and spotless, going down to the grave. A boy's heart, empty of joy. Nelson Horsley's word of hope, a gossamer thread. Easily snapped.

"…we therefore commit her body to the ground…"

Kevin Macklin, forlorn. Josie, a pretty pink handkerchief screwed into her eyes. Joe Macklin's gimlet eyes searching the heavens. He staggered as the coffin was lowered. Gnarled hands held him. Loss that should never be insulted by rational explanation. A wound that could only be darned.

Adam closed in on the open grave. The last man standing. His Mum's arm slid through his, to draw him back to life.

"Terrible lad, terrible." Hoping to comfort. "There'll be a day, son, when someone else will come along…"

"You talk bloody rubbish!"

Annie cut to the quick. In her loving heart she already knew sorrow. Now it had become a life-threatening tumour. She knew that she had lost her son. A shard of opaque glass obscured him from her adoration.

"Now we see but a poor reflection as in a mirror…"

Rose Hanson, a pale shadow behind Doris and Isabel. Her compassionate expression imprinted itself on Adam, as he ran. Escape the rhododendrons mocking him with their call to duty.

*

Stratford-Upon-Avon. Adam, and two sixth-form companions, on a weekend trip with Rose Hanson. Crammed into her sports car, they had travelled southwards. A sight-seeing halt in the village of Upper Slaughter. A 'Doubly Thankful' village. Not one inhabitant lost in either of the two World Wars.

That evening. 'Midsummer Night's Dream', directed by Peter Brook, in the style of the old Commie fraud Berthold Brecht. Adam relished every minute, though contemptuous of the braying middle classes at the interval. Poseurs airing their critiques for all to ingest.

"Miss, may I borrow your programme?"

On the landing of the B & B.

"Of course, Adam. Let me have it back in half an hour. I need to scribble some notes while they're fresh in my mind."

"Shall I bring it to your room?"

"Number six."

Rose sat before the dressing table mirror in her dressing gown. She was almost ashamed to look at herself. Then she said out loud,

"I love Adam Sampson." Challenging her reflection, she added, "There, I've said it."

Why? Why him? The one-sided conversation was internalised. Rose had spent twenty-five years in teaching; she was forty-six. No other child had remotely aroused these feelings in her. She forced her educated mind to consider the question rationally. There was another passion in her life. Her duty to educate children to the best they could achieve. Especially those destined for factories and shop counters. That's what the visit to Stratford was about. She wished the RSC had been performing 'Coriolanus': *"There is a world elsewhere."* Aspiration, perseverance, achievement. Why Adam? Yes, she discerned the promise in him, but more. Across six years she was often dumbstruck with astonishment. He enquired endlessly; enthused remorselessly, and he was such an honourable little boy. Whatever failings he may have; falsehood wasn't one of them. She feared for him. If he were to carry the burden of truthfulness lifelong he would be in for a hard time. Wiping her makeup off, she smiled wistfully:

"...to thine own self be true,

And it must follow, as the night the day,

Thou canst not then be false to any man."

She had her doubts about old Billy Shake'. No, not really. He was a man of his day. Imbued with the Christian spirit. A carrier infected with Hope for a better world. Embodied in the wisdom that each individual must persevere in good and dutiful conduct. Rose felt the keenest regret that it was in hope for the world's redemption from selfishness, and meanness of spirit, where her doubt lay.

When Hazel Macklin had died. Dear Lord, was it three years since? Adam hadn't hidden his loving sorrow. Rose's admiration for him was boundless. Her shoulders drooped. She knew that she was envious of his relationship with the dead girl, and she compelled herself to say it out loud.

"Why can't I be loved like that?"

Adam lay in his pyjamas, on top of the bed.

"The course of true love never did run smooth."

"Come in number six, your time is up."

"What?"

"She wants the programme back, Sammo."

"Cheers Judd. Eh, while I'm gone, stick a cork up Huddy's arse. It reeks in here."

"Dead right. Anybody takes two sniffs of that is greedy!"

Adam padded down the softly-lit corridor. The door opened the instant he knocked.

"Come in Adam. Let's not disturb anyone."

In her quilted dressing gown and fluffy slippers, she resembled a marginally younger version of his Mum.

"What do you think, Adam?"

He was befuddled. She waved the programme that he had passed to her.

"'*The course of true love never did run smooth*'. Never got beyond that." He was a live wire. "Nothing has to stay the same. We can change, we can choose..." He faltered.

"Remember when we talked about Brecht? Man can change himself. That's what the Communists say."

"Have they got all the answers then, Miss?"

"Their history reeks of blood and misery."

A fierce desire to know welled up within him.

"Nelson Horsley believes he knows."

"I don't get you, Miss?"

"He's a devout Christian."

Adam shook his head. "He said some things when Hazel died..." His words spilt to the floor. "Are you a Christian, Miss?"

She was not evasive, but trusting to his intelligence.

"We *can* change ourselves, but I don't know if we can do it relying on our strength alone. I can't see the picture clearly."

Adam boiled with volcanic intensity. He jabbed a finger into the glabella; that space between the eyebrows.

"There's something here; something I should know, but I can't reach it. If my head split open it would be there to grasp and cherish forever. Nothing will ever be right until that happens."

Her words assembled in the ether, before vaulting into an elegant step.

"...let your adorning be the hidden person of the heart with the imperishable beauty of a gentle and quiet spirit..."

Tears wet his cheeks. "My spirit isn't quiet or gentle." The indecent villainy of lost love no longer staunched.

Rose Hanson wrapped him in her arms. Her voice resembled Hazel's, chiming in his ear.

"It's beyond my gifts to open up that hidden treasure. In the years ahead you'll know times of joy and happiness, and arid days of misery. Life fluctuates for us all. Train the muscles of Will, defend Reason with it, and never cloak your

Honesty and Integrity. Some will let you down and hurt you. Get back on your feet, and fight on. Persevere until the end, and never stop searching."

She released her hold upon him, reluctantly. The warmth of his body lit a furnace inside her.

"Love, Adam. Scrambling to find the path home on a mountain covered in mist. If you're lucky enough to walk out into the Sun give thanks. Try to put away yourself and serve whoever chooses to walk beside you."

Rose was desperate as she sought firm ground to escape the maelstrom of her feelings. Adam stooped. Kissed her on the forehead, and left the room. The stifled sound of heaving sobs receded as he went further down the corridor.

There is no scandal to relate. The rest of Adam's schooldays passed in warm complicity with her, and with his other teachers. On the final day he shook hands, and expressed his thanks. He knew that he had been privileged. Taught by men and women of integrity in an anonymous school; one amongst thousands in the nation. Active dispensers of real honour. Not ornate curlicues in flaking gold, on an ancient piece of wood, in a dead language. Their dedication steered his life's course.

Ted Sampson entered the back bedroom.

"Are you awake, Adam?"

"Who was on the 'phone?"

"I've a bit of bad news, son. It was Mr. Horsley. I'm sorry to say Miss Hanson passed away last night."

"Dead?"

Open curtains revealed a glorious August day.

"What did she die from?"

Ted shook his head. "I don't know. She was never the strongest looking of bodies, was she? I'm sorry to be the bearer of ill tidings. She thought very highly of you. Sometimes, I think she was as proud of you as we are."

"When's the funeral?"

"They'll let us know. Do you want to go?"

"For certain."

"Okay. Must be off. See you tonight."

Adam plumped up his pillows, and reclined. A head empty of meaningful thought. Annie's face popped around the door.

"Get your glad rags on. Egg and bacon's cooking." She stood in profile. "Ee lad, you don't seem to have much luck with women." Her heart raced in fear, at her candid revelation of the tacit truth.

Adam swung his legs out of bed. He walked towards his mother, and fastened himself to her in an indissoluble grip.

*

Blaze

Doddabetta is the highest of the mountains in the Nilgiri range. Nine kilometres from Ooty, with a beautiful reserved forest area around the peak.

"This is an interesting ride," Anna being wry. The upper stretches of the road are atrocious. "Should be fun on the way down. Oh look, rhododendron trees."

Adam grins. "They always remind me of the old churchyard in Ridgate."

"Does that upset you?"

"Got over it way back. Here we are. Once we're parked we could queue for the telescopes in the Observatory, if you want."

"It's your birthday Gramps. Whatever you think best. My goodness, the place is packed."

"It's popular with locals, as well as tourists."

Patience truly is a virtue in India. Small talk passes between them as they wait for a space.

"What's it to be then? Observatory, or a wander?"

"Let me treat you to lunch, Gramps. We can decide after we've eaten."

Anna strides towards the stalls in search of food.

Canny older folk know how to employ their peripheral vision. It is wiser than outright staring. Adam follows the progress of his granddaughter, whilst confirming his suspicion. He has clocked the vehicle behind them on the tortuous climb to the summit. During the interminable wait for a parking space he weighed up its occupants. There was nothing discreet about them. He realised that the three men wanted him to know of their presence.

Anna returns, laden with food. "Here we go."

"Goodness me, Anna! There's enough food to feed the Army on the Rhine...when we had an army on the Rhine. Settle yourself there. I won't be long."

Adam has spotted two policemen strolling amidst the tourists. He wanders casually over to them. Deliberately, he draws their attention to something which brings the three 'watchers' into their eye line. He asks an innocuous question, as any tourist might do. His pursuers assume differently, and disperse amongst the crowds.

"What was that all about, Gramps?"

"Oh, there's something I've never been able to discover about one of the distant hills. It's an old mystery. I wondered if they might be able to shed some light on..."

"...and it was a warning shot to the guys who've been following us."

"You're too clever by half, as Mum would have said. Eat."

A modicum of the feast is consumed in silent fellowship.

"Amazing view, Gramps. How frequently do you come here?"

"Every couple of months." He peers at the Nilgiris across the vast distance, and she sees delight and wistfulness in his face. "Do you know what the name of our home means, Anna?"

Anna practices her Hindi. "*Uttar Aanand Kare Kee Pahaadiyon*. Not a clue."

"Top hole, bloody fine effort," he declares, in imitation of Billy. "*Hills of the North Rejoice*! After I qualified as a P.E. teacher, I spent part of each summer holiday in the Lake District. The Nilgiris don't entirely fulfil my lingering passion for them, but they resonate in my gut. It satisfies a need once in a while."

"Is it worth queuing for the Observatory?"

"Not really. There's one chap in charge who insists upon showing you Ooty bus station through his telescope."

Anna spits crumbs, choking on her laughter. Adam's hearty pat on the back soon restores her.

"Do you ever miss home, Gramps?"

"England? I'd lie if I said never." He returns from a second's abstraction. "I was going to ask you the same question. It's been a week since you arrived."

Anna places her food on a broad stone beside her, and consumes the vista before her instead.

"The anger isn't gone, but it's dissipating. Being with you and Mishka is comforting. Seeing the work that you do together for the children is amazing." Uncertain if she should speak her next thought. "Listening to your story each night is...is...I don't know what? There's something liberating going on, and I can't figure out what it is? Hazel and Rose Hanson – such terrible loss inflicted upon you as a child."

Adam looks sharply at her when she says 'loss'. They study each other for a long while.

"Oh! I see, I see. I've suffered loss as well. Those two youths who raped me…"

"Not just them, Anna. Sudden violence and violation is despicable, and unfathomable to those who haven't experienced it. Only you can make choices and decisions about what you will do next. It would be unpardonable of me, or anyone else, to even suggest how you should feel. What else brought you to Ooty?"

"My utter disenchantment with my country, and its people. Lost in a stagnant sea. No tides or currents of civility to sweep away the detritus and filth produced by apathy. The rape was the straw that broke the camel's back."

Adam recognises in his granddaughter not merely a fierce intelligence, but the double-edged blade of keen self-perception.

"Innocence. I've lost my innocence. That's why you been relating your 'plain tale from the hills' to me and Mishka. It was ever thus, you're saying. So where next?"

Adam remains resolutely silent. It is not for him to tell.

"Two paths, Gramps. I...I think that's what you're pointing to." He smiles in affirmation. "There's a broad highway I could take. Cynicism. Uncaring, unfeeling, selfish..."

"You're anticipating the next part of my tale, my darling. Perhaps it's no longer worth telling..."

"Oh no, Gramps. Neither Mishka nor I will tolerate that. We want your *'Tales of the Arabian Nights'* before bedtime." She speaks softly. "I need to hear."

"What's the second path?"

"I could stop being a hypocrite." A quizzical look comes over her features. She is looking into herself. "I said it didn't I...to that frightening man, Khan. What was it I said?" Anna mines within. "Hold fast to your innocence, even when you're beset by all that bestial mankind can throw at you." She looks to Adam.

"That's the top and bottom of it. Another of my Mum's summary, and invariably accurate, judgements."

Anna bouncing on the rock. "We do so want to hear more about Great-Granny. Mishka is as fascinated as I am. If it's not too painful."

"Hold your horses. Mum comes back, eventually. Hey, I'm eighty years old, and despite a lifetime of stubbornness I'm still alive and kicking. One thing I have learnt is that wearing the Spanish ruff isn't that comfortable, or necessary to achieve good."

"Wearing the what?"

"It's from a translation of Rostand's play 'Cyrano de Bergerac'."

"Can't say I've ever heard of him."

"Cyrano was his creation. A 17th- Century French Musketeer with an enormous nose. He placed honour and duty above all else. So much so that he promoted the suit of a young man to the woman he loved, Roxanne. Cyrano thinks he doesn't deserve to be loved, and so he is unyielding in his creed of virtue. He wears the Spanish ruff. It keeps him upright and stiff-necked."

"I don't approve of hair shirts."

"Then don't wear one." Anna, startled by his bluntness. "Still, Cyrano wasn't wrong to persevere in treading the path of nobility. Come along young lady. I think we've seen enough here. I want to share my birthday with my wife as well. She bakes a mean cake."

Hand in hand they meander to the car park.

The car pootles down the mountainside at a pedestrian pace. Partly due to the volume of traffic, but also the necessity to negotiate lethal switchbacks. Adam glances into the rear view mirror. He sees the minibus that shadowed them up. It is escorting them down. When they emerge from a severe bend they see that the traffic ahead has thinned, creating a gap. Adam accelerates a tad. Another sweeping bend approaches. There is a violent impact, as the minibus jolts the car off the road.

"Are you alright, Gramps?"

He lifts his head, from where it lies against the steering wheel. A minor abrasion.

"That was expertly done," he muses wryly. "A warning, just a warning."

"You've got to report…"

"Later, later."

She looks at her Grandfather with deep concern.

"I promise, darling, I promise."

The traffic behind has come to a standstill. An excited crowd surrounds the vehicle. A face at the open window.

"Will your engine start, sir? We can push you back onto the road."

The engine fires, and a swarm of eager men ease them back onto the excuse for a highway.

"Thank you, thank you." They pull away.

Above the murmur of a dispersing crowd, someone shouts, "Go carefully, *Achchhe Pita*."

"Who was that?"

"Another 'friend' I expect. Just to press the point home. Come on, let's get to the bungalow."

"We're not going straight home, Gramps. Drive to the Orphanage..."

"But Mishka will be..."

"She will be waiting for you at the Orphanage."

The clouds have gone from Anna's brow, and her smile is as wide as the horizon beyond.

"What are you naughty girls up to?"

"A cunning plan. Cooked up by your two favourite women."

Good humour is restored. Adam thinks that old Rudyard K may have been right. Meet with triumph and disaster equitably, and you can accomplish anything.

"Orphanage it is. One thing, Anna. Not a word to Mishka about our mishap. I will tell her, but let's not spoil the party. It is a party, isn't it?"

"Mind your own beeswax. I remember you using that one of Great-Granny's when I was small."

Joy fills the beat-up old car.

"Happy birthday to you, Happy birthday to you,

Happy birthday Achchhe Pita, Happy birthday to you!"

Sixty children, in serried ranks, cheer the kind old man, whilst the adults gathered around him applaud. Mr. Devi, Chairman of the Orphanage committee raises his arms.

"That was very fine singing, children, well done. Now, what do you think? Does the *Achchhe Pita* deserve a special treat for his eightieth birthday?"

The excited children roar, "Yes sir, yes sir."

Mishka ushers two children forwards, from where they are hidden amidst the clamouring crowd. The girls do not exhibit shyness. Shining delight is in their eyes. Between them they carry an object, shrouded lightly in muslin. It is handled as if it were the *Koh-i-Noo*r diamond. Mined in India, but part of the British Crown Jewels. In Persian, the name means *'Mountain of Light'*. For Aasmi and Talika, rescued recently from the clutches of traffickers, that describes the Orphanage; they have been brought out of the Stygian inferno of slavery. The lot of so many girls and women throughout the world.

Mishka whispers. They ascend five steps onto the verandah. From their newly-acquired store of English they recite in perfect unison:

"Happy birthday, *Achchhe Pita*. This is for you. Thank you."

Overcome. They rush down the steps, and wrap themselves around Mishka.

Adam stares at the covered object. Looks at the sea of faces. Expectant. Smiles. Miles and miles of smiles.

"Remove the cover, Adam. *Jaldi, jaldi!*" Glee and delight in Jitendra Devi's tone.

"It's a bit…"

"You hold it, Adam. I shall reveal."

Jitendra, a successful purveyor of fine sarees and benefactor to the Orphanage, is a showman. He entices the children to an unbearable pitch of tension, before he removes the covering with tantalising languor.

"Oh my goodness! I don't know what to say. *'Rosa Osiria'*." He raises the rose bush high above his head, "My dream rose."

Mishka and Anna have joined him.

"Each child gave a little something, from the money they earn growing vegetables for the kitchen." Mishka.

Anna. "The widow's mite, Gramps. Plus, a contribution from Jitendra."

Adam stares at his prized rose. All he can say is, "Black, with red edges." He repeats himself, trance-like.

"Say something to the children, *pyaare*."

He raises his quivering voice for all to hear.

"Pride of place in my rose garden…pride of place. You are all so very kind…"

Jitendra steps in, as Adam restores himself.

"So, it is time for food. It is time for English birthday cake. Baked by Mrs. Sampson herself. I don't suppose any of you are hungry?"

A cacophony. "Yes we are," overwhelms his mischief, in Hindi and in English.

"Okay, okay, my starving little *bandaron*. I am thinking one more thing, before we eat."

To everyone's astonishment a flash of indigo blue glides above the assembly ground in flight. Gone into the trees, borne on a gasp of delight.

"Oh my, oh my!"

"What is it Jitendra?"

He indicates first the rose in Adam's hand.

"We are visited by rarities today, Adam. That, my friend, was a Nilgiri Flycatcher. As rare as hen's teeth, as you English say." Jitendra addresses the children. "A Nilgiri Flycatcher, *bandaron*. Most unusual. A good omen. What I was going to say was that we are very privileged to have amongst us a good man. Good men, and women, are also rare in this troubled world of ours. We must take great care of the *Achchhe Pita*. As Mr. William Shakespeare has written, there are seven ages for men. I hope that our good friend will not mind me saying, but he has

123

reached the seventh. He serves us, and we will serve him."

Adam chuckles inwardly. He recalls the end of that famous speech, from *'As You Like It'*. He is not quite ready for *'mere oblivion'*.

"Such a pity," Jitendra continues, "that we do not have someone who can provide a blessing on this day."

Mishka's voice resounds in the clear mountain air.

"But we do." She looks pointedly at Anna.

Anna gazes beyond everyone. Is there a sign in the distant hills? What better way to restart her ministry, wherever it may lead, than to bless her beloved Grandfather, and these children and the loving and generous people who provide for them. She steps forwards, and takes Adam's hand, then Mishka's.

"Lord of the Universe, I call upon you to bless each and everyone here on this day of loving celebration. We thank you for the gifts of food and drink before us. May the Spirit enter into us, and fill us with joy. In the name of Jesus Christ...and of *Kushmanda.*"

Chattering youngsters led away to satisfy their voracious appetites.

Mishka kisses her hand. "How do you know about *Kushmanda*, Anna?"

"Been sneaking a look at Gramp's books."

"Well, you couldn't have chosen a better goddess. You know, Hindu people believe she created the world with her divine smile? I do not believe that it could have been wider or happier than those I see today."

"Bishop Arthur wouldn't approve." Adam put his arm around her waist.

"Bugger Bishop Arthur! Whoever he may be."

"Billy, really..."

Anna interrupts Mishka's admonition.

"My sentiments exactly, Billy. Come on. I want some of this famous cake."

From indoors singing erupts.

"What's the song, Mishka?"

"It is a birthday song from a Bollywood film. I suspect it was taught to them by a very naughty rickshaw driver!"

Billy traverses the mountain road in stately fashion. "Damn fine fireworks."

"Indeed they were. Rounded off the best birthday I've ever had. I love fireworks. Always have done."

"I remember, Gramps. You always used to put on a display in your garden when I was small. Mum cooked yummy food, and Dad was grateful that he didn't have to do the job after a hard day's work."

"First time you've mentioned them. They'll be wondering where you are."

"I won't have been missed. They're in the Caribbean. Funnily enough, I think they're due home today, or is it tomorrow? Need to check my time zones."

"It is today, Anna."

She looks quizzically at Mishka, wondering how she can know.

"Shall I tell her Adam, or will you?"

"I had an email from your mum this morning, wishing me a happy birthday. She mentioned that she and Dave were home. They had a great time in St. Lucia."

"Did you...did you tell her...?"

"Not my place."

Mishka. "Mother's worry, Anna. It would be a kindness..."

"Now then, Mishka. Anna will choose the right time."

"Oy, oy, oy! Worry! My mother would give me the rounds of the kitchen if I went missing for more than twenty minutes when I was a boy. Not to mention a damn good crack across the back of the legs. She is a treasure to me..."

"If I know you, Billy, I expect you deserved it. Once a naughty boy, always a naughty boy."

"Thank you Mishka. You are quite correct. She had a slap like a midwife."

Laughter is stifled.

"What in the name of the Holy Ghost is that, guvnor? The sky is on fire."

The rickshaw gasps up the drive to the bungalow. Consternation, as they tumble out of their taxi.

"Oh Gramps!"

"*Pyaare*!"

Two women hold fast to an ashen Adam.

"Maadarchod."

Mishka ignores Billy's exclamation of *'motherfucker'*.

Adam detaches himself, and walks towards his rose garden. A fierce blaze illuminating the night sky. An eternity of deathly hush, then his shoulders droop. The solemn band weep before the burning bushes. Crackling thunder disrupts their mourning. Indian rains, sudden and brutal, thrash the fires.

An old man looks to the heavens, and drinks in the nectar of life.

"Too late," he screams above the storm, "but it saves us a job."

Purposefully, he strides to the rickshaw, and reaches within. They see him emerge clasping his gift; the precious *Rosa Osiria.* Adam lifts the plant high, once more, and walks towards his ruined land. In the rich and vibrant tone of a younger man he swears an oath.

"I swear by my Almighty and Loving Father I will not be defeated. In the name of my Saviour, Jesus Christ, I dedicate this gift, given in love, to the renewal of the blackened earth. Desecrated by the malice of evil men. I will persevere; I will run the race. No matter the cost."

The four of them relish the life-giving force of the tempest that drenches them.

On the other side of Ooty, secreted in the hills, two men sit with drinks. The house is large, and well-appointed. Ilaiyaraja Khan luxuriates in the comfort and prosperity of his home, built on procuring the misery of children.

"Was it a good party?"

"They showed him much honour."

"I am so pleased for the *Achchhe Pita*. Birthdays are important to sentimental Westerners. I hope that other events did not distress him too much."

"He had a quiet word with me about the incident on the road from Doddabetta. I shall, of course, make enquiries."

"May I pour you another drink?" Khan may be a gangster, but he values the old-fashioned virtue of hospitality. As he pours, he looks at his *'Serpenti Tubogas'* watch. The 18kt rose gold case seems appropriate, under the circumstances. "Our friend, Adam, should have discovered the housewarming present my boys clubbed together for by now." He presents the cut-glass tumbler to his guest. "If he is wise that will be an end to it."

His immaculately-dressed visitor sips the fine cognac.

"Regrettably, I think you are optimistic."

Khan smirks. "I am a good judge of character, Rasool. May he live out his days in peace, but I will not have him interfere with my business. If he does, then there will be a price to pay. A sum so vast that he will be bankrupt."

"How is the 'Palace of Delights'? I haven't had time to visit recently."

"It thrives, but new stock is always required. The jaded appetites of men need the constant tonic of fresh choices. Our good neighbour's Orphanage impinges upon that. Forgive me, Rasool, there are business matters which I must address."

Rasool downs the remainder of his drink. Shakes hands. Clasping the door handle, he pauses.

"What is it?"

"I respect your business acumen, Ilaiyaraja..."

An impatient wave gestures for him to come to the point.

"He is a man beyond our experience. A quite remarkable fellow, in his own way…"

"…but misguided."

Sycophantically. "Most certainly misguided. I do not think this will be the end of matters. I have spent much time beside him. He is a man of adamantine will and conviction."

Khan straightens his cuff.

"Excellent pun, Rasool." Checking the time on his ostentatious watch. "Then I shall be forced to escalate our actions, in order to persuade him. Perhaps the granddaughter?"

Rasool is alarmed. "Do whatever you feel necessary to protect your interests, but I recommend that you leave him and the young woman alone. They are still Westerners, and I'm not sure if I could deflect the problems that would come our way if either of them were to be harmed. My authority is limited."

Khan reflective. "Indeed…indeed, you are correct. Shame about the young woman. She is delightful. I had the pleasure of observing her in the Upper Bazaar. A bottom like the moon over the Ganges." Lascivious laughter pollutes the room. "A pity she is not twenty years younger. She would realise a fine profit for my organisation. Safe journey, my friend."

The driver salutes his passenger, as he emerges from the splendid property. He opens the rear passenger door for him.

"Home or office, sir?"

"Home, Jamal."

In the back of his official car Police Inspector Rasool Sharma reclines in comfort. So far he has lent Adam some good will, as instructed to by Khan, to create a facade. Now it is time to distance himself.

"How did you meet, Mishka?"

The measured insertion of the needle punctures another hole in the material. Adam has insisted that they remain indoors whilst he toils in his garden of ashes. Quite suddenly the needle is suspended.

"Weeping, Anna. He found me weeping in the street. That is unremarkable. The streets of India are filled with women like me in despair." She begins to sew once more. "It was the blood. My bloodied nose, and the blood seeping onto my ankles that made him approach me."

Anna is as motionless as an Easter Island statue.

"When Adam spoke to me I was frightened. I thought that he wanted what other men had wanted from me. When I had the courage to look up I knew that I was wrong. Sorrow and love were etched across his face."

"What happened then?"

"He took me to a doctor, and from there to the Orphanage. Whilst the doctor was patching me up he spoke of the children, and said that they were in need of another helper." Mishka's expert sewing makes her hands fly. "Our love for each other came from working beside one another. Finished. Get changed, and we will present you to your grandfather."

Adam works slowly. Clearing a circle in the midst of the ruined rose garden. Mulching and watering the hole he has dug. Two days have passed since the devastation. On the first his women had insisted that he rest. Now he works; dogged and determined.

"Pyaare."

"Just a moment, darling." Bent low he continues to water the parched earth. "What is it?"

He turns to see two women in their sarees. One drapes a piece to cover her face. Regally, she reveals herself. A shout of delight.

"What a surprise. You look wonderful, Anna. I..."

A small lorry enters the drive. Six muscular young men leap from the open back. Apprehension. The sound of a cranky engine *"phut phuts"*. Billy's rickshaw swings round the static lorry.

"Sorry I am late, ladies and guvnor. A minor mechanical difficulty. Adam, my friend, may I introduce my nephews – well, half of them."

"Billy, you have the better of me. What...?"

The eldest of the party steps forwards.

"Sir, we would be honoured if you would permit us to assist you in the restoration of your garden?"

Adam doesn't know what to say, until his women link his arms and tell him.

"Yes is the word you're looking for. Yes, please."

Adam bursts into life.

"Drinks, a drink before we make a start. No wait!" He stoops and picks up the *Rosa Osiria*. "First we dedicate this token of rare beauty to the task ahead."

A circle forms. The weather-beaten hands of an old man place the rose in the earth. He invites two pairs of feminine hands to join with his. Tenderly, they press the earth around its base. Baritone voices sing around them.

"Baar baar haan, bolo yaar haan

Apni jeet ho, unki haar haan..."

(Again and again, say this my friend

May victory be ours and defeat be theirs...)

The lusty note of an engine, accompanied by the sick splutter of a tired rickshaw fade with the twilight. Much has been accomplished. The young men have been fed and watered, and now they are gone. Payment has been refused. Madan, the eldest, spoke for them all.

"*Achchhe Pita*, whatever you would give to us, please donate to your Orphanage."

Adam rests his whiskey and soda on the plain side table.

"Billy told me that all his nephews are godly people. It cheered me no end. Only one of them is Christian, like Billy, but all follow paths of peace according to their creed."

"That's something I've never quite understood, Gramps."

"What's that?"

"Over the years I've watched numerous TV programmes, back home, and whenever the British Empire is discussed it's always the same diatribe. The terrible missionaries oppressing the native peoples."

"There is some truth in that, Anna, but it's way off the mark in India."

Mishka interjects.

"Actually, Anna, the old East India Company did everything it could to keep the missionaries out. Business first. Before 1813 no British missionaries lived or practised in India."

"You're very well informed, Mishka."

Wife and husband exchange smiles.

"Do you like history, Anna?"

"I do, very much…"

"…and where does this enthusiasm come from?"

"From someone sitting not a million miles from where we are."

"Me too. I caught the bug from Adam. He thought that it would be good for me to know more about my own country."

Adam snorts into his drink.

"Would that the trendy ignoramuses in Britain learnt a bit more about their past. Even more important, taught it in the schools without bias. Good and bad is the story of every country on the planet. There's light and dark in the history of all nations. Light that lifts our feet to walk jauntily through life, and darkness that forces us to trudge painfully along. That's in the DNA of every individual, and individuals make nations."

Anna hesitates. Her dear old Gramps has passed through a horrible trial in the last couple of days. She takes the plunge.

"Where has the darkness been in your life, Gramps?"

Mishka shocked. "Anna…"

Adam chuckles. "Now, now, Mishka. I'm old, but not that feeble. I think my little dumpling wants a story."

"Not if you don't want to tell."

Adam sips steadily from his glass. They dwell in anticipation. He rises and pours himself another *chota peg.*

"You will not like me!"

A rejoinder of "What?" is exclaimed.

"The next part of my life is filled with successes and excesses. Underpinning them is the unedifying principle of 'Self'. You may not like me afterwards." Before they can respond. "But I will tell you."

*

West

Salisbury Cathedral may be observed from the cardinal points of the compass, whichever approach to the city you take. The 123 metre spire keeps the cathedral in view. Adam had stopped in the city for a bite to eat. The pub he patronised had the higgledy-piggledy roofline of old England. When he left he noticed Faux-Medieval script on a board.

"Go in peace. Go gently pilgrim."

Adam was journeying to his first teaching post. Brindle House, a co-educational boarding school located close to the nearby town of Wilton. Teaching in a private school was not a political choice. It was simply the first job he was offered.

He secured his helmet, and mounted the Kawasaki 500 that had carried him from the North. An uneventful journey on a beautiful Late-August day. The rucksack he bore was huge, containing most of his worldly possessions. Adam had spent his maintenance grant freely during teacher training. Not much had been reserved. Anyway, he would be sharing a furnished property with another teacher, set within the grounds of the wonderful Brindle House. When the pay cheques rolled in there would be ample opportunity for more conventional accumulation. The engine fired, and he was back on the road.

Wilton's heritage dates to the Anglo-Saxons. If people know it at all it is for the manufacture of carpets. Wilton House is the home of the Earls of Pembroke. Their shapes and shifts over the centuries mean that they have done very nicely, thank you. Public schools abound across Wiltshire. Brindle House was a later addition to the club, founded after the Second World War. Adam exited the city on the A36, joining a stream of holiday traffic. Passing through Bemerton, he was on the Wilton Road. "Nobbut a cock stride" from Wilton, as his Mum liked to say about short distances. He was heading for Fugglestone St. Peter on the fringes of Wilton. The school lay a mile or so beyond, in countryside to die for.

He processed along the Avenue with ever-increasing excitement. Away from home, the North left far behind. A new life, free of constraints. The training years had seen him take wing. A flight of friends, alcohol and sport. The car creeping out of a drive, to his left, was forty metres away. He decided to give a warning toot on the horn. The rickety old Citroen sprawled across the pavement, the tip of its nose breaching the roadway. Serenely, Adam swept onwards to his destiny. Like the proverbial bullet, the car shot forward. A shriek of "Noooo!" rent the air, and Adam catapulted over the bonnet, turning a somersault in the process. He hit the tarmac back first, and slid to a halt fifteen metres down the road. Nobody had the grace to raise a card to declare "A superb 9.9!" A grizzled old geezer loomed over his supine frame.

"You stay there, my lovely. We'll soon 'ave you some help."

Old Scrotum, the wrinkled retainer, dematerialised like a rootless spectre condemned to prowl the Earth eternally. He was replaced by a most fetching lady, who knelt beside Adam and took his hand. His balls had connected with the petrol cap on the 'Kwacker', and started to throb.

"It's alright, my love, the ambulance is on the way. Where does it hurt?"

No way could he tell this elegant and attractive lady that the family jewels were giving him grief. They weren't helped by the caressing touch of her hand, and the musky scent dazzling his senses. For the next eight days he walked like Big John Wayne. A shadow came to his rescue.

"Is he moving at all, Lucy?"

A man knelt, and draped a picnic blanket over him.

"Can you wiggle your toes – what's your name?"

"Adam. Yes, they're doing a jig."

She exhaled the laughter of relief. Adam raised a hand to scratch an itchy nose. Lucy noticed the free turn of his head, and undid the chinstrap.

"When I remove the helmet, Roger, place the blanket under Adam's head."

Roger hovered, like the Angel of Death. A rather inappropriate analogy. A snow-white clerical collar glowed against the pristine blue sky. The clamouring bell of the ambulance rent the air. In two shakes of a lamb's doodle (Annie Sampson was never far away), he and Lucy were in the back of it. She was still holding his hand, and a priapic summons fell into Adam's lap.

"I was a nurse before Roger and I married, a Sister. Roger is a quite dreadful driver. I'm so sorry."

Adam's grey cells went into overdrive. So, taken out by the vicar.

"Wouldn't mind taking his missus out."

For one ghastly moment he thought that he'd spoken out loud. The muttering, however, resided in the canyon of his overheated imagination. He risked a forensic examination. Lucy had a smile that was responsible for climate change. Her big blue eyes were complemented by the most kissable lips God ever created.

"Nearly there, old son." The driver's partner sat in the back with them. "Soon have you checked out to see what's in working order."

Adam thought he detected the flicker of a grin. His hands emerged from beneath the blanket and folded over his groin. Lucy's eyes locked with his. It was a case of mongoose and snake. The vehicle drew to a halt, and the back doors opened. Lucy stepped down. Driver and mate manoeuvred the stretcher.

"By gum, you're a big lad, aren't you?"

For one terrible second, Adam thought that the resemblance of the blanket to a wigwam had been noticed. They wheeled him into Casualty, and straight in to a cubicle. Lucy stood well back. As he was leaving the grinning ambulance man leant over him. Accompanied by a leery wink he whispered,

"She is, isn't she?"

Adam rocked a little with laughter.

"You'll be right as rain in no time, old son. Turning tricks before you can say 'Jack Robinson'. Mind how you go, and get yourself a car. Bloody dangerous, motorbikes." He came close once more. "Far more comfortable as well. You'd be amazed how convenient they are for all sorts of antics. Tarrar."

"Lovely to see you smiling, Adam. You don't mind me calling you Adam?"

His hand reached out purposely. He wanted to touch her. Fingers clasped.

"Not at all Lucy."

"Where were you travelling to you, before you were so rudely interrupted?"

"To start my very first job."

"Oh my goodness. I hope this isn't going to cause you problems."

"It shouldn't, term doesn't start for another week. Reckon I'll be fine by then."

"You're a teacher?"

"Newly-qualified."

"Hang on, young man," she said. "If you were heading in that direction there's only one possible place you could be going to…"

Together, they exclaimed: "Brindle House!"

"Yep, joining the P.E. department."

She looked mortified. "So, so sorry. You really do need to get back on your feet for that job." Lucy peeked at her watch. "I must go. Don't worry, we've given the police our details, and they'll pass yours on to us when your fit to tell them. You mustn't be concerned about your Kawasaki. We'll make sure everything is paid for. Best be off. Roger will need a hand with the police – again. God bless you."

Her hand seemed to woo the curtains, as she parted them. She stopped to look back at him. He could only distinguish her pliant silhouette. The intimate Sun, behind her, produced ripples before his eyes.

"You know, Adam, there's every chance that we'll meet again."

The virgin soil of an erotic Utopia was splintered by a brisk voice.

"Now, young man, what have you been up to?"

Adam blushed scarlet as Sister Ratcliffe pulled back the sheet.

"Lucky that rucksack cushioned your landing."

*

Women fall in love for many reasons. When they decide to marry they take a longer view. Safety is paramount. Lucy sat naked on her bedroom stool, drying her hair. Roger was everything to her. He wasn't a great lover, but her early adult years had provided sex enough for a lifetime. Except...except she knew that the periodic tsunami of erotic feeling was about to sweep over her. She never knew when it would happen. Six months, nine, a year. Come it would, and she knew that she would have to purge it in a furnace of fury. Sometimes she could extinguish the fire with the aid of her box of tricks, secreted safely away from prying eyes. Once, since she and Roger had married, she had betrayed him. Her dearest friend had died in an accident, and later that year she had gone to London to visit Dan, the widower. Roger had insisted she stay overnight somewhere. Lucy returned late the following evening, after nearly twenty-four hours of hedonistic sexual indulgence with Dan. It didn't entirely quell the rumbling fault line within her, but it made life tolerable. Guilt did not consume her. She loved Roger. His kindness, his grace. *His* love did not stem from the collar around his neck; they were the essence of the man.

Lucy peered into the mirror and was startled. For a nanosecond Adam's face stared back at her. She felt so cold, even though the summer sun blazed outside, that she quickly put on her dressing gown. Looking out of the window, she murmured to herself:

"Where on earth did you come from?"

She could see Roger watering the flower beds. It was nice little vicarage set on the outskirts of Wilton. The other side of the town from where they had sent Adam flying from his motorcycle. She pictured him lying in various positions: on the road, in the ambulance and in the cubicle. At each stage of the journey to the hospital she had observed his character emerge, as he realised that he wasn't badly injured. It wasn't all she observed. Her past life had given her an intimate knowledge of the ways of men. Lucy wrapped her arms around herself, "I like him." She returned to the stool, and examined the thought in the mirror. Frowning, she couldn't quite fathom the attraction. He must be ten years younger than her. A jolt upset her equilibrium as she realised the kernel of his allure. There was something of Roger about him. Her husband was forty-five, and that young man could only be twenty-one or two, but they shared a look. Neither could hide their feelings. In Roger's eyes she always saw love that was unafraid. It streamed from him. Flowing like a river that knew its source, and knew its end. Her frown expressed concern for Adam. She had seen that same love, but confused and mingling with lust. It was the core of him that he could never disguise. An overwhelming pity rose within her, because she recognised love throttled by fear. A dam of hesitation held it in check. She didn't want to think about it any longer. Shaking her hair free from the towel, she moved to the open window.

"Roger, Roger!"

Her beloved husband waved a hand.

"Give me ten minutes to get dressed, darling, and we'll go out for breakfast."

Roger beamed at her, and gave a thumbs up.

A quarter of an hour later she descended the stairs. Foresight made her pause halfway down.

"When I meet that young man again, I must be careful. For his sake."

*

Wendy Gunnerson made a sudden and unannounced entry into his bedroom. He had been standing at the window counting his blessings. Adam had survived what could have been a nasty accident. Now he was safe within Brindle House's vales of advancement and prosperity. To the right, he could see Abel Goodrich's manicured lawns. The west wing of the Palladian mansion was visible through the trees. Early Sunday morning. A ground mist lay soporific over the bucolic scene; a harbinger of autumn. The sun was not yet warm, but it would be. It would shine like a beneficent father watching over his sleeping children. As the shape-shifter moulded the mist, Adam saw a hare sitting bolt upright. He laughed aloud, recollecting that hares are symbols of ambition, fitness and virtue.

"Wuhay! Nice budgie smugglers. What are you laughing at?"

Wendy, as affirmed by Abel Goodrich, was a fine big lass. She was also the School Secretary and shared the house with Adam, and Des Jones who had lately arrived. Following the accident, she collected him from Salisbury General. Wendy tended him over the next few days with carnivorous delight. More than once she offered a blanket bath. When Adam declined she would exit his bedroom, her shin length skirt sweeping a path before her, singing raucously.

"Get your gums around my plums, doo da, doo da,

Make a luncheon of my truncheon, doo da, doo da day!"

Wendy was five feet seven inches, and fourteen stones of muscle. Her summer blouse revealed the forearms and biceps of a farm labourer in prime condition.

"What time is it, Wend?"

"The sun will soon be over the yardarm."

"My God, it's a bit early for more ale."

"Lightweight. Get your threads on boy, and I'll treat you to breakfast in the village."

Wendy drove her sporty number through the lanes with gay abandon.

"Nice motor Wend. Quite fancy it…"

"Have we time?" she cackled. Innuendo was her stock-in-trade. "Pass your test, and you can have one. Keep you off those bloody motorbikes. Don't fancy a funeral – I can't afford the wreath on what 'Quackers' pays me."

Adam lay back, allowing the burgeoning sun to bathe his face, whilst his ponytail flew out behind him. A pleasant thought emerged. That ambulance man and Wendy shared a similar view of what you could get up to in the back of a car. Lucy.

"Who is she?"

"I beg your pardon."

Wendy shifted gear with a grinding thrust, to match her throaty laugh.

"I know that look, shit legs. You've got someone on your mind – and possibly your groin! Here we are. *'Widow's Memories'* for me this morning." The allusion to sausages was not lost on Adam.

They sat over their second mug of tea, whilst Wendy assaulted her toast and marmalade.

"Right Wend, get me up to speed again. Who am I meeting at this barbecue?"

"Dear God! Did you take a crack on the head when you fell off the 'bike? I've told you twice already; gormless northern git."

"Kiss my arse!"

"Yes please." You couldn't win with Wendy.

"Details woman, details."

"Right. Number one. Rodney Porter D.S.O. - dick shot off; Headmaster, accompanied by his delightful missus, Pippa. Think Trevor Howard and Celia Johnson in *'Brief Encounter'*. Two. The Bursar. Major Donald 'Quackers' Muir O.B.E. – other bugger's efforts - with the Bride of Frankenstein on his arm; she runs the local coven. Sally, biology and vegetable plot, and a few of the other inmates who teach here. Your esteemed Head of P.E., Des Jones, will run the bar. I fear that you two single gentlemen will cause riot, mayhem and dampness amongst the sixth form girls. Last, and deservingly least, Estate Manager Harvey 'shit legs' Edrich and his wife. She's as dim as a nun's night light, but they've managed to produce two rather charming teenagers. I suspect dark practices on a barren heath, lit only by the harvest moon."

"Don't hold back, Wend, say what you think."

"Knock that brew back. I said I'd give Abel a lift with the barbecue."

Adam grinned. "Fine looking man Abel. Speaks well of you."

Wendy blushed alcoholic red. "Kiss *my* arse!"

"Can I think about that?"

Wendy grabbed him, and jostled him towards the door.

"No, no," he squealed, "no tickling. I'm in a delicate condition."

"'ere Wendy," a shout came from behind the counter. "Put that young man down. He needs a woman with experience."

"I'll save a bit for you to spread your marmalade on, Betty, or a sausage for your mustard! Great breakfast. Tarrar."

Rodney "Oh Mr." Porter was not 'away with the fairies', as Wendy had suggested. He enquired after Adam's health, and then expatiated upon the school's liberal tradition. His accent resembled that of Wimbledon commentator Dan Maskell. 'Catch' came out as 'cetch'. Pippa, his spouse, was charming and gracious. A Tory lady of the shires who smacks of the firm mummy and the coy temptress. Almost certainly a goer, in her younger days. Wendy handed him on to Sally Humphreys, whilst she withdrew to manhandle hot dogs.

"Gird your loins, Adam. I suppose I'd better present you to the Bursar."

It is a curiosity of public school life that retired military personnel are deemed adequate for the post of resident accountant. Perhaps the distinction of rank recommends financial acumen and probity. Major Donald 'Quackers' Muir considered himself a wit. Sally remarked later.

"Well, he's half right!"

Fruity Morningside tones lilted on the still air of the Grove.

"Ah, the young man who will be engaged with physical jerks. We've certainly a few of those in the Upper Remove. One or two pieces of paper for you to sign. My office, Monday morning, ten sharp! You will then enjoy a tour of the premises, accompanied by my *aide de camp* Harvey Edrich."

The 'Commandant' strode away, salt and pepper hair receding into the distance. Joyce, his wife, threw a piercing look backwards at Adam.

Her moon face hung upon an over-pronounced lower mandible. A lumpen woman, looking permanently out of temper. Military wives revel in an over-conscious sense of their husband's status. They feel it is conferred upon them by proxy. Would Adam be useful to them? The brevity of her glance found him wanting.

Sally guided him towards the barbecuing genius of Harvey Edrich. Wendy wielded a nine-incher on her fork.

"Wuhay! Harvey – Adam, and vicky versa. Fancy a large one, Sal?"

Sally began to sing. *"Anything you can do I can do better…"*

Harvey Edrich remained po-faced.

"Pleased to meet you, Harvey."

The Estate Manager didn't look up.

"Saw you talking with Abel Goodrich yesterday."

"He was pointing me towards Wendy in the Office."

"Wuhay! Must buy him a pint."

"Don't like my lads interrupted when they're working. Burger or hot dog?" Before Adam could fathom the source of such rudeness, Harvey addressed a body behind him. "Afternoon Chaplain. Burger or hot dog?"

Adam looked up at Sally's shapely six-foot frame. Her eyebrows lifted.

"I think a beef burger for me, please. What will you have, darling?"

A silken voice, as chirpy as the birds singing in the Grove, said,

"Hot dog for me, please Mr. Edrich."

Adam felt his bowels melt, and turned to face the new arrivals.

"Goodness gracious! Yes, yes, of course. I'm so glad to hear that you're on the road to recovery. I don't know how I can begin to repay you for my appalling ineptitude…"

"Adam, darling, this is Adam."

He felt the pulse drumming in his ears. She had remembered his name.

"Of course. Sorry to have forgotten. Rather a traumatic experience we went through together. Slipped my mind."

"That's alright, Roger."

"Gracious, you remember my name. I feel quite ashamed."

"I heard your wife…" he hesitated, "Lucy call to you, whilst I was lying prone." He felt the need to elevate his status. "Actually, supine."

Roger was puzzled. Then it dawned on him.

"Oh, quite, quite. You know, I rather admire that Adam. So important to be precise with words."

Wendy approached. "And lo, she came from the East bearing gifts. Here you go, your Grace, one burger for the use of."

"You are a dreadful woman Wendy Gunnerson. Elevating me above my station."

"We all need a bit of boost to our spirits now and again." Waving a monstrous hot dog, she advanced on Lucy. "Here you go, my gal, get your laughing tackle round that." A sparkling hint of complicity passed between the ladies. "Permit me to formally introduce, Mr. Adam Sampson M.M. – motorcycle maniac. Lying flat on your back is no way to meet the School Chaplain, and especially not his wife."

Wendy was sailing close to the wind. Lucy didn't know what was more troubling.

Suppressing the desire to guffaw at her old friend's innuendo, or dismissing the burst of desirable images shooting into her womb.

Roger piped up, "A pair of fine biblical names, Adam Sampson. Mankind's first procreator, supported by the strength for the task."

"I'm shocked, your reverence. What is the Church of England coming to when men of the cloth are risqué?"

Roger looked nonplussed, then it dawned. "Oh, I say Wendy. I didn't mean…"

He laughed along with the rest of them. As it tailed off, Lucy's honeyed voice said smoothly.

"And gorgeous long hair as well." She stared at him boldly. "Better make sure Wendy doesn't shear you, Adam." For good measure she added, "The goatee beard works well in tandem."

"Whatever tickles your fancy."

Wendy received a thump in the back from Sally Humphreys.

"Come on Wend, I need another drink. Adam, you look like you need a stiff one." Sally addressed Roger. "Poor lad has been in the lion's den, meeting everyone. Excuse us." She gave Wendy a pointed look.

They each took an arm, and frogmarched him away.

"Harvey, another pint?"

The barbecuing demon raised a thumb.

"Nice to see you again." Adam threw the remark over his shoulder to Lucy and Roger.

"Put your tongue back in, Sampson," Wendy smirked.

The two women tightened their grip on him.

Sally mused. "The vicar's wife. Well, well, well."

"You dirty little boy!"

"Stop it you two. I don't know whether I'm coming or going."

The remark made them squeal even more.

"Hey Des. Three reds, and a pint for Ada Camp."

Barman Des Jones poured; Adam enquired.

"Who's Ada Camp?"

"Fill him in Sal while I deliver his pint."

"Harvey Edrich." Adam looked bemused. "Bursar...*aide de camp*...remember?"

"Oh, yeh, yeh."

Wendy came bustling into view. She reminded him of his Mum so many youthful years ago. Standing amongst new friends in the sunshine he felt the soothing warmth of a home he thought long lost.

"Did he get it Sal?"

"Eventually."

"Ignore the pair of old trollops mate." Des Jones glugged from the bottle. "You know Wendy's nickname? The Titanic – all hands went down on her."

The screeching noise drew looks from far and wide. Adam revolved a slow three-hundred and sixty degrees. Lucy was nowhere to be seen. In the languid heat of an English summer, the smoke from the barbecue was almost too lazy to rise. Hope in Adam's heart soared into the heavens. Bright days ahead.

*

Vanessa Goody was Deputy-Head teacher. Carping, crusty, a repository of cant, and by common consent deserving of another title beginning with 'C'. In her early-forties, her skin was graveyard white. It sagged in visible and, thankfully, invisible places. Her haircut was so severe that a butch lesbian would have declined to adopt the style. She worked extremely hard, but possessed an insuperable problem. Her entire existence revolved around the pupils. The view of female colleagues was that her manic devotion was a surrogate for the life she desired, but had not the courage to grasp. Adam would witness this, *ad nauseum*, as he progressed through his career. Single male teachers are also prone to this inhibited and stifled life. It was something he was determined to resist. The demands of public school life are heavy. It's so easy to engross yourself in teaching, trips, and incestuous socialising. If you are fortunate, the day is never realised when the cavern of despair opens and you discover that there is nothing else.

Sally Humphreys stood beside the photocopier, whilst Adam was trading banter with Wendy.

"You should be charitable to Abel. He's got hidden depths."

"There's something living in his beard. I swear…" Wendy reacted to the office door swinging open.

"Ah so!" Vanessa exclaimed her habitual catchphrase to fill awkward silences. "Adam, I see that you are free before lunch. The Headmaster and I would like a word in his study." She became coy. "I was wondering if you might also spare me some time after tea?"

"For what, Miss Goody?"

Sally and Wendy buried themselves in work to stifle their wickedness.

"Oh, do call me Vanessa. We're almost at the end of your first year. Would you be able to drive me into Salisbury? I need to proof read the School Magazine at the printers. Perhaps I could treat you to afternoon tea, as a reward for your kind services."

Wendy was almost apoplectic. Sally gripped the photocopier to control her impression of a Quaking Aspen.

"I'm so sorry, Vanessa, but we have house cricket matches at four-thirty."

"Ah so. Right. Headmaster's study then in an hour." She hurried from the room.

Wendy leapt to her feet and faced Sally. They each put the palms of their hands together, and bowed obsequiously. A pair of pantomime Chinese ladies exclaimed.

"Arrrrrr...se'oles!"

"Wuhay! Fill your boots."

"Dip your bread!"

"Sod off the pair of you."

Sally opined. "She fancies you rotten, does the Desperate Deputy."

Wendy stuck her oar in. "A diversion down one of the lanes, and you could flash your sticky wicket at her."

"Give over you two. It'd be like throwing a banger up the Blackwall Tunnel. Eh, I've had an idea. Give Maggie Ansell a call, and tell her she can get back into 'Goody Two Shoes' favour by giving her a lift."

"Not a bad idea, my lad. Since she found our esteemed Matron pissed as a fart she's been less than friendly."

Sally added. "Maggie will be three sheets to the wind by four this afternoon. Could be an interesting ride into Salisbury."

"Right. Basketball in the Gym. See you later. Boozer tonight?"

"Do bears shit in the woods?"

Sally grabbed Adam's arm. "Wonder what the old man wants to see you for? Not been furgling the Sixth Form have you?"

Wendy coughed, and took an inordinate interest in her pencil sharpener. Sally's antennae vibrated. She loomed over the Secretary's desk.

"You know something, don't you?"

Wendy rearranged her desk, nonchalantly.

"Maybe I do; maybe I don't." Her rubicund cheeks glowed, and she smiled at Adam affectionately. "Nothing to worry about. You may learn something to your advantage." Then she looked sad. "Unfortunately, it will be to someone else's disadvantage."

Adam thought that he had come a long way in the last year. Indeed, he had, but it wasn't always the right way. Callously, he quipped.

"*C'est la vie*, or as the French say, 'That's life!' See ya."

"There we have it then, Adam. If you are agreeable, you will take over as Acting Head of Department with immediate effect. Subject to a satisfactory probation period, of shall we say a term, you will be confirmed in post.

Adam was thunderstruck, and lost for words. Vanessa spoke.

"Of course, it has come early in your teaching career, but we have observed you closely since you arrived at Brindle House. We have absolute confidence in you."

"May I ask what's happening to Des…I mean Mr. Jones? We live together – well, you know that – I mean, he hasn't said anything about leaving."

Rodney Porter looked pained, and Vanessa Goody was glacial.

"Ahum." Rodney cleared his throat. "Affairs concerning other members of staff are confidential. It would be indiscreet…" his words tailed off.

"Let me assure you, Adam, that Mr. Jones, Des, will be fine. We have given him the very best of references. He speaks highly of you, both as colleague and as friend."

"May we have your decision, Adam?"

"Yes, yes Headmaster. My answer is yes."

Rodney Porter rose, and hands were shaken.

"You will receive the usual HOD allowance, with immediate effect. Perhaps you'd be kind enough to join Vanessa in her office for fifteen minutes? She will brief you on the wider responsibilities of the post."

"Do sit, Adam."

Vanessa arranged herself decoratively on the magisterial chair. The Georgian window behind her was a portal for sunlight to flood the room. At his moment of triumph, Adam visualised Nelson Horsley staring out of his office window on that bleak January day. He was dazzled by the sunshine, and a phantom silhouette took shape. A kindly man held hands with an elfin girl. They smiled with pleasure and approval.

"Adam, Adam!"

"I'm so sorry, Vanessa. Have to say I'm rather overcome by the swiftness of events."

During the past year many changes had borne fruit. Adam's accent and manner of speech had undergone a minor transformation. It wasn't affectation, merely the product of exposure to people who had once been beyond his ken. He was startled, and swore later to Sally and Wendy that he had heard Rose Hanson declare:

"There is a world elsewhere."

"Perhaps now is not quite the time to go into the details of running a department. I'll consult my diary, and make you a proposal. Donald Muir will prepare an amended contract." Vanessa sashayed round to the front of her capacious desk. She hoisted herself on to the edge of it, crossing her ankles. Her pleated tartan skirt draped above the knee.

"Not bad legs," Adam concluded. "Oh well, she's got one good point."

"At seven-thirty this evening, I'm hosting a wee drinks party in my apartment. It will be an opportunity for you to meet some rather influential people from the surrounding area. Dame Jocelyn Farrow will be there. You know her work? One of our leading sculptors. Naturally, Jeremy Morton, our poet in residence will be present. When isn't he, if free drink is available?" Her false laugh was covered by a hand, like a Georgian lady brandishing her fan. "How dreadfully indiscreet I am. The Brigadier and his lady have kindly consented to pop in for half an hour…"

"I'm afraid that…"

"…and one or two others. Oh yes, Roger Birch and his wife will be there. He was enquiring after you the other day. Still anxious for your health after that most unfortunate accident. His eyesight is quite dreadful. Sometimes, I think, he can't see what's under his nose." Another staccato laugh.

"Thank you. Yes, I'd be delighted to accept your kind invitation."

He hadn't seen Lucy up close since the week before Easter. She had attended the school's Easter service before they broke for the holiday. Most of the time he was too damn busy to think about anyone. Periodically he caught a glimpse of her in the distance, collecting Roger in her Triumph Stag convertible.

"Ah so. Goodness gracious. Nearly lunchtime. Will you join me in the Refectory for a bite?"

Adam suspected that Vanessa could give Wendy a run for her money in the innuendo stakes.

"If you'd forgive me, there's rather a lot to take on board. Think I'll draw breath for a while."

She uncrossed her legs and stood foursquare.

"Quite so. Off you trot then."

Adam held the door handle.

"I don't suppose you could enlighten me, just a little, about Des…"

Vanessa straightened papers on her desk. Assuming an imperious pose, she said:

"Shall we say, one or two discrepancies in his accounting procedure for the departmental allowance. Not to worry, we'll see you don't go short."

He was halfway through the door when her siren tone held him.

"Remember Adam, my door is always open – to you!"

Tilly Ashton popped up the instant he entered the crowded room, in the West Wing of the great house.

"Hi sir, what can I get you?" Her wide-eyed smile enveloped him.

"Glass of red please, Tilly."

A bevy of sixth form girls, supplemented by a couple of boys, were serving drinks and canapés. Adam maintained surveillance on Tilly's long legs as they devoured the room. Engrossed in their bronzed beauty, he failed to notice his First XV Captain, Josh Meyer, sidle up against him.

"They go all the way up to her arse, sir!"

"Shush, you're a naughty boy, She's coming back. Here, let me have some scran, I'm famished."

"Here we are Mr. Sampson. It's the good stuff the old witch keeps hidden."

"Tilly, Tilly, Tilly, you and this young man should be thoroughly ashamed of yourselves. You both need spanking."

Three pairs of eyes locked in merry complicity.

"Give me a whistle when you need a refill, sir. You know how to whistle, don't you?"

Together, the sixth-formers declaimed, "Just put your lips together and blow."

"Thank you Lauren and Humphrey. Now sod off, and get on with your duties. By the way, you scrub up well. Like a dog's dinner, as my old Mum used to say."

Vanessa grasped him, linking his arm.

"Come and have a word with the Brigadier. He's anxious to meet you. I believe that he once played for Blackheath. The same club as Dr. Watson, you know."

Her face was impassive, and her tone sincere. On second thoughts, he decided it was best not to tell her that Sherlock's partner had been added to the roster of one of Rugby Union's most famous clubs by Arthur Conan Doyle. The Brigadier was a decent sort, only half-raising an eyebrow when Adam mentioned the introduction of Rugby League training methods into the boys' Union sessions.

"You made a very good impression Adam." Her grip tightened, asserting proprietorial rights. "Let's have a chat with Dame Jocelyn. Oh God, quickly, Jeremy Morton's heading in our direction."

Adam had been collared by the erstwhile poet in the School Office one morning. Ten o' clock and reeking of sherry.

"Do you know my work? Printed on sheepskin. Adds a certain *frisson* for the reader. The foreword is written by my dear chum David Lemming. You know his films. Did I ever tell you about that most amusing scene in *'Gather Ye Rosebuds'*? Got his rapier caught in his codpiece, and…"

"Jeremy."

"Yes Wendy, my darling?"

"You recited the frigging story six times in the pub last night."

"Ah, yes. Rather forgetful these days. Well, must tootle along." He paused in the doorway. "I say Wendy; hope you don't mind me asking again. No chance of shag one of these days?"

"Give over Jeremy. The state you're in you'd need a stirrup pump to get it up."

"Right, right...cheerio then. I'm quite well known, you know."

Adam's attention refocused upon the famous sculptress. She was rolling a ciggie, between barking coughs.

"That's a fine looking specimen you have on your arm, Vanessa. Fancy posing for me, young man? Ten quid an hour, and as much Burgundy as you can glug." Her trombone voice bore the authentic note of the county set. She laced her conversation with an imaginative range of epithets and obscenities. He liked her.

Adam was in transports of delight. Dancing angels skipped even more lightly when he saw

Lucy Birch enter the room, with Roger in tow. He saw his chance.

"Would you excuse me. The Chaplain and his wife have arrived, Vanessa. I should take the opportunity to set his mind at rest." She looked puzzled. "That I'm fighting fit after our little set-to in the Avenue."

It dawned on her. "Very thoughtful of you, Adam."

"May I replenish your drinks?"

Dame Jocelyn thrust a scarred hand between her legs. "Got a bottle of the good jollop here. Jeremy Morton sniffed out your stash, Vanessa, and that's not a euphemism." She roared at her own wit. "That man could nose out a pint of shandy in a warehouse stacked with Chanel No. 5. Here gal, let me top you up. Put a bit of lead in your pencil – well, in your eraser."

Adam slipped his arm from Vanessa's. The last words he overheard were flattering.

"Wouldn't mind a gander at that chap in his posing pouch."

Vanessa was all a flutter. "Oh, Jocelyn, really!" A wistful look over her shoulder revealed that she was inclined to agree.

Before he reached Rev. and Mrs. Birch the former moved away. He found himself alone before Lucy.

"Love the shirt, complements your jeans."

Off duty. Adam wore a loose collarless white shirt, and ice blue jeans with sandals. Comfort for a warm summer evening. God, what was it with these women? He was aware that he was a presentable young man, but didn't regard himself as especially handsome or debonair. Possibly, it was all in his imagination. What Adam didn't fathom was that they were not attracted solely by his trim young figure, but by his openness. It was a rarity, in their environment, to come across someone who spoke so passionately and unguardedly. There were times when he said things that might be best left unspoken, but it portrayed him as daring. Older women imagined the *frisson* they might get from handling him, not a piece of sheepskin – unless it was the rug they were entwined upon.

"Your dress is beautiful..." She didn't reply, "...and I'm in love with your car."

"I see you've adopted more comfortable transport these days."

"Yes, took everyone's advice, and transferred to four wheels."

"The GT6 is a gorgeous little car."

"How…?"

"Wendy! Heard about your promotion too. You are on the up."

"The jungle telegraph, eh. I only accepted eight hours ago. "Wendy!" came simultaneously from both their lips.

"We had a brief chat with her on the way up the drive. She's off to the pub."

"Adam, my dear chap." Roger held a glass of white wine. "Here you are, my darling. Sorry it took so long. Got waylaid by Jeremy Morton, poor chap. Not a happy fellow. How are you Adam? Oh yes, congratulations."

"I'm fine. Thank you. Long since recovered from our coming together."

"I am relieved. You know, we must get to know each other better. Dinner perhaps. Bring Wendy Gunnerson along, or Sally Humphreys. Anyone you like. Give Lucy your telephone number. Afraid I've landed her with being my social secretary. The parish and school combined leave little time for admin. Evenings such as these are a rare delight. We have limited opportunity to get out together, other than for church socials. Lucy spends an awful lot of time on her own."

"How do you occupy yourself?" Adam was curious and aroused.

"Oh, I'm pretty content on my own. I get out and about. Play a bit of Squash. Do you play, Mr. Head of P.E.?" Her mockery was in good faith.

"More a Badminton man."

Roger enthused. "You go to that club as well, don't you darling? What a marvellous opportunity."

Adam looked quizzical.

"Go with her, Adam. I appoint you Lucy's official coach. Give her a pointer or two."

Neither demurred.

"What else do you get up to, Lucy?"

"I'm especially looking forward to next Michaelmas term. Fiona's starting a choral society for pupils, staff, and anyone else who's interested. I love to sing."

A chocolate brown voice intoned.

"Goodo Lucy. Glad to have you on board."

Fiona Dyson Bell loomed over them. The Head of Music was six feet one-inch-tall with a shock of snow white hair. A tender and amiable person. Superb at her job.

"Do you warble, Adam?"

His old choirmaster, Tommy Greenwood, came to mind, and he blurted out, "Not since I was a choir boy."

"Were you indeed." Roger beamed his approval. "Are you a Christian, Adam?"

Lucy pulled him out of a hole. "Darling, rather unfair to put Adam on the spot at a social gathering."

"What are you Adam? Baritone, I'd guess."

"Sounds about right, Fiona."

"Then I want you on the team. Won't take no for an answer."

Lucy said nothing, but she linked Fiona's arm and they looked at him expectantly.

"Ok. Yes, that would be great. Gosh, look at the time. I said I'd divide the evening between here and the pub. Or rather, Wendy issued a command."

"Do you always do what women tell you, Adam?" Lucy was being provocative.

"All the time." He paused, and became serious. "Yes. I think I always have." The thought distracted him, briefly. "So nice to see you both again. Bye for now."

He fled from the apartment before Vanessa could snare him. Roger cried out, "Don't forget the Badminton."

Halting in the doorway, he stood and stared. Josh Meyer materialised once more, grinning with youthful insight.

"Nice."

"Married."

"More of a challenge than an obstacle. Night sir."

*

There is a time for everything. A time to accede, and a time to deny. A time to advance, and a time to retreat. Women decide those times. Man inherits the delusion of power. No more than the accident of elemental physical strength. Lucy did not pursue Adam for his telephone number. She could live without the finer points of Badminton.

Choral Society rehearsals began in September. Handel's 'Messiah'. Custom dictated that the hardened soaks repaired to 'The Black Bear' for lubrication of the vocal chords, post-rehearsal.

Adam's self-confidence was stratospheric.

"Join us for a drink."

Her sumptuous smile was entrancing.

"Not tonight, but we've months and months ahead – together."

When Adam came to manhood he had unknowingly constructed a tower for security. In anatomy, the fibrous pericardium protects and secures the heart. He had adopted similar armour. It was an emotional palisade, the sort built by the Ronnie Ogles of this world. Adam didn't become brutish and coarse, like Ogle, but he adopted an extravagant devil-may-care abandon. He lost touch with the beautiful innocence for which Hazel and Rose had cherished him. As a teacher he was cavalier in meting out justice to transgressors. Yet he could not stand outside himself in this moment, and admit to the adulterous injustice searing his heart. Little more than the pangs of sexual hunger gnawed him, and he was determined to eat.

Two weeks into rehearsal she sat in the car outside her house. She could see the light glowing behind the curtains of the office. Roger was hard at work. She did not possess a scintilla of doubt; she loved him alone. The last week had been excruciating for her. When the itch came upon her it had to be scratched.

"I love you Roger."

She pulled out of the drive, heading for Brindle House.

At the onset you sustain the pretence of being part of the group. Soon you gravitate to a cosy table. We're just good friends. A half hour before closing time he escorted Lucy to her car.

"Thanks Adam. I should really stop parking in this spot. You never know who's lurking about."

"Only me, I'm afraid. Your luck is out tonight."

Her gloved hands were warm in the sparkling chill of the lustrous October air. A smell of dying leaves was pungent, but the intoxicating fragrance she wore was overwhelming. Lucy took the collar of his overcoat. A lingering kiss confirmed for her that he was the right choice. Her open car coat gave him access to treasure. Adam's hand insinuated itself beneath her jumper and massaged her breasts. She withdrew from him gently. Her hand stroked him from shoulder to wrist. Fingertips palpated each other.

"Soon…soon."

The Triumph Stag zoomed away. Incongruously, he thought, "She needs a new exhaust."

Adam catapulted back into 'The Black Bear'. "Large rum and coke, please." He plonked himself beside Sally.

"What is SHE drinking?"

"Rum and coke."

"Never seen you on the hard stuff. Had a shock?"

His idiotic grin was a three-part novel. Sally lowered her voice.

"Don't go diving in! If you'll pardon my unfortunate metaphor. Word gets about. There's always one beady-eyed toe rag ready to spill the wotsits. Consequences, my darling, never without consequences."

"Wuhay!" Wendy trolled over from the Ladies. She parted Adam from his drink, and took a sip. "Mmm, nice. Celebrating or something?"

The inane smile never left his face. Wendy caught Sally's glance.

"Time for one more before closing."

Wendy strode towards the bar, singing as she went.

"If I could read your mind love,

What a tale your thoughts could tell

Just like a paperback novel

The kind the drugstore sells..."

There wasn't a shred of cruelty in Wendy. She refrained from finishing the verse about heroes failing. The final two lines would be especially crushing.

"...And you won't read that book again

Because the ending's just too hard to take."

Wendy fancied Adam something rotten, but she wasn't stupid. Nor was she jealous. Women know women. She already knew the ending, and she wanted to weep for the man behind her, who was just a boy.

"Oh my goodness," she gasped, "oh my goodness!"

"It's a good job I can breathe through my ears."

She yanked his hair. "I've got to have you now, please."

"Fiona says Tempo is everything. *Larghissimo* – 24 beats to the minute…"

"Faster maestro, faster…"

"Ah, ah, ah. *Adagio* – slow and stately."

An urgency raised the pace.

"Allegretto…Vivace…Presto…" Timpani hammered in their hearts. *"PRESTISSIMO!"* Her dilated pupils poured lava. Adam's were wet with tears. He was wanted. Somebody wanted him.

"God, I thought the bed would collapse. You don't disappoint, young man. Every time a winner."

It was December, and there would be a hiatus in their liaison. Christmas. Lucy made it clear that Roger needed her support throughout the busy season. Shame really, because the house was all his. Des Jones had been replaced, or rather Adam had. His new assistant was married and lived off the grounds. Wendy's mother had recently suffered a mild stroke. She had gone to live with her mum, further down the valley. Occasionally, she stayed over, but kept out of the way. She knew, but nothing was said.

Adam was engaged in a mild post-coital sulk. It was disappointment at the month of abstinence ahead.

"I'm not a performing horse, you know."

Lucy knew perfectly well how he felt. She sat upright, and folded her arms about him.

"You are a great fuck."

"Bear comparison do I?"

"Beg pardon."

"To your former suitors."

"Good grief, you sound like a 1930's film."

"Yep. Hitchcock's 'The 39 Steps'. I am the suave Robert Donat, you are sexy Madeleine Carroll – with better legs."

"You're always going on about old films."

"Grew up with them."

"What about the latest movies?"

"Grubby and cynical."

She rolled him over, pinning his arms over his head.”

“You’re an old romantic. A big softy.”

“Not for much longer!”

A fit of the giggles consumed her, but she maintained her grip.

“Top three films – go.”

“’Colditz’ – bravery and honour; ‘Goodbye Mr. Chips’ – love lost to tragic death, and ‘MRS. MINIVER’ – the perfect family who suffer loss, but are noble and steadfast. They live happily ever after.”

She released him, and lay on her back.

“Ye gods and hellfire. That sure is an odd view of the world.”

He quivered. “Why can’t people be honourable and dignified? What’s wrong in two people pledging themselves, and being faithful to one another?”

Lucy felt the most excruciating pain. She was an apple, and he had thrust a knife into her core with his rhetorical questions. They lay beside one another, holding hands. He tranquil from his eloquence; she beating the pain, and propelling

Roger to the nether regions of her mind, but not from her heart. The furnace of sex still glowed strongly within. She knew that her relationship to this sweet and innocent child had weeks, perhaps months, to go before her inner flame subsided. Every atom told her that she should end it now. The pain for him would be horrid, but she justified the continuity of their relationship with, "…it will pass." Lucy never knew that she was feeling the same sorrow for him that Wendy Gunnerson had experienced. She had to steel herself to look at him, surreptitiously. He lay motionless, eyes closed; a portrait of bliss. She realised why she couldn't abandon him yet. Sex was fantastic, but tremors of love for him swayed within her. She was alternately elevated and horrified.

"Why are you crying?"

Lucy clasped him so tightly he felt crushed. She told him the truth… and she lied.

"I'll miss you so much."

Adam assumed she referred solely to the Christmas period. She did, but she was also speaking of the time beyond when she would see him no more.

*

"Bloody hell, Barry, look at the size of you. Did you eat all the crusts in your house?"

Christmas Eve in Ridgate. The Horse and Groom was heaving. Adam there to see his father. It wasn't the best start to the Festive Season to learn that his parents' marriage was over. Negotiating the clamouring mass at the bar, he spotted Isobel Harris *neé* Holmes. The gigantic bloke with her was Barry Wetherspoon. There were old school friends in every direction.

"Nice one Sammo! Come and join us. You remember Izzie."

"Good to see you both. The old feller's waiting for me over there."

"Great bloke your old man. Bit of a dark horse." With that he resumed his clumsy seduction of Isobel.

Adam foxtrotted through the crowd, wondering what Barry meant.

"Hello son. Was that Barry Wetherspoon I saw you with? He's a wrong un. Too handy with his fists."

A lady was seated with his Dad. Forties and slim of build. Fair, with kind and homely features.

"I'd like to introduce Irene, my friend. Pint is it?"

"Rum and coke, please Dad."

"Keep Irene company."

In the brief interlude together, Adam learnt that she and his father had met in Ridgate Library. She was a visiting supervisor, carrying out an inspection. When she asked him to answer a few questions for her survey he replied, "Quid pro quo, Irene. If you meet me for a drink tonight." Irene was unmarried, and captivated by his charm. The rest was history. Ted Sampson was stopping every few paces to exchange banter. His eyes sparkled with joy. Adam rode a seesaw of emotion, rising for his Dad and descending for his Mum.

He returned to his unloved mother. They watched television in silence. It was eleven o'clock.

"Mum, do you want to come with me to Midnight Communion? I'd like to see the old stomping ground."

Annie was impassive. Her eyes never left the television screen.

"No, you get yerself going. It fills up as soon as the pubs shut. They tell me the new vicar does a half decent job."

"Sure you won't come?"

"I've not much time for Him up there, these days. He went quiet when last I called on Him."

Her brusque pain stirred his heart. Adam wanted to hold his mother, but the touch of a younger woman consumed him. He was afraid of losing the sustaining memory of Lucy. When he closed the gate he could see Annie through a crack in the curtains. Defeat and resignation were etched across her face. She sat immobile. Canned laughter shrieked from the television in mockery.

The graveyard rhododendrons held no fear for him. A mass transfer had taken place, from pub to St. Barnabas. Sentimental folk memories reaching out like a shepherd's crook to yank frightened people back to treasured places, where security and comfort was once certain. Christmas Eve in Ridgate participated in the national ritual. Folk gathered in the sacred space.

When closing time was called they left it, and went to church.

"Adam! It is you, isn't it?" An elderly chap laid a hand on his shoulder. "Na then lad, you've surely not forgot your old choirmaster?"

"Mr. Greenwood."

"Ee lad, you look as fresh as you did all those years ago. You've got a bit big for your cassock. Do you still sing?"

"I'm in the school choral society. We're performing 'The Messiah' at Easter."

"Champion lad, champion. Sorry to see the parting of the ways."

Adam knew he was referring to his parents.

"Hope the Handel goes down well. Merry Christmas."

The service began. Adam didn't know why he was there. Did it have meaning anymore, or was he as sentimental as the rest? He prayed earnestly for his parents. Seeking God's blessing, he gave thanks for the treasure he believed was stored up for him; lifelong union with Lucy. When they sat again he smiled. Ellen and the Colonel. His boyhood dream would be realised.

On Boxing Day, he lunched with his Dad and Irene. His mother had been invited to the Macklins. He rang their doorbell. Joe Macklin responded to the chimes.

"Come to collect a parcel," Adam said. "Happy Christmas Joe."

"And the same to you Adam. You'll have a drink before you escort her ladyship back to the mansion?"

Josie clasped him to her capacious bosom, and squealed. "Ee Annie, what a handsome young man you brought into the world. Best Christmas present ever. I'll keep him in the loft for special occasions."

For a nanosecond the sparring partners of yesteryear floated breezily on the air.

"Mek sure he washes his hands and face. He was always a dirty little divil!"

"A bath every night. Six sharp!"

The two old girls snuffled merrily into their Advocaat. Josie drew breath.

"Are you courting, Adam?"

Blushes overwhelmed him. He bought some time by glugging his scotch. Best not to reply, "Yeh, shagging the vicar's missus."

"I prefer to spend my money on myself, Mrs. M."

"Like father, like son..." Josie shot a warning look at her husband. "One more for the road, Adam."

Joe sought out the bottle, Adam's eyes were riveted on the sideboard. A photograph of Hazel held pride of place. Taken on the day of the Rose Queen. There was no jolt to the heart. He thanked Joe for the refill. Without anyone noticing, he lifted the glass a fraction to Hazel. Within his heart he spoke softly to her, and thanked her for the love she had given. He swore to her that he would give the same cornucopia of affection, unstintingly and everlastingly, to his Lucy.

"We'll be off then, Josie. Lovely dinner. She's a grand cook is Josie."

They were halfway down St. Barnabas' Road when his mother blurted out,

"By gum, that woman could talk the hind leg off a donkey!"

His laughter was hysterical. The seismic tremors of tension were released. Earthquakes are destructive. This one swept away the bondage of past. Motorways were transformed into highways of promise, as he drove home. Adam had been wooed by a brave new world, and he had accepted its hand. His allegiance was pledged to a bronzed and beautiful woman.

*

Roger Birch was not without a sense of humour. He and his wife arrived home at a quarter to one in the morning. Midnight Communion had gone well in his charming village church, on the outskirts of Wilton.

Lucy scarce contained a smile when she entered the bedroom. Roger was lying on top of the bed, *au naturel.* It didn't displease her. She lay beside him, snuggling up against his warm body. There was no frenzy in his face. A serene look of love lit his features.

"Well it is Christmas Day," he joked, "you won't begrudge me opening one present early?"

A throaty laugh reverberated around the room, and she knelt beside him whilst she drew her nightdress over her head.

"There we are, darling, done. Don't want you getting all fingers and thumbs and tearing the wrapping. It cost a small fortune."

She enjoyed Roger's lovemaking. It was never furious, or perfunctory; neither brisk nor business-like. His tenderness and consideration moved her deeply. The demands he made upon her were infrequent. He enjoyed caressing her, but it was part of something bigger. A component. Like the humour and interests, they shared. All combining to unify two people in love.

Lucy lay in the dark, listening to his shallow breathing. His left hand still lay upon her breast. Why would God not spare her from this raging fire that had burned within her for so many years? She thought back to the years after university, when she had been a single woman. What she had done in that time seemed unreal to her now. Her activities had given her a living, and appeased the incessant roar of the flames. Roger knew everything. Once he had asked her to marry him, she felt honour bound to be frank. Lucy remembered the day, vividly, when she had told him that for five years she had worked as a high class prostitute. Roger was looking straight at her, and his gaze never wavered. Nor did he hesitate.

"I love you. I have no idea why you might love me. I ask you again. Marry me."

No religion quoted at her. Not a scent of judgement. Nary a shadow of doubt in his face, or in his voice. Her love for him, had never wavered, but she had never smashed the nugget of lingering doubt. She couldn't fathom why he loved her. Her sexual fires lay dormant for longer periods, but they were never extinguished entirely.

"Oh Adam," she murmured softly, "what am I to do?"

Term ended on Maundy Thursday. The only outstanding event was the choral concert. It was Good Friday, and Roger was otherwise occupied.

Lucy and Adam exhausted themselves together throughout winter and early spring. Today was no different, a kaleidoscope of arms, legs, mouths and tongues.

"Put some music on. Let's dance."

"I'm a bit out of practice."

"Let me show you a few moves. Only fair, you've shown me a few. God, how can a P.E. teacher not be able to dance?" She laughed noisily.

"Don't laugh at me!" His vehemence stunned her.

She studied his back, as he shook violently.

"I'm so sorry, Adam, so sorry."

Lucy knelt before him. There weren't any tears, but his face was ashen and he looked so miserable. She felt sick inside. The realisation that this was the moment poured black pitch into her throat. It must be ended now, and it was the worst possible time.

"Once...years ago I danced with a precious girl...I left her, and I shouldn't have. Never saw her again. I...I can't dance."

In faith and hope he told her everything. About Hazel, then Rose, and his inability to reach out and help his mother.

Lucy heard words from someone who had convinced himself that he was unloved. It was familiar to her. The tsunami that had loomed above her, perpetually, cascaded over her, but she stood firm. Dry land, she was standing on dry land. Gone. Fire, that grim-faced destroyer, was completely extinguished. The boy in front of her had flooded her with his bitter tears of honesty. Now she knew fully that she was loved. By Roger. All that remained was the parting. It had to be cruel. She released his hold, and went over to the C.D. player. Joe Cocker sang. Lifting him to his feet, she gathered him into her arms.

"Body to body. Then you'll make quiet love to me."

Adam lay there with a sense of restitution.

"I want you to listen to me, Adam, without interruption."

There was no purpose, or merit, in telling him about her former life as a prostitute. She would keep it terse.

"My elder sister, Dawn, gave birth to a little girl, Annabelle Lucy. When she was three she was hospitalised with pneumonia. We spent weeks beside her, then she was gone. The post mortem revealed a small heart defect. That's when I became a nurse."

She trusted to his intelligence; she would not patronise him with the obvious. Lucy knew that he was snared in a cocoon of perfection. He had to fight his way out of it, and accept life in all of its imperfections. Adam knew what she was telling him. In nature, new life springs out of death and decay. You must grasp hold of it, or live a solitary life. He lifted his head, as she whispered to herself.

"Dear God in Heaven, I loved that child as if she were my own." She drew upon her cigarette. "Always intended to have kids."

Illusion still pressed upon him.

"Have them with me!"

Steel doors closed within her. The flaming compartments were under control. She would not let them flare up again.

"Can't be done," she said harshly. "I'm infertile."

Adam was a torrent of excitement, grasping her limp hands.

"Then we'll adopt. When we're married, we'll adopt."

She pulled him upright. Her hands gripped his shoulders.

"Adam, I am never going to marry you!"

"…but…but…you don't love Roger."

"BUT I DO! I will never leave Roger."

She lay back on the bed, and spread her legs.

"Now Adam, now you can fuck me!"

She was entirely confident of her power over him, and without fear of what he might do. Lucy knew that his honourable soul was tormenting him, because he wouldn't acknowledge the ugliness inside him as well as the good. Perhaps if he took her in anger he would begin to understand. Shiny armour is bound to tarnish. She wanted to scourge herself for what she was doing, but she knew that they had to part on these terms. Lucy saw his body slowly inflate until every muscle was taut. She knew what was coming. Adam's enraged face stared down at her. He gripped her wrists and forced them into the mattress. Each powerful thrust didn't hurt her body one bit. His terrible hurt and reproach, unhidden by anger, stabbed her again and again.

Lucy dressed quickly, and opened the door. It would have been improper, so she rejected the rites of consolation. "Thank you, Adam."

When she closed the garden gate his fists were beating on the front door. An unstoppable high-pitched howl burst from him and rent the Good Friday sky, like a curtain being torn. Lucy flew to her car, barely able to see through the mingled tears of loss and freedom.

Another year concluded with summer shenanigans in 'The Black Bear'.

"So Des Jones was stitched up?"

Wendy gulped a huge draught from her pint. She waggled the empty glass, and it bobbed to the bar in Abel Goodrich's hand.

"Five years fiddling invoices, and getting Edrich to flog stuff on. I watched the governors escort him from the premises. *Schadenfreude*, my dear; wet myself. Thanks Abe." She took the glass and slurped the top off.

"Why wasn't he handed over to the Old Bill?"

"Adam, Adam, Adam." Sally shook her head disapprovingly. "Distinguished majors do not get fingered."

Wendy choked on her pint. "Pleeease! I'm trying to keep this down."

"Distinguished?"

"Officer, gentleman, and public school. Chaps can't be prosecuted for trifling embezzlement. It'd be the end of civilisation."

Adam cooed. "Hardly trivial. If I hadn't checked my accounts so closely the pair of buggers would have thieved *ad infinitum*."

Wendy gurgled. "Ooooh, I love a bloke who can go on *ad* infinitum. Are you up for it Abe?"

The grizzled gardener smiled benignly. "Straight on, and steady with the helm. That's my motto. Mind you, Wendy, I does like a firm hand on my tiller."

Laughter exploded beyond their table.

"So, why didn't they prosecute Harvey Edrich? He's lower down the food chain."

Wendy shrugged. "They may have considered it, but knowing that slippery sod he'd have taken 'Quackers' down with him, and that would mean the school as well."

"It's taken Rodney Porter down. Now we're in the doody with Vanessa running the show."

"Aha! Five years at Brindle House, and the boy has grown in wit and wisdom. That is why I'm moving to pastures new. *'The wind is in the East'*, as Dickens remarked."

Wendy chirruped. "I don't know anything about Dickens, Sal. I've never been to one!"

The evening drifted to a merry close. Adam and Wendy remained, closeted in the snug.

"What are you doing this summer?"

Adam sunk lower into his chair.

"Not a lot. I'll spend most of the time here. I love the place."

"A word in your shell-like, my lovely. Our new headmistress is not overly-pleased with you."

"What have I done?"

"Cost her mate his job. Your super sleuth secretary discovered that her brother served alongside the errant major. They were great buddies. She put a big word in for Donald Muir when he applied to be Bursar. Watch your step. Right, you can walk me home."

It was a peerless night sky. They strolled arm in arm down the lane.

"You and Abel seem to be hitting it off these days."

"He's a funny old soul. Mother loves him to bits."

"How about you?"

"He warms my cockles."

They continued in silence, until they reached the gate. Wendy spoke lightly.

"Haven't seen you breaking any hearts recently."

Adam remained mute.

"You didn't come to the farewell do. Roger was there, she...Lucy wasn't. Looked me firm in the eye, he did, and said she was indisposed."

His face was in shadow. "You reckon he knows?"

"Uhhu."

"Best make a move, Wend. The coach leaves early. Bloody cricket tour." He pecked her on the cheek. An owl hooted. "Don't suppose you know where his new parish is located."

"How would I know?"

"Bollocks Wend! You could give MI5 a run for their money."

"London. Somewhere in London. That's all I know. Cross my heart and hope to die...etc, etc." She watched him search the night sky for a sign to guide him. "Adam, it's been three years. Give it up." Her heart melted when she saw the schoolboy smile light up his face.

"I have Wendy; I have...but it never goes away entirely. Goodnight."

She leant on the garden gate, and watched the brilliantined darkness swallow him. In most things he was the same old Adam. Bloody good at his job, and a real laugh to be around. He had become irascible though, and it was the children who bore the brunt. The lads still flocked to him. They were achievers, and they recognised that 'Sammo' would lift them to the highest level. The change was fear; it infected his presence. Boys were afraid of him. Quite a few staff felt the same. Respect he had, but very little love. He was encased in chain mail, and it entrenched his defiant loneliness. Wendy shivered. His loose and virulent tongue did not endear him to authority.

She cried out, as she marched into the hallway. "Mum, I've made up my mind. The answer is 'yes'."

"About bloody time. You've kept that poor man dangling long enough."

"Cup of tea?"

"Bollocks to that! Two bottle of pale ale under the sink."

Wendy and Mary Gunnerson sat long into the night, planning a wedding.

*

The shemozzle flared up the following Easter. Adam still sang in the choral concert. Song released him from his inner dissatisfaction. Fiona Dyson Bell invariably chose pieces with a religious motif. He appeared indifferent to them. He was content that the fever within subsided when he sang.

"Adam, would you mind giving me a hand with clearing away when the others have gone?"

It was tradition for Vanessa Goody to hold a select post-concert soiree in her flat. Adam didn't mind lending a hand. It was an opportunity to swill a couple more glasses.

"Just put them in the kitchen, Adam. Anywhere will do. Would you excuse me a moment?"

He stood looking through the window, admiring his little house in the distance. A familiar voice spoke, but in an odd girly tone.

"Adam."

Vanessa was clad in a black Basque, with matching stockings. His glass hovered; he swigged the contents. Then he laughed. Laughed and laughed until tears splashed on the oak floor.

"You bastard! You bloody bastard!" Her complexion was anaemic with fury. "I know all about you. Couldn't keep your pants on when the Chaplain's wife crooked her little finger. That little tart!"

Adam had never contemplated violence against a woman, and he never would again. His right hand clasped her throat. The air itself shrunk from fear of him. Releasing his grip, he set the glass on the table, and strolled away. She could hear his malicious chortling, as footsteps receded down the corridor.

The Times Educational Supplement is the teacher's trade paper for jobs. Adam's application to be Director of Sport at High Heath School, Hampstead was received with favour. Six years earlier he arrived at Brindle House in Wendy Gunnerson's car, bearing physical scars. It was another August day when he left. The GT6 didn't contain much more than what had been in his rucksack, way back when. Brindle House meant the world to him. His departure was enforced by circumstance. An additional layer of discordance was cemented to his fractured spirit.

Luminous

St. Stephen's Church Ooty lies on the road to Mysore. Its origin is linked with stellar dates inscribed on the sarcophagus of English history. The foundation stone was laid on April 23rd 1829 – St. George's Day – to coincide with the birthday of King George IV. In 1830, on November 5th, the Church was consecrated by the Bishop of Calcutta. We do not know if they celebrated with fireworks. Tipu Sultan's palace, on the island of Srirangapatna, contributed timbers to the construction. In 1947 it came under the Church of South India.

Anna contemplates the painting depicting the Last Supper, displayed on the Western wall. She has re-entered through the panelled doors beneath. Mishka and Billy are with the children. It is the Orphanage's practice to shepherd their charges on regular trips to points of interest, in and around Ooty. Know your past; know yourself. They have seen the inside of the church, and now they are eating and playing in the graveyard at the rear of the building.

She focuses on the image of Christ. Lost, losing, but out of that loss comes immeasurable gain. Her grandfather is superimposed upon the painting, where Simon Peter sits. So far, his remorseless tale has catalogued an unbroken thread of loss throughout his life. Anna thinks of the people of her parish, back in Buckinghamshire. Many of them prosperous, but not all. That isn't the point. Irrespective of their bank balance, no-one is immune to loss. Names spring to mind. Those bereaved of husbands, wives and children; others in poverty of body and spirit, marriages broken. The last thought causes her to close her eyes so that the walls will cease to shift around her. Called to ministry. The call remains strong and vivid within her.

"But what about me?" she implores of Christ, on the night before His Crucifixion.

"What did you say, Anna?" She has not noticed Billy's silent entry. "Am I disturbing you?"

Assume the unruffled exterior. "Not at all Billy. Are we ready to leave?"

"Not yet. The children are playing. I thought I would take the opportunity for prayer. Will you join me?"

Anna breathless. "I don't know if I can." Her head droops in shame.

Billy takes her hand, and draws her into a pew. Sitting beside her. His penetrating stare sees through and beyond her hair, fallen across her face.

"Why did you come to India, Anna?"

She knows it is futile to pretend. Oh yes, she could trot out tales of holidays and wanting to visit her grandfather, but Billy could not be fooled. This simple and jolly man is a keen observer of life. That much she has learned in a short space of time. Suddenly, she laughs. Perhaps it is a gift given to all taxi drivers.

"I'm a fraud, Billy, and a coward. I've run away."

He is tempted to ask who she has run away from, but holds his counsel.

"I've run away from the people I love, and from the people I should be serving."

Anna looks to Billy expectantly. He remains silent. She knows that she must speak the words out loud.

"I am fleeing from God, because I don't possess the courage to own to myself."

Billy rests a hand on the Bible lying on the thin shelf of the pew in front.

"Then you are the same as the rest of us. Embroiled in the war with self. Shall I tell you what shape that conflict takes?"

Her look implores him to give the answer.

"It is the demon of perfection."

Anna is puzzled.

"The idea that we should be perfect; a denial of our imperfection. If we own to our faults we think that we must live in perpetual shame, and what a burden of misery that would be. This is wrong thinking. When we confess to the bonds of our unwholesome thoughts; to the fetters of our cruel words and the slavery of our actions, concealed guilt is cast onto a pyre where it can be burnt. We do not step from the flames cast in perfection, but we are cleansed and reborn to follow Him. We become a forgiven people. No matter how many times we stumble, His hand will raise us up."

"Billy, it is you who should be His minister."

His laughter echoes around the empty church.

"Oh no Mrs. Anna. You are wondering, perhaps, how such words come from the mouth of a not-so-humble rickshaw driver? I got scholarship to top-notch, bloody fine school." He raises a hand to the painting. "Sorry guvnor. Might have gone on to big things, but this is India. Families need to be fed. Not a bad life, sitting down all day long. You are not so different from your grandfather. He has walked through the fire, but God be praised he has emerged."

"What do you know of him, Billy?"

"We have been friends for over twenty years. In that time, he has revealed much of his life to me, in dribs and drabs. Do I use the English expression correctly?"

"You do, my friend. Gramps has been sharing his story with us over the last few weeks." Her hands reach out, and she takes the Bible from Billy. "I have not been entirely honest with him. It isn't that I've lied. More the sin of omission. Billy, will you listen to my story?"

He places his hand upon hers. Together they hold the Word.

*

If the tabloids got hold of it, they would have a field day. 'VIVACIOUS VICAR IN THE VESTRY'.

Anna had taken the initiative. The tension between her and the Churchwarden was unbearable. She drew Peter to her, and kissed him. His lips lingered lightly upon hers, and a world of trouble was in his face.

Peter Goodman fumbled with a folder on the table.

"Anna, I'm at least twenty years older than you, and...married."

She would not be denied. "Peter, don't tell me that you haven't longed for me to kiss you. I've been yearning."

His head shook from side-to-side in bewilderment at himself.

"No, no, I can't deny it. We've been falling in love with each other, haven't we?"

Anna closed her eyes at hearing his words, and rapture made her luminous.

His next words extinguished the light.

"It's not possible Anna. I can't leave Sophie."

"Do you love her?"

He was not the sort of man to tell tales out of school, but there had always been an inner impulsion to be truthful and honest.

"Not any more. I'm not sure now if I ever did."

Anna was too wise to say what the whole parish thought about Peter and Sophie's relationship. She had no need. His pent up feelings could be released at last.

"She cares for nothing but her status. The house, the cars, money, if our friends are the 'right sort of people'." He paused. "And the humiliation. I'm an idiot, or so I'm told in private, and increasingly in public."

If Peter had simply been bringing his troubles to his minister she could have counselled him. Now the Rubicon had been crossed detachment was no longer possible. She took his face in her hands.

"You are the gentlest, kindest and most compassionate person I've ever met. That's why I love you, Peter."

His despondency was heart-breaking to see.

"Sophie is still my wife." He looked Anna squarely in the eye. "I took an oath before God. I cannot be unfaithful to Him."

It was her turn to fumble with papers and registers.

"Of course, of course Peter. I...I must get over to the vicarage. Home group tonight; bit of prep to do."

She loaded her arms with books and folders.

"You can't manage that lot on your own. Let me help."

They strolled across the churchyard in silence, and down the drive to the front door.

"Bring them into the study, please Peter."

The small room was packed from floor to ceiling, and they bumped against one another spilling everything out of their arms. Then they were embracing, and kissing one another in a torrent of joy. Peter was fifty-eight years old, but he still found the strength to sweep his beloved Anna off her feet and carry her to the bedroom.

*

Sophie Goodman swept onto the terrace. Her garden was in vibrant bloom. She gestured summarily to the two young women bearing salvers.

"On the side table."

Her lady friends were scattered across the lawn, savouring their Pimms. Sophie clapped her hands, and they came running.

"Lunch girls, lunch!"

When they were seated one of her acolytes popped the question.

"I say Sophie; will we get a glimpse of your handsome husband before the sun goes down?"

The bevy of girlfriends giggled in unison. Sophie assumed an elegant pose of reflection.

"Handsome Joanna? Peter, handsome? Yes, I suppose he is, though not quite the good looks of yesteryear. Always looks a bit down in the dumps these days."

Meaningful looks passed between one or two of the company, which weren't entirely flattering to their hostess.

"Where is he, Sophie?"

"Hannah, my dear, where he always is; canoodling with the Vicar."

Joanna affected a look of horror.

"My goodness, I do hope not. Can't have scandal in Manor Green."

Sophie's reply was devil-may-care, with a *soupçon* of waspish delight.

"My dear, I don't think Peter has the energy these days, nor the inclination. He's at the other end of the Drive going about his good works." She changed the subject. "Are we all happy with the plans for the coffee morning?"

The group rejoinder confirmed the decision taken in committee.

Hannah's curiosity got the better of her.

"What are Peter and Anna Wilbey up to today?"

Sophie lay her fork on the edge of her plate.

"Hannah darling, you seem to take an inordinate interest in the activities of my husband." Her delicious mockery made Hannah blush. "You're not smitten are you dear?" She allowed her domination to bring the table back to her. Picking at her chicory she continued. "Churchwarden and Vicar are engaged in the thrilling task of surveying the graveyard." She leant back, and sipped from her glass. "I don't know what that young lady would do without my Peter."

Rosemary Ferris piped up. "Whatever do you mean, Sophie?"

"Oh, you know, he keeps her on the straight and narrow. The young lady does seem to have some rather fanciful ideas. I'm not sure she apprehends that we are simple folk in a simple English village, and that's how we intend it to stay."

*

The district committee of St. Giles, parish church of Manor Green, was more astonished than outraged. Surprisingly, it was Mary Beccles who took it most calmly.

"How much do they reckon it's worth?"

"Probably not less than a quarter of a million pounds at auction."

"Thank you Peter. Well I think that it's money that can be put to good use. I like the idea, Anna."

Mary outranked them all, as the village's longest resident. She had been born in her cottage seventy-six years before this gathering took place.

Ann Waters' mousy voice spoke plaintively. "We've had it such a long time. It seems a shame."

Mary took up the theme. "It only comes out at Easter and Christmas. Think of the good we can do with the proceeds, Ann. At the end of the day, it's just a lump of gold with a few precious stones in it."

Tom Carter interjected. "Will we be allowed to sell it?"

"Peter, would you detail the procedure?"

"Certainly Anna. We will need to bring this before the Bishop and the Diocese…"

An excited Anna cut across him. "Given the purpose to which we intend to put the money, I think we have a good chance of convincing them. Sorry, Peter."

Tom put his two pennorth in again. "Will we need planning permission for 'doing up' the Old Barn, and changing its purpose?"

Peter tapped his pen on the Minutes Book. "Most probably Tom. Given the scale of the problem the council has with homelessness, and their shortage of money, I should think that they might look favourably on the project."

Ann raised her hand. "What about the Village? How will they react to selling the 'Cross of St. Giles' to fund a shelter for the homeless on their doorstep?"

Mary Beccles was forthright. "I remember the days when there was standing room only in our church. We only see the villagers in here twice a year now, and they're coming in fewer and fewer numbers. I don't know that their opinion matters. Besides, remember who St. Giles is..." A few of the committee looked puzzled. Mary filled them in. "...the Patron saint of beggars and cripples."

Anna took up the reins. "Thank you Mary. I think that we should anticipate some opposition, but with perseverance and God's good Grace I believe that we can win through."

"Shall we put it to the vote?"

Nodding heads responded to Peter's question.

"All those in favour...carried unanimously."

Anna and Peter embraced in the quiet confines of the Vestry.

"So, you've done it," Peter said.

She was all aglow. "Some way to go, but we're on the road. Come with me, darling."

Hand-in-hand, they descended into the Crypt. Anna unlocked the secure cabinet, and withdrew the 'Cross of St. Giles'. It had been donated to the Church in 1149 by the original Lord of Manor Green, Sir Eustace Chetwode. An act of thanksgiving for his safe return from the Second Crusade.

"This way Peter." She carried the heavy golden icon raised before her. Anna knelt before the tomb of Sir Eustace. "Hold it with me, Pete."

He was beside her, and they joined hands on the Cross.

"Almighty Father, bless our enterprise in providing for the poor and dispossessed. We give thanks for the life of Sir Eustace Chetwode, and for the gift he freely gave, many centuries ago. May our service join with his in ministering to those in need. We ask you this in Jesus name. Amen."

As they climbed the stone stairway she whispered. "A quick drink at my place?" She couldn't see his face in the gloom.

"Sorry Anna, best get home. Been away longer than I said I would."

*

Rachel Burton was never malicious, just garrulous. Not a quality desirable in a Curate. She had come late to ministry, in her mid-fifties. Her previous job had been as a youth worker. The toil and toll of many years had served only to strengthen her Christian belief. Rachel was the jolliest of women. An abundance of good will and smiles poured from her in an unending stream. It was nurtured in her unshakeable conviction that goodness could be hunted out of the thickets of the most despicable or despairing person. It was her mission to ride to hounds every waking moment. In her boundless enthusiasm she was incautious. Rachel did not stand back and assess the wisdom of who she shared thoughts, feelings and information with.

"What a wonderful husband you have, Sophie."

Rachel and Sophie Goodman were enjoying a post-service cup of tea in the Church Hall. The latter cocked an eyebrow in amusement. Sophie tolerated the Curate for the sake of good form.

"What on earth has he been up to now?"

Rachel blundered onwards, her rubicund cheeks aglow.

"Well, I've only just returned from holiday, as you know…"

"Yes, how was Israel?"

"Wonderful, wonderful. To walk in the footsteps of the Lord…"

Sophie couldn't bear a blow-by-blow account. Her idea of a great holiday was a five-star hotel in the most fashionable resort of the day.

"You were about to tell me why Peter is a treasure?"

"Ah yes. A more than apposite word. Anna brought me into the loop on my return. The committee has decided to sell the Cross of St. Giles to restore the Old Barn."

Sophie was as alert as a fox upon hearing the baying of hounds.

"Mmm? Is that a good idea? The Cross brings the tourists in. Anyway, restore the building to what purpose?"

Rachel lowered her voice. "That bit is still confidential, but you are the Churchwarden's wife. Probably no secrets between you." Rachel's corncrake laugh echoed around the chancel.

Sophie eyed the Curate, and considered a biting retort. She kept her counsel, inwardly scornful of this naïve old maid.

"We're applying for planning permission to convert the barn to a shelter for the homeless. Isn't it marvellous? All down to Anna and Peter. They're a marvellous team."

"Goodness me, Rachel, look at the time. People for drinks. Super service."

Guests had departed, and Peter was in the kitchen.

"What's going on between you and Anna Wilbey?"

The crystal wine glass froze in his hand.

"If you think the Village will stand for her crackpot plan, you've another think coming. Do you realise what a homeless shelter will do to property prices? It's out of the question."

Marriage could only be one of two states for Peter. A Holy Joy or a Holy Terror. His relationship with his wife had evolved into the latter. Not as portrayed in films with shocks, frights and a happy ending. No, it was the more informal and insidious trouble of the soul. When you realise that you are joined to someone with whom you have nothing in common. The horror, which Peter endured, festered in the compost of self-imposed duty. On that recent day, pregnant with consequence, he had told Anna that he was married. Then he had succumbed, and found respite from his unhappiness in her arms. He had taken an oath on his wedding day, and it mattered to him. You could ferret into his childhood, excavate his relationship with his mother and father, and you would find nothing to account for his resolve. The adamantine creed was simply the core of the man.

"Who on earth told you...?"

Sophie smirked, "Oh come on, Peter. Even you're not that dim."

Her disdain for her husband was surprising. Peter had been a very astute businessman. So successful that he had been able to retire early, and devote himself to the church he loved. It was in that community he sought ethical values.

He shook his head. "Anna really is going to have to speak with Rachel. Listen Sophie, this project is really important. Please don't make waves."

The time was forfeit when such an appeal might have worked. Husband and wife each had their principles. Their differences were lodged betwixt Peter's bond with community, and Sophie's harness to the primacy of the individual. She took a fresh bottle from the wine cooler, opened it and poured herself a glass.

"Cheers!"

The battle lines were drawn.

*

Manor Green 'society' does not produce people who blab after their fifth gin. A select company was on parade at the Old Manse. They had foregathered after morning service. Anna's intentions were the subject of a discreet discussion.

Jacob Bland believed himself to be the most successful businessman in the Village. He and his wife occupied the Old Manse. Consequently, Jacob conferred on himself 'Lord of the Manor' by proxy. The insubstantial reality of his claim to the defunct title could be traced through the tacky quagmire of hubris, if you could be bothered. Sophie Goodman didn't quite grovel at his feet, but her ingrained habit of complimenting Jacob shined his shoes. To be fair to the lady, she was not alone in deferring to his status.

"Jake, darling, this really is too much to bear. We simply cannot accept the young woman's proposals. It will be the ruination of our way of life."

Penelope Bland was less taciturn than her husband, and couldn't resist a sly dig.

"Sophie, darling, I do think you're being less than fair to our dear Vicar. After all, she's something of a novice. What is she? Thirty-four, thirty-five? You yourself said that Peter has a hand in the affair. I do hope that Anna hasn't been led astray by an older man."

Looks were averted, and took an absorbing interest in champagne and canapés. It provided respite during which half-smiles and smirks could be aired.

"Good God, Pen'! I trust you're not suggesting hanky-panky. Old Pete? He's as straight as the Poplar in the churchyard. Now, if you were talking about someone else on that committee – no names, no pack drill – he's about as straight as a roundabout!"

Jerry Newman was always outspoken. He didn't care a fig about the Blands, or anyone else. When it came to wealth he was in there with the best of them. He also retained a good deal of inside knowledge about Jake Bland's dealings in the City. Penelope gritted her teeth. It frustrated her no end that she had to entertain people like the Newmans. She suspected it would take the merest scratch of the surface to reveal their true family name – Neumann. However, money sticks with money.

"Getting a bit side-tracked, Jerry." Jake defended his wife obliquely. "We're all in agreement that our excellent Vicar must be dissuaded from her miscalculation. Came from the best of motives, I'm sure. Sophie, my dear…"

She became the second lady in the room to clamp her incisors together. The way he said, "My dear," was intensely patronising to her ear. She gave him her most glittering smile.

"…I feel that you're best placed to have first crack. Get Peter to spell it out for the young lady. Very damaging for the growth of church life in the Village."

Sophie felt uncomfortable, with every eye in the drawing room on her. Nonetheless, she spoke honestly.

"Peter is very keen on the Vicar…" She became flustered. "I mean on the Vicar's idea. I fear that he isn't open to persuasion."

The hostess nimbly filled the silence.

"I say, everyone's glass is looking a little peaky. Come on, refills, and we can chat as we drink. Okay darling?"

Jake Bland admired his wife's social dexterity, and beamed his adoring approval at her. When glasses were replenished, he repaired to a corner with Jerry Newman.

"No need for silly pamphlets and protests, Jerry. Softly, softly catchee monkee."

"Quite so Jake. Attending Lodge next week?"

Jake laughed. "Catch your drift, Jerry. Is Tommy Henshall home?"

"I understand that the Chairman of the Planning Committee – I do beg your pardon – the Master has returned from his cruise, and will be presiding. You still in touch with Bishop Arthur?"

"Lunch party next Sunday. He and Deirdre will be joining us. One of Pen's ideas. Raising funds for the children's playground. Let me show you the grounds, Jerry. They look an absolute picture."

"It's dead in the water, Anna. Please don't punish yourself. You did everything possible."

She leant against the Vestry safe, despondent and confused.

"Why Peter? Why would they gang up on us like this? The 'Shelter' wasn't to satisfy my ego, or yours. It was to fulfil a desperate need."

"What did the Bishop say to you?"

"Oh, it wasn't him in person. He used the Archdeacon to convey his message. She was stupendously good. Said that Bishop Arthur praised me to the skies for proposing a shelter, but there was no way he could see the Diocese approving the sale of the 'Cross'. Even his hands were tied there. Ingrid Lovat conveyed his regrets beautifully."

Peter felt defeat eating into his bones. He had already shown Anna the letter from the council. Their application had fallen at the first step.

"People know people, Anna. That's just how it is. Word in the ear; nudge of the elbow, and the 'right' people make the 'right' decision. Naturally, it's for the good of everybody. It just so happens that 'good' is exclusive to *their* interest."

Anna was getting angry. "How dare they come and sit in these pews. Not one of them has a shred of true faith."

He looked at her in astonishment. Peter had always known that she was an idealist, but not that she was so unworldly. Contrary to popular opinion, ministers were some of the worldliest folk he'd ever come across. The best of them fulfilled the biblical injunction to be *in* the world, but not *of* the world. When they achieved that state they were at their most powerful. Status and intimidation meant nothing to them. He wasn't sure what he could say to her.

She continued to rant. "They have money, position and power. All we were asking for was a few crumbs of decency. An opportunity for them to exhibit the sense of honour and duty that they prattle on about so much."

Peter rested his hand on top of hers. Now he understood.

"Duty Anna, I know all about duty. It's a terrible task master. If you think that you're going to find your reward in this life, for being dutiful, think again." Some old words spilt from his lips.

"Straight is the line of duty, curved is the line of beauty.

Follow the straight line you will see the curved line ever follow thee."

She clasped his hand. "Who said that?"

"Can't remember. If we believe in the Way of Christ, all we can do is persevere. No matter how painful."

"You were selected for Lay Ministry training. Why didn't you see it through?"

A strange gurgle came from his chest. "I don't get on very well with the hierarchy of the Church of England. Being boxed and tied up with a pink ribbon isn't my style."

"I think you mean having a blue stole around your neck."

"I'm an outsider Anna. Always have been, and those on the inside won't stand for it. You get one invitation to step over the line and side with them. If you decline they smother you with indifference."

She drew the man she loved to her. "Why don't we live on the outside together?"

Peter didn't want to let go of her just yet. This would be the last time he would touch her.

"It can't be. You see, we're both bound to what we hold most dear. We have to do our duty."

They clutched each other fiercely. The door of the Vestry opened just as he cried, "Oh my love!"

Rachel Burton had a knack for getting the wrong end of the stick.

*

Who knows why some people run off at the mouth, whilst others keep a confidence? Some are plain malicious, and delight in causing trouble. Others are less easy to explain. The knowledge they bear inflates until they can contain it no longer. Perhaps the satisfaction they get from sharing illicit information gives a relieving vicarious thrill. Rachel Burton fell into that category. When she could contain herself no more she always began with the classic line.

"I shouldn't be telling you this, but I know you won't tell anyone…"

Ann Waters, from the church committee, was her bosom friend. Rachel related the doings in the Vestry over coffee, at the single mums and toddlers morning in the church hall. In the space of a fortnight it had circulated around the Parish. Only Mary Beccles took a Christian view. The savvy old countrywoman read the runes, and came to a charitable conclusion.

"Don't suppose a vicar should behave like that, but she's only human. Anyroad, it takes two to tango. Mind you, can't say as I blame Peter. That wife of his leads him a hell of a life."

Sophie Goodman was glacial with her husband.

"If you think I'll give you the satisfaction of a divorce, you're very much mistaken. Life will go on as usual, and you will play your part. I shan't say anything to your little popsy. Under the circumstances, she's highly unlikely to be with us for much longer."

Her icy tone changed to sheer spite. Sophie picked up Peter's Bible from the dining table.

"I had a look at the passage you're reading next Sunday. Luke 14 isn't it? I was very moved by verse 27: 'And whosoever doth not bear his cross, and come after me, cannot be my disciple...'."

She looked at him with an intense hatred.

"I hope you have strong shoulders, Peter."

Penelope Bland summoned Anna to the Manse. She went in trepidation. Six weeks had passed since *'The Affair in the Vestry'* had become common knowledge. The only open reproach had come from Anna's lips.

"Why didn't you speak with me, Rachel? It's all such a mess."

Rachel dabbed at her eyes. She was inclined to be lachrymose at the merest hint of sentiment, never mind a full-blown crisis.

"Please forgive me Anna. I'm such a fool. I can never control my tongue. Proverbs is full of people like me." Rachel Burton knew her Bible inside out.

"*A perverse person stirs up conflict, and a gossip separates close friends.*"

She sobbed even harder.

"I don't deserve your friendship, Anna."

"Come here Rachel." She hugged her Curate and stroked her hair. "We'll always be friends.

You're very important to me. I love you, as a sister."

"Forgive me, forgive me."

"Of course I forgive you. As my Gramps used to say, 'It'll all come out in the wash'."

Anna parked in front of the Old Manse, wondering what the Blands wanted. She was nervous about the reception she would receive. In the weeks past many had kept their conversations with her brief and terse. Only Mary Beccles and Tom Carter had been true to themselves, and to their Faith, chatting to her freely as of old. Mary referred to the 'business' just once.

"It's a nine-day wonder, Anna. Wagging tongues won't go on for ever." Mary was also a realist. "Though I'm sorry to say, my dear, that you'll probably get moved on to pastures new. God moves in mysterious ways. The Church of England is more predictable. There's plenty in Manor Green who'll miss you."

Jacob Bland was the epitome of graciousness when he answered the door.

"Do step into the hallway, Anna. Pen will be with you shortly. Would you excuse me? Rather bogged down with paperwork."

He left her alone. She was acutely aware that she had not been invited into the drawing room, or kitchen. Normally, a cup of tea would already be in her hand.

"Anna, my dear, so sorry to keep you hanging about."

She held up her flour-dusted hands, before wiping them clean on her pinny. Anna almost guffawed, as the image of Pontius Pilate flitted through her mind.

"Endless baking for the Village celebration. Which rather brings me to the point. Jake and I have the most enormous favour to ask of you."

She explained that her son and his friend had turned up for the weekend, unexpectedly.

"We have an absolute houseful – no room at the Inn!" She brayed at her flaccid theological wit. "Now you roam around alone in that rambling old vicarage. Oodles of room." Penny was at her most charming. "Would you mind, awfully, giving the two young men a bed for the night? I'm sure you'll enjoy their company."

Anna put it down to her imagination. Was there a malicious twinkle in her eyes, and in her choice of phrase?

"Yes, yes Penny. Only too glad to help out."

Jake Bland was in the doorway. "Thank you Anna. Got us out of a tight spot." He put his arm around his wife's shoulders, and they beamed at her.

"Well...I'll be off then. Lot's to do. Oh, what time shall I expect the boys?"

"The young men will be dining with us. Would 10.30 this evening be too late for you?"

"No, not at all."

"Justin and his friend Hugo will be punctual. Jacob will see to that. Bye then."

Anna's guests arrived at ten-to-eleven. They were already the worse for wear from drink. She offered them coffee, but Justin's winning way cajoled her into opening a bottle of wine. The rape came without preamble, and little was said during the ordeal. Anna remembered only one comment. Hugo thrust into her violently.

"So, you like old men, do you? About time you tried some young cock!"

After Anna had spoken with Jacob Bland the next day he conveyed the information to his wife, before their guests arrived. Penelope Bland stood stock still over the dining table. Then she gave a short toss of her wavy hair.

"Suppose what she says is true. Johnny Carstairs would tear her to shreds in the witness box. After her shenanigans with Peter Goodman she's no threat whatsoever." She placed the fork with gunsight precision. "You should have a quiet word with those two young men, Jake."

"I'll have 'em on the carpet in my study."

"Oh do leave it until just before they leave tomorrow. Let's not spoil their weekend. Speaking of departures. Have you had a word in Bishop Arthur's shell-like?"

"All in hand darling. Arthur knows the score. Think he'll act accordingly."

Penny reached up to her husband, and her arms made a chain around his neck.

"Tigger, you are wonderful." She kissed him lingeringly.

*

Billy hasn't moved throughout the telling. Anna raises her head. There is no condemnation; no judgement. Loving friendship is in his face.

"We should return the children to the Orphanage. Come Anna." His hand has never left hers. They turn and bow to the Cross. "You say that Adam knows nothing of this?"

"Not the whole truth."

They emerge into the late-afternoon sunlight.

"Should I tell him?"

Billy stops, and faces her. "That is your choice. He will not be shocked; he will not condemn you. Your grandfather will love you even more."

"As you do."

He throws his head back and roars. "Well of course I do. Can't be a top-hole Christian if love is not in your heart. Come along Mrs. Anna, our little princes and princesses are waiting. They will be ravenously hungry. Let's get them home."

Two assistants are huddled with the children on the pathway. One of the ladies runs towards Billy and Anna.

"What is it Nadia?"

"Reyansh is missing. We cannot find him anywhere."

"You have searched the grounds?"

"Yes."

"And you made it quite clear to the children that they must not stray out onto the road?"

"Yes."

Anna interrupts. "When did you last see him, Nadia?"

"Some of the boys say he was loitering by the entrance, talking to a girl."

"Then as Sir Arthur Conan Doyle has said, *'Once you eliminate the impossible, whatever remains, no matter how improbable, must be the truth.'* Nadia, you and Indira stay with the others. Come Anna. The roadway."

Billy looks to his left, but Anna spots her 'ray of light' first. Billy is chasing after her as she runs towards the boy, and the two girls hovering over him. Reyansh's mouth is smeared with the remains of a pastry. One of the girls proffers another *Gulab Jamun*, and the greedy little boy reaches for the golden delight, whilst the other whispers sweet promises in his ear. Anna pulls his hand away, and clasps him tightly. Her eyes are fixed upon the two young girls. They are aged beyond their years, and fearful. Not of her. A man and his bodyguard walk towards them from a shining car.

"Good afternoon Anna. How very nice to see you again. Thank goodness you have found the little chap. We were passing by, and saw the poor fellow looking lost and hungry. How is your grandfather, in the best of health I hope? Do convey my greetings to him...and his lovely wife. Have a pleasant journey back to the Orphanage. Good day." Khan raises his hat. His bodyguard rounds up the two girls.

Billy's ire explodes. "We know what you are, Khan. *Ben chod*!"

Khan revolves slowly. His malevolent gaze falls upon Billy. A restraining hand rests on his bodyguard. He lodges the memory for another day. It is not good business to allow yourself to be called a *'sister-fucker'* with impunity.

*

"Hi Mishka, hi Gramps. Any chance of a drink? What a day!"

"Something wrong, Anna?"

She quickly relates the incident with Reyansh.

"We will not allow it to spoil a very special day. Stay with your grandfather while I fetch you that drink. He will bring you even greater refreshment."

"Wait there dumpling."

Adam retreats down the corridor, in the direction of the bedrooms, and reappears in a trice.

"A visitor to see you."

"Mummy, mummy!"

Alexandra Wilbey advances into the room, and clutches her daughter to her. Each wipes away tears of joy from the other. Anna searches over her shoulder.

"Is daddy here?"

"No darling. He's rather busy. Been promoted to Chief Superintendent. Come and sit with me."

"Take her onto the verandah Alex. Mishka and I will join you with the drinks."

Mother and daughter sit side-by-side.

"How did you know I'd be here, mummy?"

"Dad and I have been Skyping each other. He didn't tell me to begin with, but I wormed it out of him."

"What else has he told you?"

"Not a sausage. Here, drinks. Your old Gramps Is not one for blabbing."

Anna comes to an immediate decision.

"It's about time I told the whole truth, and nothing but the truth..."

"Not just yet. Mishka has prepared a superb dinner, haven't you darling? Let's celebrate this wonderful day. My three favourite women in the whole world, together at last. Drink up. I feel a party coming on."

"...and that is exactly what I told Billy."

They sit around the dirty dishes, replete and pensive. Alex Wilbey takes her daughter's hand. After a minute, she rises and collects her handbag from an armchair.

"May I smoke?"

"Only if you give me one."

Mishka is outraged. "Adam, you know what the doctor said."

"Problem Dad?"

He grins. "Old age and poverty, as my Father used to say. Well...old age." Adam strokes

Mishka's arm. "Just the one, my darling, I promise."

Anna looks at her mother with curiosity. She appears totally in control of herself. No extremes of emotion. Alex knows what they are thinking; what they are expecting from her.

"You know, Dad, I'm eternally grateful to you and Mum. I had a proper upbringing. You came to Faith much later than Mum, but between the two of you I was instilled with good values."

She draws lazily on her cigarette. Then addresses the assembled company.

"I can't say I envy you your faith. The demands it puts on you are awesome. I admire you though. Is there a God? Maybe...maybe not. I don't buy into that crap about it being a crutch for weak people. Those of you who truly believe are the toughest bunch in the world. If you weren't you'd give up the race." She looks at Mishka. "I don't know if there's such a thing as Karma." Her laugh is brittle. "Tell the truth, what do I know?"

Anna adopts a look of mock-seriousness. "Zero, zero, fuck all, blank!"

Mishka's hand flies to her mouth. "Goodness me, Anna! Where on earth have you heard that?"

"From a very lovely rickshaw driver."

Mishka giggles. "I really must have words with that naughty fellow."

Alex brings them down to earth. "There is one principle that seems to hold good in this world."

An amused Adam stubs out his fag end. "Do tell."

"What goes around, comes around. You've all been wondering why I didn't fly into a rage when Anna told us what happened to her. You know Dave and I live at the other end of the county, but news travels fast; especially on the police grapevine." She lights another cigarette, which Adam eyes enviously. "Dave told me about a fortnight ago. Just swapping the day's events over dinner. Justin Bland is dead. Road traffic accident. Apparently he'd passed his test, and begged his father to buy him a flash sports car. Daddy was having none of it, but the boy worked on his mother and she twisted her husband's arm. The usual story. Showing off to his girlfriend, and ploughed into a sandstone wall at sixty miles an hour."

Anna broke the spell. "The poor Blands; poor boy."

Alex Wilbey was a remarkable and intelligent woman. She understood her daughter's response, and was filled with an intense pride.

Anna muses to herself. "A child lost, and a child to be born."

The exclamation explodes from all points of the table. "What?"

"I'm pregnant."

Alex leaps to her feet. She seems afflicted with St. Vitus' Dance, as she smothers her girl in kisses. "I'm going to be a granny, a granny." She whoops and whoops, whilst Mishka and Adam embrace Anna. It is Mishka who silences the celebration.

"How do you feel, Anna?"

"Excited, frightened – a little confused about where it will all lead. But I will love my child dearly."

Mishka is nervous, but knows the question must be asked.

"And the father?"

"You mean, is it one of those boys?" Her face is a picture of delight, and she takes her mother's hands. They swing round and round. "It's Peter's, it's Peter's!"

"We'll leave the table for tonight. Come on, settle yourselves in the lounge. Champagne, and more champagne."

"I say Dad, champagne in the Queen of the Hill Stations. They'll be making you Viceroy next. Oh, I am sorry, Mishka."

"Not at all Alex, I am not offended. As Billy says, there is no need for the chip on the shoulder. We are the coming nation. Sit, sit."

"There we are. Now, a toast. To mothers and daughters, grandads and grannies, husbands and wives, but most of all to children."

"*Pyaare.* Only one word is necessary. Family."

Adam reclines. Finally, he is nearing the loving peace he has sought throughout his life. The elusive force dances tantalisingly before him.

"Births, deaths and marriages eh? You can't wack 'em." The old North of England accent trips a fandango.

Father and daughter read each other's mind, and begin to sing.

"The wheels on the bus go round and round,

Round and round, round and round.

The wheels on the bus go round and round,

All through the town…"

They dance a reel as they sing. Suddenly, Adam stops and clutches his throat. A sob is stifled.

"Dad, Dad, are you alright? Come on, sit here next to me."

"Sorry. I just had a flashback. Singing and dancing with my Mum in the kitchen, when I was five-years old."

Alex kisses her Dad tenderly, and holds his head on her shoulder.

"I hear that you've been up to your old tricks."

He stares at her, puzzled.

"Storytelling."

"Oh that. Yes, but not quite the tales I used to tell you at bedtime."

"I know. Sounds like you've revived *'This is Your Life'.*"

"Good grief. How do you remember that? Was it still on the telly when you were a tiddler?"

Alex picks up her drink. "So, is the tale told, or is there more?"

In her eagerness, Anna presses her Grandfather onwards. "Oh, the final chapter, Mum. Mishka and I can't wait to hear."

Adam reaches for the bottle and refills glasses.

"Not sure it's a good idea to continue. What's gone before had an ulterior motive. It was told for your benefit Anna. Call it, opening a window to dispel illusions."

Alex affects a gaiety that doesn't convince. "Good. We brought her up too well."

Her Father looks at her sharply. "What do you mean?"

"Sorry Dad. Have I offended you? What *do* I mean? Anna was brought up the same way I was. The difference is I went out into the working world early, and discovered the fear that infects so many people, and makes them mean. I didn't abandon what you and Mum taught me, but I saw – I see – the world as it is, not what I'd like it to be. Anna darling, it's not you alone, it's your generation. You seem to stay at school forever, cocooned in a world of high-minded principles. That's what I meant, Dad, and that's why I'm glad you told her, and Mishka, your story."

Alex peers into her champagne. "Tell the final chapter - for me Daddy."

He drains his glass, and puts it firmly on the table.

"We never involved you, did we? Never bitched about each other, or involved you in a tug-of-war..."

"...and neither of you explained, Dad. Not you, not Mum. I'd like to know."

Adam speaks hesitantly. "It is the most unedifying part of the tale. Shall we have another bottle of champagne – oil those wheels?"

*

South

Charles Ulric Mycock was a dab hand at shattering illusions. Adam had accepted the job of Director of Sport at High Heath School, Hampstead. Surely, here his values and principles would be validated. A top class public school must be imbued with integrity.

"Still pretty warm for September."

Discussing the weather is the default position for a stout-hearted Englishman upon making the acquaintance of a stranger.

"Yeh, imagine the humidity factor inside those tights."

Charlie drew Adam's attention to the far side of the morning tea trolley, in the Refectory. An ungainly and lumpen women was swabbing her crimplene trousers, where she had spilt tea down them.

"Who's that?"

"Assistant matron. Tell you what mate, if I had to fuck that I'd want two double-strength industrial bin liners. One for her and one for me, in case hers tore." He proffered a hand. "Charlie Mycock, and you're Adam Sampson."

"Pleased to meet you, Charlie. So what do you do here?"

"As little as possible. Teach maths and…"

"Hello sir. Good holiday?"

Adam was surprised that Charlie didn't tell the boy off for interrupting.

"Not bad mate. How was yours?"

"Scuba diving in the Caribbean. Lost quite a lot of weight. What do you reckon?" The boy, about fourteen, pirouetted.

"Yeh, you look a lot trimmer – but the shadow of your arse weighs thirty pounds!"

The youth laughed, and gave Adam the once over. His face resembled the painted mask of a clown.

"I'm in your set, sir. See you."

"Who's that Charlie?"

"Ricky Johnson. He's latched onto me; cos I'm knobbing his mother. She takes me out for some great meals, and I slip her the high hard one. Quid pro quo, Sammo, quid pro quo."

"He gives me the shivers. Looks at you as if he wants to interfere with you."

"Get used to it. Hampstead is full of jousters."

"Jousters?"

"Fudge packers, sausage jockeys."

Adam changed the subject. A person's sexuality was inconsequential to him.

"Before we were so rudely interrupted, you said that you teach maths, and...?"

"Head of Pastoral Care for Middle School."

The lunatics had taken over the asylum.

*

North London has more public schools than public lavatories. Prep schools alone outnumber the angels who serve in God's Legion of Light. Their clients are people who purchase privilege. Of itself, that does not guarantee intelligence or talent in their offspring. It facilitates formative years for networking to be sown into the ground, and made fertile in adulthood. Childhood inculcates into them a sense of entitlement. It stays with them throughout their lives. Cyril Connolly, formerly of Eton College, wrote some rather unflattering words in his book, *'Enemies of Promise'*.

"...the experiences undergone by the boys at the great public schools...are so intense as to dominate their lives and arrest their development...the greater part of the ruling class remains adolescent, school-minded, self-conscious, cowardly, sentimental, and in the last analysis homosexual."

Adam was seduced by the school motto: *"Libertatem per Tolerantia'* – Freedom through Tolerance. At interview he had been awestruck by Headmaster, Oliver Frinton. He was six feet three inches tall, with the build of a plague-wasted cadaver. The sort you see illustrated in a Gerald Scarfe cartoon. Oliver had a curious accent. Ostensibly, he sounded pukka; out of the top drawer. Periodically, the elocution slipped to reveal his true background. He was a dry cleaner's boy from Wapping who had reinvented himself. Still, the money was astronomical, compared to what Adam was earning at Brindle House, and he was a coal man's son. Who cares? Time would reveal the deceitful nature of Oliver Frinton. He was worthy of his nickname, *'Kipper'*; two-faced and spineless.

Adam took a top floor flat in West Hampstead, across the Finchley Road. He was able to walk to work. High Heath School was located on the edge of the Heath, halfway down Spaniard's Lane. A convenient location for teachers, who like to drink. In the direction of Highgate there was the 'Spaniard's Inn'; cosy and discreet for assignations. Backtrack towards Hampstead, and you had 'Jack Straw's Castle' – still a pub in those days. The first time he went there Charlie gave him a pithy summary of the environs.

"See that dip in the Heath? *'Gobbler's Gulch'*. That's what the gay guys call it. Tell you what mate, after dark when all the fag ends are alight it looks like the fairy glen."

The school was a disappointment to Adam. The boys were complacent, and brimming with disdain for anybody unlike them. Rudeness and inattention were endemic. They lived a lie of decency and honour, and Oliver Frinton massaged their egos. Adam had to be fierce and aggressive with the boys in order to make any progress. He became despondent, and there were days when he was tempted to walk into the traffic on Finchley Road, rather than duck and dive across the highway.

Ironically, it was Charlie Mycock who put it into perspective. The closing assembly at the end of the year was for prizes, cups and paeans of praise. Adam and Charlie were lounging against the wooden panelling of the packed assembly hall. The Headmaster leapt onto the podium.

Charlie breathed, "Now let's all suck each other's dicks!"

Illumination flooded Adam's brain. That was it. Everyone was complicit. Adam finally comprehended the game. Despite the heat of the day, and the respite of a long summer holiday, ice solidified along the length of his spine. He knew that he was incapable of joining in; he confessed to himself that he was an outsider.

*

Replenished by lunch, Adam strolled into the Senior Common Room to browse the papers and shoot the shit with whoever was there. Men hid behind their newspapers in acute embarrassment. Muffled crying came from a corner. Art teacher, Caroline Merry, was dabbing her eyes whilst Matron comforted her. Charlie Mycock appeared like the Demon King, from the kitchen.

"Coffee Sammo?"

Together they disappeared into the inner sanctum to put the kettle on.

"What's wrong with Caroline?"

"You know that fuckwit Zach Jerome?"

Adam knew the boy well. He had an air of dumb insolence that would have consigned him to the glasshouse, if he were in the army.

"What's he done?"

"Left a painting on Caroline's desk."

"So?"

"Twat he may be, but a good artist. Supposed to be a cracking likeness of Caroline." His eyes glittered. "Spread-eagled over a vaulting horse, with her hands tied behind her." The Head of Pastoral Care for Middle School was salivating. "That's not the best bit. He's drawn cocks going into every orifice. If I could get prints, I'd make a fucking fortune."

"Has Kipper hauled him in?"

"That's why Caroline's pissed off. Two-day suspension."

"He should be expelled."

"Think, Sammo. JEROME."

"That's the name of the squash courts."

"Yep. His grandpappy paid for them, and his old man contributes to the upkeep, amongst other things. The Jeromes go way back at High Heath."

"So he gets away with it? His family is more important than the welfare and dignity of one of our colleagues?"

"That's about the size of it, buddy. Wonder if she'll let him put it in his GCSE portfolio?"

"For fucks sake, Charlie."

"Aaaah, she'll get over it."

"Thanks for the coffee. Got to go, department meeting."

No such meeting existed. Adam sat in his office, staring at the dregs in his mug. Four years had passed since his arrival. He had made a difference, he knew that, but he thought that the cost might be too high. An iron carapace protected him from slings and arrows, but it also obscured what was finer in him. Beyond work he floated on a cloud of food and drink; roistering with like-minded individuals. He had turned thirty earlier in the year, and the lifestyle was beginning to pall. Inspiration wouldn't be found in the bottom of a coffee cup. It occurred to him that the only tlme he breathed freely was when he took his solitary walks in the Chiltern Hills. They were his Sunday obsession; communing with nature. Despite the trials he encountered, he knew that he could not leave High Heath. The one positive was that the school gave him freedom to innovate and initiate. He couldn't give that up. What he could do was move out of London, and he knew his destination. Each Sunday he took the Metropolitan Line to Cranchurch in Buckinghamshire. From the station he would take off into the hills. He would go and live there.

*

"She is coming, my own, my sweet,

Were it ever so airy a tread,

My heart would hear her and beat,

Were it earth in an earthy bed;

My dust would hear her and beat,

Had I lain for a century dead;

Would start and tremble under her feet,

And blossom in purple and red."

The unfettered ferocity with which Ashley Cross day-dreamed was cataclysmic. Longings bound her fast to childhood. When she came down to earth her unhappiness was more pronounced. She always visualised the woods first. Summer light dappled her face, as she peered through the foliage at the family home. Mum hanging washing on the line, and her Daddy striding from the shed brandishing his garden fork. He would stop to peck his wife on the cheek, and they would laugh. A house filled with laughter and joy. Easter or Christmas Day; Harvest Festival or Bonfire Night in the village – the idyll was unchanging. Above all, Daddy. Ashley loved her mother dearly, but she worshipped her father. His pronouncements on any subject were the final word, and woe betide anyone who challenged him. Not that he aired his views in the manner of a fierce Victorian gentleman. Nor did Richard Carpenter react aggressively to those who might cast doubt on his opinions and conclusions; his wife and daughter were sufficient unto the need. Richard's patriarchal dominance emanated from a softly-spoken tone, and an eternal smile. His party trick, in perpetuity, was to make everyone feel special. So sunny was his disposition that it could be years before you noticed the price you were paying. Ashley was unable to settle her bill, because the luxuries of his attention never ceased to rain down upon her. He made love a debt.

She came out of her fantasy, and her eyes swept the crowded church. Her cake stall had done good business. The Saturday afternoon shoppers in Beaconsfield had come and gone at a steady flow. Tony would be there soon. The one thing she could rely on her husband for was punctuality. It was part of his minor public school credo. He had gone to some God-forsaken place in the North, where chaps were instilled with the right virtues and values. When she had met him Ashley had been eighteen and he twenty-two. He seemed so urbane and sophisticated. Tony's sports car clinched the deal. Marriage was blissful. Tom, their son, arrived and they doted on him. Trouble began to brew when the boy turned nine. Ashley wanted to work, maybe just a part-time job. Unlike her father, Tony *did* turn all Victorian.

"No child of mine is going to be a latch-key kid."

That was that.

She weighed the cake in her hand. The last one on the stall. Now, who could she entice into buying said Lemon Drizzle? Her eye was caught by the rear end of a slim young man with long hair, standing in front of the altar.

"Hi. Were you wondering about the Bishop's Chair?"

Adam was entranced by the depth and sincerity of her smile.

"Oh, yes," he lied. "It's...it's...big."

Her laughter resounded around the cavernous church. It resembled that of a little girl skipping merrily, without a care in the world. She had also recognised it herself, and was startled. Where had it suddenly come from?

"They say Disraeli gave it to us. I'm Ashley. Want to buy a cake?"

Her lips were parted ever so slightly. They seemed wet and inviting.

"Sure, yes. There's lots I need to buy. Just moved into the area. Setting up home, and all that."

She fished. "Won't your wife take care of that?"

"Haven't got one of those."

"New job?"

"Old job. Putting distance between work and play. London in the day, and Cranchurch for rest and recuperation."

"What do you do?"

"I'm Director of Sport at High Heath School in Hampstead."

She never took her eyes off him.

"Well, I'd better be off. Shelves to put up. Oh, sorry, I'm Adam, Adam Sampson."

As they shook hands he felt the cool metal of her wedding ring.

"Nice to meet you Adam, really nice."

She waggled the cake.

"A snip at £1."

"Thought I'd got away with it, Ashley."

She watched him all the way out of the door.

Adam mentioned the encounter to Charlie Mycock. He was, as ever, trenchant in his response.

"Probably got a knob for a husband, who couldn't find his talleywacker with a six-man search party. Fill your boots! What you doing on the train?"

"The GT6 is in dock. The old girl's creaking these days."

Charlie kicked off into a detailed description of his liking for 'old girls'. Allusions to grease and other lubricants leapt from the ravines of his overheated mind.

It was early Saturday afternoon before Adam could get into Beaconsfield to collect his repaired motor. He heard the altercation as he stepped onto the Broadway.

"How am I supposed to get out of there? You've jammed me in; it's as tight as a nun's."

The middle-aged man haranguing Ashley Cross was the worse for wear, by the look of him. She appeared frightened and tearful.

"Excuse me…"

"Who the hell are you?"

Adam had intended to be polite, and defuse the situation. The old temper rose within him.

"Someone who's going to tear you a new asshole, if you don't mind your manners."

He stood toe-to-toe with the aggressive motorist. The man was grossly overweight, and none too steady on his feet. He assessed the younger man in front of him, and thought better of the situation.

"Only want to get my car out of the space," he grumbled.

Adam kept up the front.

"You could get a sixty-seater coach out of there, if you weren't as pissed as a fart."

Aggression reared its head again in the complainant.

"How dare you. I haven't been drinking…"

Fortuitously, a police patrol car had drawn up on the other side of the road.

"Oh, right pal. Let's go and ask him for his opinion."

"Think I'll walk." Mustering his dignity, the man faced Ashley. "My apologies, madam."

"That's alright, Jeremy."

Through bleary eyes he peered at her.

"I'm Tony Cross' wife. Tony…Rugby club."

"Good Lord, yes, yes. Old Tony. Good man old Tone. Right then, yes, must be off."

He tottered in the direction of the wine bar. Ashley and Adam stared at each other.

"I do so hate conflict and confrontations. Thanks for rescuing me."

"You make me feel like a shining knight…but where would we find one at this time of day!"

With the tension broken he tried his luck.

"Tea, coffee? Jungs?"

She accepted, and they walked the short distance to that excellent shop. Adam soon learnt about husband and son, and their home in Chalfont St. Giles not far from her parents.

"I must go, Adam. Thanks again. You've completely restored me."

He leant forward and kissed her on the cheek, to which she responded.

"We must do this again." His words fell as summer rain into her ear; refreshing the dry and arid air.

She breathed an almost inaudible, "Yes."

He pulled a business card from the back pocket of his jeans.

"Got my home number on, as well as work. It's half term next week. I'm free whenever…"

Her face was filled with checks and counterbalances.

"Bye."

With the sun roof open, the GT6 roared along the road to Cranchurch. Adam heard his Mum singing, and he joined in.

"Come into the garden Maud,

For the black bat, night, has flown,

Come into the garden Maud,

I am here at the gate alone;

And the woodbine spices are wafted abroad,

And the musk of the rose is blown…"

It might be said that Alfred Lord Tennyson knew a thing or two.

*

Illicit affairs are not worth relating, unless Charlie Mycock is your audience. They serve to satiate his prurient interest. Once Ashley accepted Adam's proposal of marriage events moved swiftly. His first meeting with the Carpenter clan took place in Milton's Indian Restaurant in Chalfont St. Giles. In 1665, during the Great Plague, John Milton beat a retreat from London to take up quarters in the village. His cottage is almost opposite the eatery. Whilst they waited for Ashley's parents and brother to arrive Adam mused out loud.

"Do you reckon Milton ate here regularly?"

She laughed at his silly suggestion.

"Probably came in for takeaways."

He launched into an impromptu sketch for her amusement.

"Good evening Mr. Milton. Table for von?"

"Takeaway, please, Sanjeev. Lamb Balti – to take away the sins of the world; pilaw rice – flavoured with a grain of mustard seed, and garlic naan bread of life."

"Oh, oh, oh, you are a great vit, Mr. Milton." ASIDE: "Vot the fuck is he talking about, Akbar?

Here we are, JD and coke on the house. What are you writing these days?"

"An epic poem in blank verse concerning the Fall of Man; the temptation of Adam and Eve by Satan, and their expulsion from the Garden of Eden."

"Ve are Hindi. Anything in it for us?" Vot is it you are calling your poem?"

"Paradise Lost."

"Catchy. Aha! One Lamb Balti. Ven you have eaten it you vill think you have regained Paradise. Mind how you go."

"Paradise regained...PARADISE REGAINED. YES!"

Ashley spluttered into her white wine, and grasped his hand.

"Sssssh, the waiters might hear you. God, I love you."

Her demeanour changed in a trice. A demure Ashley materialised from nowhere as she saw her family approaching.

The evening went off well. Richard and his wife, Irene, were the happiest of married couples. They did not betray the disappointment they must have felt at their beloved daughter getting divorced. Her brother, David, was a pompous, pontificating pain. He did not possess his father's discretion, and opined on all subjects. David's chins resembled a three-tiered cake stand. They flowed unhindered to the nether regions of his fat gut. The sewage of half-baked knowledge was delivered, unceasingly, in mangled received pronunciation. David wanted to eschew his mother and father's modest origins.

Hands were shaken outside the restaurant. Ashley and Adam strolled arm in arm to the car.

"What do you think?"

"Your mum and dad are lovely, Ash."

"David can be a pompous ass, but he's goodhearted really."

"I'm sure we'll get on like a house on fire. Your dad is a great guy."

Girly tones tinkled on the air. "Daddy's an angel."

It was on the tip of his tongue to say, "Well, he was in the RAF, so I suppose he got his wings." Her shining eyes made him think better of it.

Richard Carpenter's garden was resplendent. A tribute to the unceasing application he gave to his passion. The marquee groaned with food and drink. No expense was spared for the wedding reception. Wendy Goodrich, *neé* Gunnerson and Abel had been invited.

"Jammy git! You've fallen on your feet."

"Yes mum."

"What?"

"That's exactly what my Mum would have said, if she were here."

"Why isn't she here?"

"Holiday in Lanzarote, Wend. Booked long since."

Abel's agricultural muttering broke in.

"Must 'ave a word with your father-in-law. See what he does with his Dahlias."

"You're looking like the cat who got the cream, Mrs. Goodrich."

Wendy beamed, but remained unusually silent. Adam patted her stomach.

"Good living as well, by the look of it."

She couldn't contain herself.

"I'm preggers! Up the duff, up the spout!"

They both shrieked with delight.

"Half a mo'." He jogged to a table and plucked a bottle of champers. "Can I announce it, Wend?"

She assented, and Adam declared the glad tidings to all and sundry.

"Raise your glasses to Wendy Goodrich, and to Abel…because he's able."

From a corner of the garden a powerful voice sang Gospel. It belonged to Richard Carpenter's old friend, Victor.

"Oh happy day, oh happy day…"

Truly, on that day, Jesus walked in the garden.

*

High Heath School was unchanging. Unhealthy attitudes were repeated *ad nauseam.* Women, especially, bore the brunt. Jacqueline Hampton was told that her place was in the kitchen. Headmaster, 'Freddie' Frinton was a legend in his own lunch hour for his conduct towards female staff. When Sarah Templeton reported to him that Lower School exam reports were indifferent he hurled a chair across his study in temper.

Adam was an 'old sweat'. About to turn forty, and in his thirteenth year on the staff. Married life kept him sane, and their five-year-old daughter, Alexandra, was his treasure. He popped into the staff room for a breather before the swimming meet. Katy Benson stood at the window in floods of tears. He took her arm.

"Come on Kate, take a pew for a minute."

She eased her six-months pregnant body into an armchair.

"He screamed at me. Frinton screamed at me."

"Why?"

"Carpeted me because of that cocky little sod Julian Marlborough."

Adam knew Marlborough. A very talented first year. Smug and self-satisfied. Not too dissimilar from his father, Hugh, who sat on the governing body.

"You know Alex Winter in my form?"

"Yes. Lovely lad."

"Marlborough makes his life hell. Alex is on an assisted place. He lives alone with his mum in a tower block too dreadful for words. I caught Marlborough, and his gang, taunting Alex with a sickening song they made up. All about his clothes, and how he lives in a skip. I gave them detention. Tuesdays – for three weeks. Daddy complained, and Frinton said I'd been too harsh. When I argued he flew into a rage, and bellowed at me."

"What did he say?"

"Don't tell me how to run my school."

"Frinton is a fanny with ears. I'll tell you this for nothing. He's got no right to shout at you, and you'll have an apology by morning."

"Apology?"

"He may be 'Mr. Twat' from Twatsville U.S.A., but stupid he aint. Shouting at a pregnant woman? You could take him to the cleaners, and I don't mean the one his dad owned."

Kate threw an arm across her brow.

"Oh Adam, Adam, I think it's coming!"

"Get yourself off home, Kate, and have a stiff one."

"That's what got me into trouble in the first place. Thanks Adam, you're a treasure."

"Yeh, I should be buried on a desert island."

"Bollocks. Give me a hug."

"Steady on. Go on, home. Apology by morning, you'll see."

"...and that's exactly what she got."

Adam concluded the tale. The Carpenters sat around their Sunday lunch table in silence.

Mother-in-law waded in, with her familiar dogmatic tone.

"Why do you have to get involved? It's none of your concern."

"When a colleague and friend is in trouble isn't it right to help them?"

Brother David stuck his oar in. "Got to look after your own first. If you're marked down as a troublemaker, you'll jeopardise your position. Where will that leave your wife and family?"

"So what you're saying, David, is devil take the hindmost. An admirable moral stance."

"Personal responsibility comes before airy fairy morals."

"But Irene, every time I come here you bemoan that *'fings aint wot they used to be'*. Grumbling about the state of morals these days is something we've heard time and time again. Children with no respect; a lack of common civility. Or do these things only apply to little people. Are the masters of the universe exempt from decent behaviour, because they're our 'betters'?"

Ashley snapped, "Adam!"

He had rustled the branches in the Carpenters' Eden. Daddy might be offended. Her face was flushed in annoyance.

Richard recited one of his interminable stories.

"When I was a boy there was an old sea captain who lived two doors down. He used to tell us boys marvellous stories. On the way home from work one day I passed him sitting on his doorstep. I was fifteen, all bright-eyed and bushy-tailed. Old Arthur asked me what sort of day I'd had. There'd been a spot of trouble at the works. I told Arthur that I intended to pass some information to the management about the furore. He took a long draw on his pipe. 'Dick,' he says, 'when the wind blows strong it's the great trees that fall; little trees bend and stay standing'."

Father's sagacity was received as if Christ had delivered the Sermon on the Mount.

Adam raised his bowed head.

"In *Fiddler on the Roof*, Tevye the Milkman accedes to the requests of two daughters to marry who they want. When Chava, his third daughter asks permission to marry outside the Jewish faith Tevye says: *'If I bend that far, I'll break'*."

Ashley volunteered them both to clear the table, and load the dishwasher. Adam was bent over the machine when the blow was struck. His head rang from the smack it received.

"Don't ever speak to my mother like that, or upset my Daddy with your smart arse remarks."

Research confirms that once a person inflicts violence upon their partner the likelihood is that they'll do it again. Adam rubbed his neck, and recalled a comment Ashley had made a fortnight before. They had been at one of her church socials, and someone asked where he originated from. When he mentioned the North a chap retorted that it was a cold part of the world. Adam laughed, and said, "We didn't have to worry about that. Dad was the local coal man."

"Mummy always said I married beneath my station."

Ashley kissed his cheek, but the barb went home.

"Hi Daddy."

Alexandra had tottered into the kitchen unheard. Adam lifted her into his arms.

"Big hug. It's ages since I had one."

He realised that applied to his wife, as well as his darling daughter. Alex was everything to him; he loved her with every fibre of his being. Mothers like to declare that they would die for their children; fathers always have done, across millennia.

Effusive thanks and goodbyes were said, and they drove home. Alex played, Ashley washed, Adam mowed the lawn. Intermittent conversation dribbled a tepid stream of normality back into their relationship. In the bedroom she took hold of him, and they made love. Married life pursued its unspoken course, but not unbroken in spirit. Adam lay in the dark, and words glowed crimson in the mirror.

"I slept, and dreamed that life was beauty;

I woke, and found that life was duty."

His was a rude awakening.

*

The timbre of her laugh made him dizzy. Adam steadied himself. He looked around the crowded Senior Common Room to ascertain its source. Leaning against the wall, with Charlie Mycock entertaining her; his eyes aglow. She was tall, slender, and possessed a magnificent pair of 'pins'. Short hair, mellow brown and wavy, accentuated her cherub face; skin pale and soft. Holly Browne hailed from the Scottish borders. She'd lived in London since she was eighteen; her accent only retained a gentle burr. Holly was High Heath's first female head of department; Drama. Adam realised why her laugh had knocked him off an even keel, and he shivered. The ghost of Hazel Macklin had walked over his grave.

'Freddie' Frinton was absent. His deputy, Stephen Sherriff, conducted the start of year inset day. Adam managed to secure a seat beside Holly, just beating Charlie Mycock to the punch. He looked over his shoulder, and caught Charlie's eye three rows back. The shape of his mate's mouth was unmistakeable: "Cunt!"

The 'Lawman' got through business swiftly, including the introduction of new members of staff. Holly was now known. The meeting broke for lunch, and Adam made small talk.

"Got anything planned for this evening, Holly? You need to celebrate this exciting meeting."

Goose bumps erupted when she laughed once more.

"Wash a few bits in the hand basin. Get them dry while the Indian Summer lasts."

Adam thought he spied an engagement ring, and pointed.

"Get that boyfriend to treat you to a meal."

Red spots lit her cheeks.

"Oh that. Granny left it to me in her Will…"

"What are you up to, you Lancashire git?"

Michael Bunbury, head of music had docked alongside. Top bloke. He had the most wonderful back catalogue of stories from years lived amongst Hampstead's gay community.

Adam mimicked one of his colleague's favourite phrases.

"How very rude! A bit rich coming from a Cheshire sod buster, so to speak."

"You coming to the 'Willy' after this shit's finished?"

"I don't know Mike. I'll get it in the ear if I'm late home and pissed – AGAIN."

"Taking it in the ear. I say. How very adventurous. Oh, you can blame me, as per. Whenever he gets shitfaced, Holly, he tells his wife it's my fault. Miserable old fart, come and join us. Ashley's put up with you all summer." He cocked a thumb at Holly. "You can bring your girlfriend."

Mike and Holly cracked up.

"Have I missed something?"

"Never mind. Yes, or no? We'll all need reviving after listening to that little Welsh cunt rabbiting on all day. Coming or not?"

"It's just the way I'm standing."

"How very vulgar. Watch out for this one, Holly. In my experience, sporting types love to 'play up, and play the game'. Our Mr. Sampson has some very funny rules of his own."

"Bugger off. Haven't you got some scales to finger?"

The three of them marched to the Refectory for lunch. An air of companionship and gaiety embraced them.

A confluence is the junction where two rivers meet. Holly Browne and Adam were those rivers. Working beside one another they developed the intimacy of companionship. Neither asked, but both gave. He saw the way her open heart welcomed everyone. Creed, colour and gender meant nothing to her. She loved humanity. It quietened his troubled spirit.

He had been a *habitué* of the King William IV for some years. Hampstead's famous gay pub was their watering hole. Now he stood beside Mike at the bar.

"You dirty get. I saw what you were up to."

Adam looked as though butter wouldn't melt in his mouth.

Mike held his hand upright to his forehead, and waggled it sideways whilst humming the theme tune to 'Jaws'. An accusation of *'sharking'*.

"Give over. I'm fifty-three and bereft of illusions."

"You'd be wasting your time anyway. She's a bean flicker."

"Sorry?"

"A rug muncher – a todger dodger. She's a lesbian."

"Holly?"

"No, the Queen Mother!"

"Well I never…"

"No, and you never will. Here, carry these drinks while I pay."

Mike showed up eventually, after passing through an avenue of banter and gossip.

"I was telling Adam you're a lezzer."

"Oh that. Does it show from the front? Got a favour to ask."

Her big eyes mesmerised Adam.

"Mike and I have decided on *'Guys and Dolls'* for Christmas. Will you be our choreographer?"

"How did you know…" He looked at Mike. "Bunbury, you fucking Cheshire Cat, you've stitched me up."

"Somebody needs to get you out of yourself. You've been a right miserable old get this last year."

Holly: "Please."

Mike: "Pretty please."

"Okay, okay, but I warn you. I'm a bit out of practice."

"Aren't we all dear. Not much prospect of pulling in here tonight. Oh, I don't know."

A muscular young man walked in, clad in Lycra.

"I say – CT. Cyclist Trade. Drink up, I need to get to the bar urgently."

Mike was off, like a rat up a drainpipe. Within seconds he was deep in conversation with our knight of the road.

Holly rested a hand on Adam's arm.

"Thanks for taking on the dance. Weight off my mind."

"Nice to be asked. I must push off. Wife and kids you know. You must meet them. Everybody ends up at our place, sometime or the other. Mike, Charlie Mycock…"

"Who?"

"Charlie. The guy talking to you in the Common Room before the meeting."

"That's not his real name."

"It is. The stars must have aligned at his birth to create that name for him. See you tomorrow."

Adam strode through the grandeur of Hampstead's streets. What a good day. He hadn't choreographed for years, but was excited at the prospect. On the train, he realised that it would mean more time away from home. Oh well, his step-son Tom was never home anyway, and Alex was growing fast and always occupied with her mates. He doubted Ashley would be bothered. She'd been secretary to the vicar for some time now, and sat on endless committees. They led a comfortable and civil existence, but they had separate lives. Religion was a topic off limits, by mutual consent. If, by mischance, they drifted onto the subject Ashley would become frustrated and annoyed. She couldn't find the words to express herself. Adam liked to argue a subject through. When he was a child this was commonplace around the dinner table, and usually ended with gales of laughter between him and his parents. Ashley expected to be agreed with automatically. At her childhood table Daddy's opinions were devoured as though they were prophecy from the Oracle at Delphi. 'Wisdom' was received without question.

*

Julian Marlborough had long ceased to bully Alex Winter. Principally, because the poor boy had left the school. He had been made to feel like a fish out of water. Alex was an outsider.

The years had been kind to Julian. He had grown into a big and strong young man, and he was the star of the Rugby team. He was an intelligent and gifted boy, but his eyes gave the game away to the keen observer. Hidden behind his perpetual smile, they were grave. You felt that if you plunged into them you might never touch bottom. Julian was still a year or two short for the main roles in *'Guys and Dolls'*, but he was wonderful as the gangster 'Big Julie'.

Holly's first experience of trouble at High Heath came on a Sunday. It was Tech. Dress Rehearsal day. The cast were trying on their hired costumes in a flurry of excitement.

"Here's yours, Julian."

"That's alright, Miss, I've got mine."

Holly looked at the label.

287

"You can't have. Perhaps you've got someone's by mistake."

"No Miss. My mother hired this for me." He held up a splendid, but bizarrely coloured outfit.

"Come and take your costume, Julian. This is the one I want you to wear…"

"Don't worry, Miss, we'll pay for that one. I want to wear this outfit."

"Julian, we've spent time and money deciding on a style and colour scheme. The one you've acquired is unsuitable. I'd be obliged if you'd put it to one side, and get dressed in this one – quickly."

Marlborough's mouth half-opened, but he caught Adam's stony gaze. Snatching the costume from Holly's hand, he stalked off.

The doors of the theatre foyer crashed open. Hugh Marlborough interrupted their coffee and conversation.

"Miss Browne," he oozed. He and his son shared the same repellent 'titty' lips. "A word." The tone was imperious. "Julian *always* wears the costume we hire for him. We feel that it gives him more confidence in his performance."

Mike and Adam sipped their coffee. A creamy mixture of curiosity and confidence held their attention. Holly did not disappoint.

"Mr. Marlborough, as I explained to Julian, I'm entirely satisfied with what the Costume Studio supplied…"

"Nevertheless…"

She stood her ground against parent and school governor.

"A production is about teamwork. It simply won't do to have one individual standing out from the rest. Excuse me, we must run the second half. We do like to get the children out on time."

Hugh Marlborough was rigid in disbelief. A slip of a girl had demolished him. His eyes caught those of Mike and Adam. He clearly detected their amusement, and flew out in a rage.

"Cunt!"

Mike chastised Adam.

"Be precise. Oily cunt!"

'Guys and Dolls' went down a storm. Julian, along with everyone else, was excellent. They

celebrated in the 'Willy' on Saturday evening, and the festivities continued in Chalfont St. Giles on Sunday. Ashley was a superb cook, and a gracious hostess. She and Alex both loved Mike for his constant good humour. Something they didn't always find in husband and father.

To Adam's surprise, Mike accosted him on Monday morning.

"What was up with Ashley?"

"I didn't notice anything different in her."

"She was a bit glacial towards Holly. Mind you, the two of you were all over each other like a rash. You hardly spoke to your wife. She does know that she bats for the second eleven?"

"Yeh. Ashley may be a paid up member of the God Squad, but she has no beef with anyone's sexuality."

Mike was pensive.

"I think she's jealous. Do you talk about Holly when you're home?"

Adam blushed. "Too much."

"Oh dear, that's it then. You may not be getting your end away, but I reckon Ashley's worked out how intimate the two of you have become. Tricky question coming up..."

"Go on."

"How are you and Ashley getting on these days?"

"We rub along."

A good friend is always frank; no matter the cost.

"Remember – sex is nothing. It can be forgiven. An affair of the heart is much more serious."

Mike had hit the nail on the head. Adam invested his life in work, and in his relationship with Holly Browne. They liked and respected each other. When the Christmas break arrived it came startlingly into focus. Christmas Day with the Carpenters; never in their own home.

It was early morning on New Year's Eve. Adam wandered into the kitchen in his dressing gown. He felt the sullen silence radiating from his wife's back.

"What's the matter?"

She leapt like a cat, gripped the lapels of his robe and slammed him into the wall.

"What's the matter, what's the matter?" she screeched in mimicry. "I'll tell you what the matter is...I don't like you."

Ashley burst into tears, and fled.

The Christmas Spirit lay like a weight upon him. It was crushing what little was left of *his* spirit. Blank eyes looked upon a wintry garden. He had no idea what to do, or what he wanted to do. Had Nelson Horsley been wrong? Was December the most desolate of months?

Half an hour passed. Ashley walked into the kitchen, chattering briskly. It was as if nothing had occurred. A chill froze Adam to the spot. He saw his mother having one of her wailing tantrums. As quickly as they started they would stop. You were left uncertain of yourself. Had it been real, or a waking nightmare? Adam was doleful. He thought that they might be the same thing.

"Mum," he murmured under his breath. "Mum and Dad."

He was due to visit them on January 2nd. He would drive North on New Year's Day.

*

Ridgate had never been Home Counties pretty, but perhaps most people retain a loyalty to the place of their birth. Adam felt the atavistic spirit grip him, as he wandered through Ridgate Park. The lake shimmered in the sharp air of a new year. He peered into the remnants of 'Big Wood', across the lake. Whoops and blazing six guns echoed around his inner ear. He squatted, and caressed the undulations of the cold land. The earth was bone hard, but the taste of the rich loam was in his mouth.

Soon he must see his ailing parents. First he would take a look at the old de Halsall mansion. Its nineteenth century magnificence was blighted by modern accretions; symmetry disfigured. Adam experienced the oddest sensation. The building looked as though it might topple any moment. Wrested into rubble by the weight of modernity. He was frightened.

"Mr. Greenwood, you'll catch your death."

An old man emerged through the front door, pursued by a care worker.

"I'm near enough to that, lass, not to be bothered. Hello young man. Are you lost? By the cut of your jib you're not from these parts."

"You'd be wrong there, Mr. Greenwood. Born and bred."

The old choirmaster had to be ninety.

"Do I know you, young man?"

"Adam Sampson, Mr. Greenwood."

A firm hand gripped his.

"By the good Lord, Ted and Annie's youngest. How are you doin' lad?"

Adam gave the old feller a summary of the years.

"Are you still singing?"

The fire in his eyes took Adam aback. He didn't want to disappoint.

"I help out with musicals. We've just done *'Guys and Dolls'*.

"Ee, that's a smasher."

He began to sing. 'Luck be a lady tonight...'. The circular motion of his hand encouraged Adam to join him.

"Best be careful. We were getting like Norman and Fred Cussiter; battling it out for supremacy."

Tommy shook with glee.

"That pair o' buggers – begging your pardon, Jessie."

The stout lady grinned. Adam knew the type. She'd heard a thing or two in her time.

"By lad, you've a memory on you. Owld Norman passed over two years since. Young Fred's running the business. I expect he'll tuck me away when the time comes. I'm ninety-one, tha' knows."

"Looking well on it."

"Young Jessie here, and her bevy of maidens, keep me on my toes. Have you not thowt of joining your local church choir? You've always had a smashing voice. I can still hear well enough to know that you can hold a tune."

Adam shuffled, uncomfortably.

"I'm not much of a churchgoer. The wife is never out of the place."

Tommy Greenwood gripped both of his hands with ferocity.

"Get yourself along there with her. Use that voice. Praise the Lord, Adam. Praise the Lord!"

"Come on now, Tommy. You've been out long enough."

"Aye Jessie, mebbe you're right. Adam Sampson...by gum. Look after your sen lad."

He took Jessie's arm, and she paused.

"Give my best to your Dad. Tell him Jessie Norman were askin' after him."

"With a name like that *you* must have a fine voice."

Tommy chortled. "'undred per cent tone deaf. We pay her not to sing."

"Don't forget now, Adam. Jessie Norman. He'll remember. I lived next door to Eunice Bickerton."

She looked over her shoulder, as she led Tommy indoors. A wry smile danced on her lips.

Tommy's encouragement to sing gave Adam the incentive for one more stop, before seeing his Mother. He wandered along the broken old path, beyond the rhododendrons. Familiar names leapt at him from the tombstones. Still there after all those years. Hysteria gripped him, and he laughed at his idiocy.

"Well they would be, wouldn't they!"

"Can I help you?" The young cleric eyed him curiously.

"Sorry, sorry, just a funny thought. Is it alright to have a quick look inside?"

"You're more than welcome. I'm Allan Weston. Vicar, for my sins."

"Not too many of those I hope?"

"None of us can ever escape from sin." He added cheerily, "But we can keep on trying."

Adam retrieved something from the recesses of his mind.

"Run the race. Persevere. Hebrews 12?"

"That's right. I've never seen you in St. Barnabas'. Do you live in Ridgate?"

Adam related his history. Even Allan Weston had heard of Ted and Annie Sampson. It appeared the parish was in a poor state. Allan was filled with sublime confidence. Hard work and perseverance would bring the prodigal sons and daughters home. Adam was nearly at his car when the Vicar's voice resounded like a clarion call. He had taken a short cut to catch Adam. Allan Weston stood clothed in the evergreen leaves of the rhododendrons.

"Hebrews 12. There's a passage just after your quote:

'Consider Him who endured such opposition from sinful men, so that you will not grow weary and lose heart.'

God bless you, Adam."

Observant bugger.

*

Captain Kirk got it wrong. Death is the final frontier, and you don't pass over cossetted in the throbbing womb of the Star Ship Enterprise.

"Whose is the motor, Graham?"

Adam's step-father ushered him indoors. He was a quiet and nervous soul, who wouldn't say boo to a goose.

"The doctor is with your mum."

Graham brewed up, while they waited for the doctor. He soon appeared.

"I'm her son, doctor. How's she doing?"

"It's pneumonia." He sucked the air out of the living room. "She hasn't got long. We can hospitalise her, but she'd be more comfortable in her own bed." Dr. Jenkins looked to them for an answer.

Graham was not the most decisive of men. "What do you think, Adam?"

"Mum's always loved her home."

Graham nodded. "We'll keep her with us. Thank you doctor."

A broken bird lay motionless. Adam was shocked by the sight of his mother's deterioration. An alien head rested on the pillow. His Mum's eyes drew waters of pity; black and empty in the face of unfathomable eternity. He knelt beside her, and stroked her wispy hair.

"Hiya Mum...it's Adam. Alex and Tom send you their love...and Ashley, of course."

The alarm clock ticked; measuring her race with time.

"Did you have a good Christmas? We did. The weather's a bit better down south. By gum, it's parky today."

Adam reverted to the style of speech she would recognise from her youth. For twenty minutes he regaled her with tales of yesteryear. "Dear Father," he prayed, "let memories of happier times flood her soul and fill her with peace." He kissed her forehead, and nearly jumped out of his skin.

"How's your Dad?" Her voice had all the vigour of youth.

"He…he's alright, I think. I'm off to see him soon."

"Remember me to him." She never spoke again, and died later in the day.

Ted Sampson was frail, and dependent upon his wife. He seemed content, and Irene did him proud. Adam informed his step-mother that his Mother had died.

"He should know, Adam. Keep it simple."

"Dad…Dad."

Ted raised his head from his chest.

"Hello son. What are you doing here?"

"I said I'd pay you a visit in the new year."

"Is it January already." The old wry humour sprang from his lips. "Life goes quickly when you're having a good time."

"Bit of news, Dad. Not the best."

"Spit it out."

"Mum passed away, yesterday evening."

Ted searched Adam's face for a long time.

"I'm sorry to hear that." His chin slumped to his chest.

Adam sat with his Father. He turned to prayer. A kaleidoscope of phrases, fragments, skittered through his mind. Bits of sermons flying over a choir boy's head. A few morsels retained. How foolish we are to judge the value of another's life. We witness the badness of others. Who are we to say that even the tiniest good they have done does not outweigh the burden of their flaws. Every life is imperfect.

When Adam arrived in Chalfont St. Giles, Ashley took him in her arms. He felt a terrible resentment. An impression suppurated within him, that his wife had always looked down on his Mum. The hurt was unbearable.

Annie Sampson was laid to rest in the churchyard. Allan Weston presided with delicacy and sympathy. It was a poor turnout. Most of her contemporaries had predeceased her, even Josie. They spent an hour or two in the Horse and Groom, to give the semblance of a Wake. An ancient Ernie Ogle was propping up the bar, and squeezed a pint out of Adam. He laughed all the way back to Buckinghamshire.

'Freddie' Frinton had to grant him compassionate leave again. Within the month his Dad breathed his last. The coal dust finally did for him. Adam sat beside him, and listened to his laboured breathing in the hospital bed. Ted's eyes held the same eternal blackness as Annie's. Yet a terrible anxiety flickered in them, intermittently.

To Ashley's surprise, Adam had asked her if he could borrow her Bible. He opened it at Psalm 23, and intoned the shepherd psalm of David.

"The Lord is my shepherd; I shall not want.

He maketh me to lie down in green pastures.

Yea, though I walk through the valley of the shadow of death, I will fear no evil: for thou art with me…"

A tiny tremor passed through Ted.

"…Surely goodness and mercy shall follow me all the days of my life: and I shall dwell in the House of the Lord forever."

Love overwhelmed him. He stroked his Father's brow, and knew that it was for his Mum also. The two imperfect people who had given him the gift of life.

The gathering at Ted Sampson's funeral was substantial. Men and women, who had been the children of his customers, turned out in force. Ted was honoured for the cheerful disposition he always carried, along with sacks of coal. Allan Weston joined the party for the Wake. He got deep into conversation with Ashley. They swapped tales of parish life at opposite ends of the country. After a while he made his apologies. Unexpectedly, he returned, and tapped Adam on the arm.

"Have you a minute, Adam?"

He drew the former choir boy to one side.

"This may sound brutal. When parents die the first thing we realise is that we are next." An ironic smile lit Adam's features. "Ah. Thing is, Adam, don't be afraid. There's so much life yet to be lived." The Vicar's eyes gripped Adam in a vice. "Choices to be made. Decisions to take. Think them through carefully, and take your time. Don't jump into anything. God bless you...and your wife and children. Whenever you're up here come and say hello."

Adam watched him go. A pensive mood stirred. Why had Allan taken the time to make that little speech? Was he just a keen observer, or...? Adam knew that someone was watching him. Ashley smiled across the room, and it melted hls heart. Had she...? He picked up his drink and joined her. His cousin Harry was regaling the company with tall tales. It was good to hear laughter.

*

Restoration is only possible when remains of the original creation are still standing. Love, in ruins, can be salvaged if both parties wish to create an edifice which is theirs alone; without intrusion from outside elements. Ashley and Adam did not succeed. Their fertile oasis had always been a mirage. An extended dalliance had been waltzed for nearly twenty years. There was merely the last brilliant flame of a shooting star, on its way to extinction. Adam went to church with his wife, and was appalled. The granite certainty, delivered by the ministers of his youth, was dumbed down. Sermons were insulting in their banality; modern hymns wallowed in the sentimental tripe of pop songs. He longed to sing those words that were rich in spirit, to elevate his heart, mind and soul. What he got was a group of wannabe rock stars, in their sixties, expressing an aesthetic preference. The quality of the cake was excellent.

Life at High Heath School took a turn for the better. Time enabled Adam to become inured to the shenanigans that went on, daily. Then, after a peaceful interlude, Jack Parker arrived.

"His singing voice is superb." Mike Bunbury beamed as brightly as the sun in Adam's garden.

"Can he dance?" Holly looked eager.

"Like a dream."

"He delivers the dialogue beautifully," she added. "All agreed? Jack Parker as the King."

Holly had made a name for herself. The Drama department was a focal point of excellence. Julian Marlborough was the undisputed, and unchallenged, king; until now.

Adam popped in to see Holly at lunchtime. She sat at her office desk crying.

"Hey, hey. What's all this about?"

She slid a piece of paper sideways. The large font read:

"YOU KNOW JACK SHIT ABOUT DRAMA YOU BITCH. FUCK OFF TO HOLLAND AND STICK YOUR FINGER IN THE DYKES!"

She sobbed on his shoulder whilst he murmured, "We'll sort it out."

He organised some coffee, and they sat reflecting.

"Someone's pissed off, because they didn't get the part they wanted."

"What are you going to do about it, Hol?"

"Not much I can do."

"Take it to Frinton."

"It could have come from any computer."

"Hardly the point. You're not the only gay person on the staff. He needs to stamp hard on this sort of behaviour. I think we can guess who produced this garbage."

"We can't prove it, and with his parental connection it would go nowhere."

Adam spoke bitterly, through clenched teeth.

"Why do they always get away with it?"

'Freddie' Frinton expressed his regrets, and instructed the PSHE department to up the ante on sexuality issues. Two weeks into rehearsal of 'The King and I' Marlborough withdrew, citing pressure of exams. There was no grief for Holly from Hugh Marlborough over his son being denied the star role, but there was for Adam. Julian was an outstanding Rugby player; Jack

Parker was better, and they played the same position. Adam rode out the Marlborough fury.

High excitement gripped the school. *"West Side Story"* was being produced, and it was Julian's final year. The peachy roles are Tony and Maria, the star-crossed lovers. There was no doubt. Jack Parker for Tony, and Sophie Palmer as Maria. Not only was Julian displeased at being cast as Riff, the leader of the 'Jets', but also at seeing his girlfriend playing opposite his arch-rival.

Charlie Mycock taught the girl 'A' level maths. He drooled over his prawn sandwich.

"Fit as a butcher's dog! Tell you something else, Adam. She's a first-rate prick teaser. Knows exactly what she's doing. The other girls don't like her. Watch out for sparks."

He proceeded to give a graphic instruction for the application of toothpaste to sensitive areas with an electric toothbrush. Charlie always deserved top marks for invention, if not for propriety.

Julian Marlborough's campaign of persecution began after half term. Holly walked into her 'A' level class.

"What are you playing, guys?"

Marlborough sat upright, a malicious grin on his face.

"It's Tiddlywinks with chocolate beans. Do you fancy a game of Bean Flicking, Miss? I bet you'd be a terrific bean flicker."

Charlie Mycock summed it up, after Adam told him.

"Marlborough's always been a cunt; he's a cunt now, and the only change in his life is that he'll become a bigger cunt!"

A fair appraisal, and a decent paraphrase from the film *'In Bruges'*.

The following week, Marlborough employed a variation.

"Excuse me, Miss. Do you know a play by Brendan Behan – *'The Hostage'*?"

"I do."

"His brother Les was also a writer."

"Pardon?"

"Les, Miss. LES BEHAN!"

For the first time since they'd known her, Holly's sparkle deserted her. A nasty, and personal, war of attrition wore her down.

It was a November evening, and Adam was wrapped in a curtain stage right.

"You're a northern twat Parker. 'Tony' was my role. Sophie says your breath stinks."

"She still flicks her tongue around my mouth, like a lizard on 'coke'. You still doing that stuff?"

"Watch yourself, Parker."

"Run and tell mummy and daddy, will you? Why does your mum always hang around school with you?"

Adam had to place a hand over his mouth to stifle a laugh. Jack Parker had cut his opponent to the quick. Holly said that the rest of the set referred to mother and son as Oedipus and Jocasta.

"Fuck you, Parker. You're all in for one big surprise."

'West Side Story' was an immense success. The ritual party, in Chalfont St. Giles, was as lively as ever. Ashley excelled herself as chef and hostess. She flitted from one group to another. Her enjoyment seemed genuine, and she gathered with others around Charlie Mycock who had them all in stitches.

It was ten-thirty p.m. when Charlie collared Adam in the kitchen.

"Great party. I'm way over the limit mate. Can I crash on your sofa?"

"Best clear it with Ashley…"

"Oh, she says it's fine. Hey, sit yourself down. I'll give Ashley a hand. You must be knackered."

Adam flopped into an armchair, glass in hand. He smiled inwardly. A great success for Holly, and she seemed back to her old self…"

"Adam! Adam!" His bleary eyes opened. "You've made a mess. Red wine everywhere." He had fallen asleep to the siren dance of her girlish laughter, two-stepping around the kitchen.

"Sorry…so sorry, Ash…"

"Never mind. Get yourself off to bed."

"I'll just get some bedding for Charlie…"

He stood beside Ashley. "We'll sort that out, mate."

Adam stumbled into the door jamb.

"Sorry Ash, sorry…"

He held onto the frame, and looked at her. She was utterly detached. There was a long, long tunnel in front of him. He could walk through it forever, but he would never reach her.

In the depths of the night he woke with a raging thirst. Unsteadily, he manoeuvred himself down the stairs. The image of himself as a boy halted him halfway. It was the night he had witnessed his Mum and Dad arguing. Seeing something he shouldn't. Ashley was sitting astride Charlie on the sofa; naked and upright. No one spoke. Visiting the de Halsall crypt, as a boy, had been less eerie. Ashley left the room. Charlie dressed, and Adam heard the front door click shut.

Copious draughts of coffee were drunk that Monday morning in the Senior Common Room.

"Holly, the Headmaster would like to see you. Straight away, please."

"Gold star is it, Anthea?" Mike whooped.

Headmaster's Secretary, Anthea Dawson, winced.

End of term assembly passed in a blur, and the staff Christmas lunch was on.

"Seen Holly, Mike?"

"Not since she went to see 'Freddie'. Probably arsing around in her office. Go and get her."

Adam collided with her, as she emerged from the Drama Studio. Her face was ashen, and she trembled violently. He took her hand.

The cheap clock in the office ticked irritatingly.

"You will believe me, won't you Adam?"

"Of course I will. I love you…"

"Oh Adam…"

"Not that way. That's always been a non-starter. You're a wonderful person. What's Frinton done now?"

Her head was bowed. "He has to act on a complaint."

"From?"

"Sophie Palmer. She says I've been making passes at her…that I kept touching her breasts when I moved her around the stage. I didn't Adam. There's not one shred of truth in her allegations."

Adam took her hands, as Nelson Horsley had once done for him when he was in distress.

"Not one word of truth. She's a liar."

"But how do I prove it? There'll be police and social workers. They always think the worst."

"Come here. Put your arms around me, and hold as tightly as you can." Words spilt from Adam, like a crystalline waterfall. "God knows where the goodness inside you comes from. I will not let you be lost. I've found in you the purest love in my life. You will not be abandoned."

"It won't make you popular."

"Psssh, when did that matter? Love is costly; I'm prepared to pay the price."

A smile, as stark as trees in a winter graveyard, flickered.

"I'll go home."

"Shall I take you?"

She shook her head.

"You call me any time; any means. I'll come running."

"You'll have to come to Scotland. I'm going home for Christmas."

Hand in hand, they walked to the school gates. She hugged him, then drifted in the direction of the Northern Line. A chill flat in Camden Town. A smattering of sleet whirled in the air. Adam watched his darling Holly until she was a dot. Her back forlorn, as she stooped into the wind.

Acrimony was muted. Some grievances spilt onto the carpet, like the red wine. On this occasion salt couldn't remove the stain, it just aggravated the wounds. Adam's last remark devastated his wife.

"I don't dislike your mum and dad, but it's about time they let you leave home!"

Her plaintive retort made him wish that he'd bitten his tongue.

"You don't know how painful it is to love someone so much!"

The divorce was agreed upon. Alex and Tom were told, without elaboration. Their parents felt a growing sense of relief that matters had come to a head. The only thing unsettling Adam was that, apart from a quick 'Happy Christmas' on the 'phone, Holly was incommunicado. He sent a few texts, but...

Adam's mobile bleeped in the early hours. He was sleeping lightly, and cursed bloody Virgin rail offers. Holly's text was long and rambling. Grief cascaded from her. She wrote of her hatred for High Heath; pride in her gay identity, and that she hadn't gone near Sophie Palmer. He texted:

"I BELIEVE YOU – TALK TO ME." She never replied.

The journey through the snows was terrible. He gazed in wonder at the beauty of the Heath before entering the building. Adam stepped into a common room blanketed in silence, apart from stifled weeping. He saw Stuart Robshaw with his arm around Mike Bunbury. Gall filled his throat. A picture of Doris Burford and Isobel Holmes clutching each other rose before him.

"She's dead Adam, she's dead."

At five that morning, the tenant below discovered water coming through the ceiling. Holly lay in the bath, her wrists slashed; the water blood red. The police informed her parents, then Frinton. His sententious tone resounded throughout the Great Hall.

"Holly Browne, our Director of Drama, has, I'm afraid to say, been found dead this morning. I can say no more. We think of her family, and of the great impact she made upon our lives in the short time she was with us at High Heath."

Anthea Dawson took Adam by the elbow, and drew him away from the tea trolley. Outrage suffused her features, and she spoke tersely.

"Sophie Palmer, and her mother, saw the Head' at lunchtime. I can sympathise with the girl, up to a point, she's very distressed…"

"And?"

"It was a tissue of lies. She's admitted it in writing. The police and social services have been informed. Barring the formalities, Holly is completely exonerated…"

"…but dead!"

She took his hand.

"What will happen to Sophie?"

"In the hands of the police. I doubt they'll come down hard on her. She was put up to it."

"Who?"

Anthea peered at him intently.

"He will be interviewed at eleven tomorrow morning. His father will be present. I do hope he'll find a spot to park his new Aston Martin. Tread carefully, Adam."

He stayed the night with Mike. Both too shitfaced to care where they were. The next morning passed in desultory fashion. Jack Parker strolled beside him, as they made for an early lunch. The playground was a nightmare of ice, so they went round the front. Caught between the outer and inner doors to the foyer, they heard voices.

"Most unfortunate Hugh, most unfortunate."

An oleaginous voice responded to the Headmaster.

"I feel sure that we can reach an accommodation. I'll set my solicitor on to it. Julian didn't actually do anything."

Adam's arm was held across Jack's chest.

"Quite Hugh...but the young woman is dead."

Hugh Marlborough's callous disdain vomited.

"Don't bleed on me!"

Adam crashed through the doors. His head butt split Hugh's nose, and he fell to the floor. Ronnie Ogle capered demonically on Adam's shoulder. Without hesitation, he 'stuck the Timpsons in'. Hugh Marlborough's nose healed before his rib.

Stephen Sherriff escorted him to the Headmaster, an hour later. He kept a good arm's length from Adam on the short journey, and mumbled,

"I'm sorry about Holly."

Adam spent the time thinking on his feet. Consequences, there are always consequences for people like him. By the time he reached Frinton's door he had one resolution.

"Let them be wary. All of their lives these smart alecs use their mouths to bully others." Let them be wary of him.

A bark greeted him.

"Sit down!"

He remained standing.

"Will Stephen be present throughout the interview?"

"Yes."

"Then I'm afraid that we'll have to curtail this gathering. Under the terms of my contract, I'm entitled to the presence of a 'friend'. I need to speak with my trade union..."

Frinton interrupted with alacrity.

"Would you be prepared to speak with me alone?"

"Initially, Headmaster."

"Thank you Stephen. You may leave us." The 'Lawman' retreated unwillingly. "I am aware of your especially close relationship with Holly – we all thought very highly of her – but your conduct in the foyer is inexcusable. Assaulting the Deputy Chairman of governors, in so violent a manner... Hugh Marlborough has agreed to desist from any action until I have dealt with you. A date will be fixed for a disciplinary hearing. I have little doubt that your contract will be terminated. As to what course Hugh will follow... I simply cannot defend you."

"You never do!"

"I beg your pardon?"

"You never defend any of your staff."

"How dare you!" he bawled.

"Don't you shout at me."

Frinton froze. The bully had been challenged. He collapsed into his chair.

"I...I don't know what you mean?"

Adam shrugged.

"It's a widespread opinion in the Common Room; staff feel let down."

A plaintive cry. A man – a leader – on the brink of tears.

"That's so unfair. I always do my best for them."

It was embarrassing, and Frinton realised. He pulled himself together.

"There's no way back from what you've done. You must know that it will end in your dismissal. Hugh Marlborough will almost certainly decide to prosecute. Everything is entirely out of my hands."

Adam knew the power of silence. He waited.

"Nothing is out of your hands...Oliver. I accept the consequences of my actions. Under the extenuating circumstances, however, I feel sure that we can find an alternative solution. Agreeable to you and Marlborough...and to me."

"I can't see how it can be done."

"Headmaster. If I am arraigned before a court, I will feel compelled to bring to public attention the history of abuse towards female staff at High Heath. Further revelations, in open court, about the conduct of Julian Marlborough, and his father's response, may add greater injury to those already sustained. Collateral damage to Hugh Marlborough, and to the school would be...unfortunate."

Frinton rubbed his chin for so long that it was in danger of being erased.

"Extended sick leave, on full pay, with a view to early retirement?"

"My divorce proceedings may be a complication."

"Your divorce...yesss. This has been a very traumatic time for you, Adam. Divorce, and the death of your dearest friend." You could almost hear the cogs whirring. "The Teacher's Pension Agency can be rather tiresome these days about granting ill-health retirement. It's the enhanced payments they have to include. Still, we could muster our resources. We have a rather eminent psychiatrist amongst the parents. If you are agreeable?"

Adam signed the heads of agreement. He gathered his belongings, and made for the school gates.

"Where are you skiving off to?"

Adam brought Mike Bunbury up to speed.

"Wish I was going with you – cunts!"

"Say the goodbyes for me, Mike. Let me know about Holly's funeral arrangements."

"You still living at home?"

"Not for long."

"Bugger. I've got a lesson. Give me a call." He hugged Adam, and exclaimed, "You beat them Adam, you beat them."

Mike was wrong. He hadn't beaten them. In the tightest match of his career he had snatched a draw from the jaws of defeat. He took thirty pieces of silver to protect himself, and in so doing he protected those who had destroyed her beautiful life. They got away with it...they always get away with it.

He hummed to himself in the empty carriage.

"...The love that asks no questions, the love that stands the test,

That lays upon the altar the dearest and the best;

The love that never falters, the love that pays the price,

The love that makes undaunted the final sacrifice."

It was a cold winter.

*

Sombre, clothed in Bible-black, Adam and Mike consumed their breakfast.

"I'll get the bill, Mike."

Paying in Café Rouge, always an interminable trial.

"Lead on MacDuff."

Flask Walk, a narrow alley of expensive shops, for the moneyed and unwary.

"Time for a sharpener?"

Jack Parker appeared behind them, looking keen in his funeral outfit.

"Hello sirs."

"Come and have a drink with us in the Flask."

"Thanks Mr. Bunbury."

"Look Mike, I'm going to the church. Straight on you say?"

"Straight on. Save me a seat."

You can't miss St. Stephens-on-the-Green. It looms forlorn on an island of dense urban land. Nearby stands *'The Wells and Campden Baths and Wash Houses of 1888'*. One for washing bodies; one for washing souls. *"Two households, both alike in dignity."*

Adam eased himself through the crush at the door. It was already two-thirds full. A sixth-form girl, sat next to him, risking surreptitious looks. Mischief and wrongdoing is never confidential in schools. His eyes wandered around the interior, catching Mike's. His friend mouthed,

"I'll be over there."

There was no way he could have saved a seat. They'd turned out in force to pay their respects to Holly.

The church was full. Consumed by the most extraordinary stillness; a collective holding of breath. In the crossing, where her coffin would stand, there was a photograph of her resting on an artist's easel. A film starlet with perfect lips and an adorable smile. She would watch them throughout her obsequies. The silence of the immobile throng nibbled away at Adam.

"Why? Why *so* voiceless? What were they waiting for – Resurrection?"

A Damascene insight provided the answer. It was disbelief. They couldn't, or wouldn't, believe that Holly was dead. He remembered Stanislavski's principle of *'The Suspension of Disbelief'*. During a rehearsal she had explained it to the cast. The contract between actors and audience. We all agree to believe that it's real. This was the opposite. Hundreds assembled for her, and not prepared to believe; refusing the closure of death.

The organ played softly. Adam recognised it immediately. Stainer's *'God So Loved the World'*. In the byways of his brain he heard the words learned in childhood.

"...everyone who believes in Him may not perish but may have eternal life."

Adam closed his eyes, and that little boy, in cassock and surplice, waved to him across a lifetime. He felt the capstone of failure. Everyone who ever reached out their hand to him, in succour and in love, he had failed them. Too late for Redemption.

"I am the resurrection and the life...Blessed are those who mourn, for they will be comforted."

She was carried in state by strong men of poise and dignity. Her parents followed. Pale complexions, without tears. At the crossing, the pall bearers raised her on high before lowering her onto the trestles. They bowed to her, and retreated to the West door.

"We meet in the name of Jesus Christ...Grace and mercy be with you."

Adam was rigid. The old priest, stooped and worn, was, unmistakeably, Roger Birch. He nearly exclaimed out loud, "Lucy's husband!" He scanned the congregation for a sign of her, but she wasn't there.

The service was peculiar. Bits of liturgy, but no sermon. A number of eulogies to adorn Holly's life. Adam stopped listening. He was caught up in the imagination of self. What was he, compared to her? Holly embodied nobility. She touched lives through her open heart. Integrity was fundamental. Faced by horrid lies, was suicide the only way to retain her values? She did her duty, but she did it with such exuberant joy. Lives were changed through the example of her life, not through garrulous inanities. She bequeathed a legacy of honour. Dishonour...he...

"Let us commend Holly to the mercy of God, our maker and redeemer."

Roger Birch. Mid-seventies? Lucy? Early-sixties? The lenses of his spectacles were thicker than Adam recalled.

The Committal.

"The Lord is full of compassion and mercy..."

Adam was once more in a tunnel. Black as a moonless night.

"...the merciful goodness of the Lord endures forever..."

The coffin descended through the wondering crowd.

"You coming to the 'Willy'?"

"Give me half an hour, Mike."

He sat until he was alone. Wandering around, he read memorials and admired the stain glass. Adam found himself before the altar.

"Hello. Are you a visitor, or were you attending the funeral?"

Roger peered at him through his unbelievably opaque spectacles.

"The funeral, Vicar."

"You were a friend?"

"We were very close."

Roger paused. "I didn't know Holly."

"She was all they said she was."

"Precious." The words were soft and moving. "I'm sorry. How rude of me not to introduce myself. I'm Roger Birch."

Adam cleared his throat. Lacking courage, he borrowed Jack Parker's Christian name.

"Jack...I'm Jack. It must be very demanding, running a parish like St. Stephen's?"

Roger laughed. "Oh, this isn't my parish. The Rector is indisposed. I get hauled out of retirement now and again."

Curiosity got the better of Adam.

"What do you do when you're not officiating?"

"A good question. Listen to music, and read as best my eyesight permits. Oh yes, my wife prods me out of the armchair once a week to help her with the garden. Lucy makes sure I don't remain too sedentary. Are you married, Jack?"

"Not for much longer. My fault, Roger. Nobody to blame but myself."

"That would be a rare circumstance."

Adam raised an eyebrow in question.

"Rarely is one person alone responsible for a failed marriage."

A wellspring burst.

"It's not just my marriage. I've got it wrong in everything. Always believed that I could change myself, without anyone's help. All I've really done is stamped about the world, supping on anger. Those I've loved, and those I never loved, have all felt the lash of my wrath."

Roger knew the power of silence even better than Adam did.

"Are you a Christian, Jack?"

"Once...a long time ago...I was a choirboy."

"That was your voice I heard, above the embarrassment of the congregation. Do you still sing?"

"Not as much as I ought."

For a moment, Adam thought that Roger might suggest joining a choral society. That would stretch irony too far.

"They say, Jack, that when we sing we praise God doubly. What do you think?"

"I haven't the right to pass judgement on what others give to God. I've broken all of His Commandments."

"Even murder? Surely not?"

"Malice in my heart is as good as murder."

Roger linked Adam's arm, and pointed to the Eastern wall.

"Do you see them, Jack? Either side of the altar." The Ten Commandments on two boards. Red background with gold lettering. "What do you see?"

"A list of what not to do."

"Ah, a common misapprehension. No Jack..." Roger's voice resounded, like that of a man thirty years younger. "None of us is called to be perfect. They are not telling you what *not* to do; they are declaring what you *don't have* to do. The Old Adam need not triumph; the new Adam is already amongst us."

A light of recognition passed between them.

"Do you ever feel worthless?"

"I do, I do!" Adam jabbed a forefinger between his eyes. "It's locked away in there, and I can't find a way to unchain it."

Roger sat in a choir stall.

"It's in your heart, as well as your mind – the two are indivisible. You're afraid of your heart. You only have to give the love that's locked away, and you will receive."

Roger held a hymn book close to his face and leafed through it, until he found what he was searching for.

"Here. Sing!"

Adam took the book, apprehensively. The two men were alone. Gently, he began to sing.

"I danced in the morning when the world was begun,

And I danced in the moon, and the stars and the sun,

And I came down from heaven and I danced on the earth,

At Bethlehem I had my birth.

Dance, then, wherever you may be,

I am the Lord of the Dance, said He,

And I'll lead you all, wherever you may be,

And I'll lead you all in the Dance, said He."

Adam faced the altar. The low winter sun broke upon the stained glass, set in the Eastern wall. Adam and Eve walked in the garden. Rays of light illuminated them, and dappled the altar cloth. The golden cross, in its centre, was a conflagration consigning impurities to oblivion. Verses and choruses rolled from Adam's mouth;

they were thunder and lightning playing 'tag' above the mountain top. He heard his own voice, distant and detached. It was overwhelmed by a harmonious melody saying,

"I forgive you...Adam."

Redemption was a river in spate. A rich harvest of Hope waited to be garnered. The snowdrops had already been; the daffodils were showing. Spring would come again. Blossom would appear on the trees, and the days would be warm. Then...then

"They cut me down and I leapt up high;

I am the life that'll never, never die;

I'll live in you, if you'll live in me –

I am the Lord of the Dance, said He.

Dance then, wherever you may be..."

Eastern Star

Thwack! The ancient sound of leather on willow.

"Reason doesn't always work, even with the most educated mind. A sharp reminder is needed occasionally, Anna. I'll say it again. Burn the hair shirt, it doesn't suit your complexion."

"Gramps said something similar. He called it 'The Spanish Ruff'."

Mishka interrupted, before Alex could reply.

"You are a priest, Anna, yet you don't know which fork in the road to take. Leave it in God's hands. Do not appoint yourself God's Viceroy."

Alex Wilbey roared with laughter.

"Beautifully put Mishka. I can see why you and Dad adore each other. Peas out of the same pod. How many overs left before tea?"

She craned her neck through the open window of the Orphanage Pavilion.

"Three. Better check the urn. Dad will want his tea."

"Oh yes, lots and lots of tea. Leave that to me, Alex." Mishka wanders to a far corner of the room, and chivvies the other ladies who are preparing food.

Anna scrutinises her mother carefully. She is looking into the distance through the window. 'Adam's Ale' wets her cheeks, as she watches her father signal 'four'; the sleeve of his umpire's coat flapping in a gentle breeze.

"You alright, Mum?"

"Yes, yes, of course darling. It just seems so very strange looking at Dad. Standing here on a hillside, so far from home, and so very happy."

Anna treads delicately.

"How do you feel about his last 'chapter'? Has it upset you?"

Alex holds her silence for a long time.

"Mum always seemed to be perfect when I was a child. Never troubled in her spirit. It's...it's sobering, having to hear what passed between them. Yet, not so surprising. As you grow older you see pitiful failure over and over again. Especially in relationships." Alex's voice sounds a note of sincere understanding. "I will not judge. They're my Mum and my Dad, and I love them. Who am I to say I know the secrets of someone's heart?" She embraces her daughter. "See, I did absorb a bit of theology, helping you with your revision."

They unfurl, and give their attention to the tea.

"Who'd have thought it, Mum. Gramps taught Julian Marlborough."

"Hmmm? Not entirely a success, given what he's grown up to be."

"Why do you say that?"

"Your Dad has one or two stories to tell. The more senior you become in the police force, the more the little secrets slither down the grapevine. Marlborough is..."

Applause crackles from outside.

"Oops. Here they come Mishka. Stand by for the ravenous hordes."

Alex walks out onto the verandah to greet her Father. She watches with pride, as he strolls beside his fellow umpire. He has explained how, two years before, he had put on his old public school act. Resplendent in suit, and old boy's tie, he had managed to inveigle the Headmaster of a private school into playing an annual cricket match against them. There had been some parental protest, but that had been managed by persuading parents that this was an opportunity to enhance their standing in the community through charitable action. Sponsorship provided much-needed funds for the Orphanage, and would be well-advertised.

"May I introduce my daughter, Professor Reddy."

The Headmaster takes her hand.

"I am most delighted to meet you...ah, you have the better of me?"

"Alex, Professor Reddy. So pleased to make your acquaintance. You two gentlemen need tea."

"Tea would be delightful, Alex. I..."

A car grinds to a halt beneath the pavilion steps.

"Alex, would you escort Professor Reddy, please. We seem to have an unexpected guest."

"Certainly, *Baap*."

She offers her arm to the Headmaster.

"Aha, I see you are familiar with Hindi."

"Not at all, Professor. I'm just showing off from my meagre stock."

Alex plays her part well, and they exit into the pavilion.

Adam walks down the steps, and holds the car door open for the perspiring gentleman. To his surprise, he recognises Inspector Rasool Sharma sitting in the front passenger seat.

"Mr. Sampson…," the rather shifty civilian begins, waving a document in front of Adam's face.

"Not here!" Sharma spits the words out as a peremptory order. "Do you have somewhere we could be discreet, Adam?"

"Follow me."

They retire to the rear of the pavilion, where Adam shoos a group of boys away. Rasool Sharma expects him to say something, but he remains silent. The sweating functionary responds to the policeman's curt nod.

"My dear sir, it is with apologies that I am compelled to serve these papers on you."

He proffers them, but Adam's hands remain by his sides.

"What is in your papers?"

The man is lost for words. Sharma intervenes.

"They are your notice to quit."

"Quit where?"

"The land on which the Orphanage stands has been sold to a third party. It is to be put to different use."

Adam's age sits wearily upon him, but his inner resolve does not waver.

"Perhaps I could meet with the new owner, and..."

The garrulous fat man cannot contain himself.

"Oh no sir, Mr. Khan would not countenance such a thing."

The man shrivels beneath Sharma's ferocious look.

Adam holds out a hand. "I will take your papers. Thank you. Perhaps you would return to your vehicle while I have a brief word with the Inspector."

The bird of ill omen reverses, like an obsequious head waiter.

"My apologies *Achchhe Pita*. I am so very sorry to have been…"

Adam's back is turned to Sharma. He studies the sloping hillside, and a snort escapes him.

"Something has amused you, Adam? I am surprised."

He does not turn.

"I was just thinking about hills."

"Hills?"

"Have you heard of a book called *'The Pilgrim's Progress'*, Rasool?"

"Indeed I have. I went to the very school you are hosting today. We received a fine education in many of the English classics."

"Do you recall when Christian stood before the *'Hill of Difficulty'*?"

"I am aware of your reference, but the detail escapes me. School was so very long ago."

Adam's recitation sends a chill through the Inspector.

"'This hill, though high, I covet to ascend;

The difficulty will not me offend,

For I perceive the way to life lies here…'

I won't bore you with the rest." He glares at the police officer. "Why Rasool, why?"

"Why what, Adam?"

The old man snorts again. "Please don't insult me, Rasool. A busy inspector of police does not accompany a minor bureaucrat to serve an eviction notice. Have you ever been a friend, Rasool...to these poor children?" The tickle of a breeze disturbs the air. "How much are you paid, Rasool? What currency does Khan pay you in?"

Inspector Sharma bridles.

"It is money...money, pure and simple. I do not take 'advantage' of children."

"Have you visited his 'Palace of Delights'?"

"Yes, yes I have, and do you want to know why? To see that the children are not mistreated. That they are fed, and clothed and not beaten..."

"For God's sake, Rasool! It might be better for them if they were hungry and naked, instead of being slaves to the appetites of evil men."

A wall rises between them. It is not built from bricks of incomprehension between the cultures of East and West. This is the dividing edifice betwixt courage and compromise; good and evil.

Sharma shrugs in helplessness.

"A man must live, and make his way as best he can; for himself and for his family."

He strides to his car, and this time the chill down his spine is Arctic, as he hears Adam recite.

"...Better, though difficult, the right way to go,

Than wrong, though easy, where the end is woe."

Inspector Rasool Sharma knows that it is not over. He does not like himself, because he is keenly aware that he is compelled to inform Khan.

A sepia tint of twilight advances upon the empty ground. Adam walks slowly towards his family, waiting beside the car. He hears the steady beat begin. The children are watching him from the Orphanage windows. What a thrill it would be to see their *Achchhe Pita* end a wonderful day for them by hitting a 'sixer'. A tired smile lights his face. He picks up the rhythm of their beat. Not the fast bowler this time. The wily spinner must be faced. He who with twists and turns, and ever-changing guile, will snare you with indignity if you do not see what is coming from the back of his hand.

Adam stops. He makes his stance a little squarer; reminiscent of his boyhood hero, England and Sussex wicketkeeper, Jim Parks. He is startled. The illusion of dying Sun and rising Moon makes him blink. Surely they cannot sit side by side, even in this foreign sky. He sees the shade of the leg spinner release the ball. It arcs through the air, and he instinctively drops to one knee to play the risky sweep shot. Three women look up from their amiable conversation. The unexpected silence a puzzle. Myriad eyes study the old man on one knee; his hands hold his imaginary bat in suspension. It is not quite the perfect stroke. Thank God.

"He has been most fortunate." Dr. Shah addresses mother and daughter in the sitting room of the bungalow. "It is a mini-stroke. Adam must rest. He has been given a sign, and he must respond to its warning, as I have told his wife. I leave it in your hands, ladies. Good evening."

Mishka closes the bedroom door quietly, and joins Alex and Anna in the sitting room.

"Drink?"

"No thank you, Mishka."

"Alex?"

"Er, yes, yes please…oh let me do it. I know where everything is. Sit down for a while, Mishka. You haven't stopped since we got Dad home."

Mishka sits in her favourite chair. The one big enough for her and Adam to snuggle in together.

"How are you, Mishka?"

She is a woman not only burnished by the sun, but by an early life forged in the poverty and despair of daily humiliation. Anna sees the same luminous smile light her step-grandmother's face that she saw on first meeting.

"I am fine, Anna. A little tired, but fine. You do not believe me? Perhaps you think I am playing the stoical wife?"

Anna doesn't know what to say. Ice clinks in a glass.

"From the first day of our marriage I have known that a time like this must come. The disparity in our ages made that certain. I will have a glass of lemonade Alex, please."

Alex pours and passes the cooling drink to a step-mother, twenty years younger than her.

"Thank you. You know, there is something else. I hope it will not sound callous. When you have foraged in the midden of life, just to stay alive, misfortune becomes ingrained. Many fall into the violence that springs from a life without hope. Violence of thought, violence of speech and action; they become sunless wells of angry emotion." She sips. "I have been most fortunate." Her smile is brighter than ever. "I was rescued by a shining knight. Praise be to God that Adam and I have enjoyed such wonderful days together." She plonks her glass down firmly on the table. "We must eat! Your father, your grandfather, he is fast asleep, and he is not gone yet. Who knows how many loving days the Good Lord will yet grant us."

"...no man knows when his hour will come..."

"What's that, Anna?"

"Good old Ecclesiastes, Mum. Never a shortage of wisdom from the Bible."

"Come, we will have something simple. There is also news which I must share with you. It is very distressing, and there is no doubt that this is why Adam has fallen ill."

There is consternation around the dinner table when Mishka reveals that the Orphanage must close. It is Alex who is most fatalistic and despondent.

"That's it then. Poor Dad. His entire being is so committed to those children. There's nothing we can do."

Mishka and Anna declaim simultaneously.

"We can pray!"

*

Adam lies in bed, propped on his pillows. Strength began to return five days after his 'incident'. They have moved his bed so that he can see his youthful rose garden beginning life anew. Periodically, he looks up from his book. *'Pilgrim's Progress.'* Day by day he rediscovers his resolve through the lucid water of its words. Each morning, after breakfast, he begins by reading the same passage out loud.

"It is always hard to see the purpose in wilderness wanderings until after they are over."

"Phut, phut."

The sound of a familiar engine. Lamenting its struggle with the hills.

"Billy."

Adam puts down his book. Awaits the appearance of his mate. And he waits. Animated voices sound from the verandah. They are not angry, but excited. A detonation of joy booms across the hillside. Adam is intrigued. There is a voice within the distant cacophony that he reaches out to recognise. It is just too far away.

The bedroom door opens.

"*Pyaare*. There are two gentlemen who wish to see you. May they come in?"

Before Adam can reply to his wife a taxi driver bustles into the room.

"My word guvnor. Not looking too bad at all. If I may be permitted to say so, in fear of my life..." he grins at Mishka, "...looking bloody top-hole number one gaffer."

The room becomes crowded with attendant family, Billy and Mr. Jitendra Devi, Chairman of the Orphanage.

Adam pushes himself upwards.

"Jitendra! How very good of you."

"Adam, my dear friend. We have all been so very worried about you. The children send their greetings, and insist that you make a swift recovery. They wish to see you at the crease once more, your bat flashing like the blade of the Cavaliers you have told them about in your story-telling. However, my friend, I come on serious business. Here."

A document is transferred to Mishka. She sits beside her husband, and unfolds the paper.

"Read, *Pyaare*."

They hold it between them. Adam's lips move with the words on the page. At the conclusion his head is bowed, and the room is mute with anticipation.

"How...?" Adam's voice tails away, bemused.

"You must thank your good lady wife for setting the wheels in motion." Jitendra pauses, but there isn't a response.

"When I was sorting through your clothes, *Pyaare*, that horrid paper fell from the pocket of your umpire's coat. I passed it on to Jitendra..."

"...and I found it to be a most curious document indeed. To cut the long story short, it was not legal at all. It was a preparatory

347

document, not properly signed and sealed. That unmentionable fellow had jumped the gun in declaring his ownership of the land on which our Orphanage stands..."

"Spiked his bloody guns, didn't we Mr. Devi."

"Indeed we did, Billy."

Adam waves the new document in the air.

"But this? How?"

The Chairman draws himself up to his full height.

"Jitendra Devi is not without influence. Once more, trimming the tale. A consortium of very fine gentleman has raised the funds and purchased the land. Naturally, there were additional expenses required to ease its passage past officialdom. I think your Mr. Arthur Daley, in *'Minder'*, calls it *'bunging a bit of bunce'*. All is secure. Rest easy, my dear, dear friend."

Mishka withdraws the agreement from Adam's hand to prevent the splash of golden tears from washing it away. He gathers himself.

"It is too early in the day for a *chota peg*, but we will take tea together. We will take it on the verandah."

He folds back the sheet that is covering him. No one demurs at his decision to leave his sick bed.

"That's the spirit, gaffer. Remember Mr. Churchill's motto, 'KBO'."

"Quite so Billy. Adam, 'Keep Buggering On'."

"Why, Mrs. Sampson, I am quite shocked."

Adam imitates the wartime leader's famous growl.

"And so we will, Mishka. So we bloody well will."

A gaggle of relieved friends repair to the verandah.

"Billy, after we have taken tea, will you please convey Anna and myself into Ooty?"

Billy provokes even more laughter. "The Memsahib has spoken."

*

Ooty is resplendent in the sunshine. Billy insists on accompanying his ladies whilst they shop.

"Phew. I've never known it as warm as this." Anna mops her brow.

"It will be my pleasure, ladies, to treat you to afternoon tea. See, there is Hem's café. Let us rest awhile and refresh ourselves."

"One more job for you and I, Billy. Anna, take a table. Billy and I will return shortly. Now sir, escort me to the Bazaar. There is something I need you to carry."

"It will be my pleasure, memsahib."

Their complicit laughter jingles on Anna's ear, as they wander towards the hopelessly crowded Bazaar.

"Good afternoon, madam."

"Good afternoon Hem. You remember me?"

"But of course. You are Adam's granddaughter. Word has spread of his unfortunate illness. How is he?"

"Thank you for asking. He is much recovered."

"All is well then?"

"Yes. All is well; very well indeed. Tea and *payasam* for three, please Hem."

"For three?"

"Mishka and Billy have just popped into the Bazaar, they won't be long. You know Billy?"

Hem chortles. "Everyone knows Billy. Refreshment coming up."

Anna closes her eyes, and permits the hot sun to warm her face. Yes, everything has turned out fine. The only cloud is the one she is still flying through. Her compass is not yet entirely stable. She has absorbed the lesson her grandfather has taught her through the recitation of his life story. Mentally, she attempts to summarise the message. That honour and duty are not to be found flourishing compactly around every corner in the world, and they never were. It is a conscious decision for each individual to take. Will I lead my life in the light, or in the dark?

She develops a thought of her own. In so doing she lays a hand upon her stomach, where her embryonic baby is growing. The world speaks of the child emerging from the darkness of the womb into the light of day. Anna realises that this is not true. The newly-born child resides in a world of incomprehension; a state of moral ignorance. She reminds herself that it will be her duty to lead her child toward the light of understanding; it is every parent's obligation to do so. A startling realisation opens the door fully on her comprehension. This is why she came to despise her own country, and fled. As the life of the Christian spirit diminished in England, so the wilful passion of children was more and more indulged. A harvest of selfish individualism was reaped to create a country that has become a house of moral ignorance. But. Who will teach them otherwise?

"Your companions are a long while."

Anna does not open her eyes. She assumes that it is Hem, delivering the tea.

"Perhaps you would be kind enough to convey my message to your grandfather?"

She opens her eyes abruptly. Khan is seated in front of her. Alarm seizes her, and she looks around frantically.

"Do not be concerned Anna. I will see that you are never harmed. I would like you to tell Adam that I shall telephone him in one hour, precisely."

"To what purpose?"

"Patience, my dear. Ah, here comes Billy. I'm afraid that you will have to drive his rickshaw. Quite a simple procedure. Billy has had an accident. He has sustained a broken arm, and one or two minor injuries."

Two men support Billy. His face, battered and bruised. Anna leaps to her feet.

"Billy, Billy. I'll get you to hospital!"

"It would be wise to delay that expedition. I'm sure that our friend will be a brave little soldier for a while longer. My message first."

A shiver grips Anna under the hot Indian sun. She looks over Billy's shoulder towards the Bazaar.

"Where is Mishka, Billy?"

The look of helplessness and shame upon his face is pitiable. Khan's mocking voice fills the silence.

"Rifleman Billy Patel fought an honourable rear-guard against overwhelming numbers…"

"Mishka, my grandmother, what have you done with her?"

"We are entertaining her to afternoon tea." His tone changes. "She is unharmed, for now. One hour, Anna, and I expect to speak with your grandfather." He raises his hat, in an act of old-world courtesy, and departs.

"Come Anna, we must hurry."

"But your arm."

"I will manage, as that *Ben chod* said..."

"We will manage!" Hem emerges from the shadow of his doorway. "My sons will take *you* home Anna, and Billy to the hospital. Manish, Arjun, now!

The telephone swells in their collective imagination. It forces them backwards, until they are compressed against the walls of the bungalow. Yet their eyes are snared by the receiver. When will it ring?

Adam grabs it. The ringtone that he and Mishka once found so amusing is now horrifying. The *'Laughing Uncle'* sounds like tremulous madness.

"Yes?"

"Good afternoon, Adam. I was so sorry to hear of your sudden illness. I do hope that you are well on the road to recovery."

"My wife."

"She is well – for the moment."

"What do you want from me?"

Deliberate silence loiters casually. Adam has enabled speaker phone. Anna and Alex hear the entire conversation.

Khan resumes.

"Life is but a matter of commerce, my dear Adam. You understand that this is not a question of ill-will; merely a transaction?"

"Let us trade."

"Please despatch your delightful granddaughter back to Hem's café. Shall we say for six p.m.?"

"And?"

"Anna will be perfectly safe, and all she will need to do is exchange a piece of paper for her grandmother."

Adam realises that Khan wants the land contract for the Orphanage.

"Of course. May I speak with my wife?"

"Certainly, brother."

An echoing voice is heard faintly by the occupants of the sitting room.

"He has agreed. Please be brief."

"Mishka! Mishka!"

"*Pyaare*. You must not excite yourself. Remember what Dr. Shah told you. I am well."

"You will soon be home."

An ominous silence spreads its burden.

"Mishka?"

"You must listen, *Pyaare*, and you must not interrupt. No one knows the time when He comes, but you know when He is close. It is time, my darling. Time for the bill to be settled. We must pay the price together. Honour the children. There can be no other homecoming. *Mere dil ka pyaar.*"

"*Mere dil ka pyaar...*"

A slap!

"Six o' clock!"

"You must call the police." His daughter drops to her knees before him, and takes his hands.

Anna knows the path husband and wife have decided to take. It is the path they chose long ago. The straight and narrow way. She takes the receiver from his hand, and lifts her Mother to her feet. Alex is reluctant to leave, but Anna walks her to the kitchen.

"We will have tea, Mother, and we will wait together."

The late afternoon turns to sunset. Still he sits on the verandah. *'Pilgrim's Progress'* lies open on his lap. He can read no more. The *'Hill of Difficulty'* is a mighty mountain, and his strength is failing. He clings to the cracks and crevices, striving not to fall.

A *chota peg* ripples in the glass that is placed beside him. Without look or thanks to its bearer he takes it to his hand. How many hours will pass before his beloved is with him once more he does not know; he will wait. Time is unbroken, except for the intermediate refilling of glasses. Three sit together, and they are One.

Twilight turns to night. The stars of the Indian sky cast shadows across the grounds. Their eyes are lifted to the hills, ignoring the shining lights of Ooty down below. The Moon is engorged, satiated by the waters of the oceans and the bones of the dead they secrete in their sable canyons.

Anna hears the engine before it cuts, somewhere beyond the drive. She touches Adam's arm. Gallows humour spills, unintentionally, from his lips, as he speaks the long dead words of his Mother.

"I was just resting my eyes."

Anna has woken her sleeping Mother.

Adam's whisper barely carries.

"Don't be afraid. They have done their harm."

The four men are creatures of the night by nature. Nature that is red in tooth and claw. Barely visible. They have consumed their sacrificial lamb. Now they return what is left of the carcass.

A quarter of an hour elapses before Adam picks up his glass. The tiniest dregs wet his lips. He comes to his feet. Already a spirit in the moonlight. One foot to follow the other. Alex attempts to rise, but her daughter holds her back.

Adam descends carelessly from the verandah, but his footing is sure. He knows exactly where they have laid her. Eyes accustom themselves to the darkness. Onward he trudges toward the centre of his rose garden. Her torn and ravaged body materialises, altering shape from outline to substance; incarnate on the earth. Adam stands over her. Mishka's face is untouched, and he rejoices in the beauty of her smile. He drops beside her. Lifting her tenderly into his arms, he embraces her. Neither is remotely aware that they are pierced. *Rosa Osiria* is a bloom of joy, but its thorns are cruel.

The ambulance recedes into the distance. The mortuary attendants will show her proper respect. Inspector Rasool Sharma has seen to that. It is barely one in the morning. The sky has closed in. Surely there will be tumultuous storms before the morning.

Anna brings two *chota pegs* onto the verandah.

"Thank you, dumpling. Where's your mother?"

"I've put her to bed."

"Time for you to sleep. Go on. I've just a few things to clear up with Rasool. Go on. It's over."

Anna holds her grandfather for a long time, and kisses his forehead before she departs. Rasool hides in the shadows, and draws on his drink. When he hears Adam say, "It's over," he knows it is a lie.

"Rasool..."

The policeman almost jumps out of his skin. He does not hear the old man creep up beside him.

"Thank you for coming, at this late hour."

Rasool finds every phrase pregnant with meaning. For whom is the hour late? He drinks once more.

"Only the one question, Rasool. Where does he live?"

The fatalism of the East consumes him. Without protestation he gives Adam the address of Ilaiyaraja Khan.

"Thank you. You are very kind."

The generous words slice his flesh to the marrow.

"There is one more matter I seek your help with, Rasool. Sit down. Let's enjoy our *peg* together."

Adam leads the awestruck man to a chair.

"This is what I would like you to do…"

Adam outlines his plan in detail, and finishes by swilling down his last drink.

He empties his glass. "You have my word that it shall be done, as you request. No one will interfere."

The time has come for goodbyes, and this worldly man does not know what to say. Adam stands beside him, his hand outstretched. Rasool

Sharma has never embraced any man but his father. He ignores the hand, and wraps his arms about the *Achchhe Pita*.

*

He kisses his granddaughter first. Lightly he strokes her hair, so as not to wake her. He knows that she will be stronger than he can ever be. Adam is pleased to have played a part in the certainty of her restoration. He would bet his life savings on where she will journey to next.

"Alex, my Alex."

The words barely disturb the air in the bedroom. She sleeps soundly, and he takes his time to study the life he gave to the world. A kaleidoscope of images cascade before his eyes. The most precious is the heart beat of her birth. His seed come to life in a wonderful human being. He almost blushes in the darkness, as he recollects how he wept uncontrollably when she emerged into the light of day from her mother's womb.

"Daylight," he murmurs.

Adam will not allow the evil he is about to do to intrude into the parting from his daughter. He permits his lips to linger on her forehead. The envelope, containing instructions for the funeral, is laid on the empty pillow beside her. Stealthily, and without looking back, he is gone from the bungalow.

The car rolls down the drive unheard. It is only when he reaches the road that Adam fires the engine. Four o'clock in the morning. He has passed Khan's house many times, over the years, ignorant of its occupant. The journey will take but a short while.

He senses the object throbbing beside him. Lying upon the passenger seat for all the world to see. The .357 magnum was bought in the darkest quarter of a bazaar far from Ooty. When he arrived in India he had been full of fear, and had acquired the handgun as a precaution. A smile as cold as a North country winter makes his face even paler in the waning moonlight. Inspector Harry Callaghan had carried a .44 magnum. *'Dirty Harry'*. Now there was a film. He ponders as he drives. In the flick they said that he was called *'Dirty'* because he was always given the shitty jobs. Adam decides that wasn't the real reason. It was because he swept up the garbage of the world, and consigned them to Hell. That's it, he kept the streets clean for good people to walk unafraid. He borrows justification. The shifting of a tectonic plate propels an ice field from the far north. It halts over his heart, and jails all pity and mercy beneath a glass ceiling. The Old Adam roams the Earth once more.

Bollywood and Hollywood impress upon us that the killer must have a cunning and labyrinthine plan. Actually, gaining entry to a house is easy. It is fifteen minutes before five o' clock. Strike around dawn, that's what the old war films used to say. At that time of day morale is at its weakest. In the surety of his strength, Khan has little security. Adam strolls carefully through the grounds. There will be a servant. No doubt already risen to pander to the wants of his master's day. He circles to the rear of the house. Good fortune smiles upon his enterprise. An aging retainer is seated cross-legged on a porch, slurping his *chai*.

"*Namaste*, brother."

The man is not quite as old as Adam, but he sees the gun and shares his wisdom.

"*Namaste*."

"What is your name?"

"Bhaskar."

"Does it have a meaning in my language?"

"In your English, it means Sun."

"Come, brother Sun, let us go together and bring some light into the world. We will go silently. Please lead me to him."

The retainer knows he will not be harmed, despite the touch of the muzzle brushing his back.

Adam has no desire to examine the interior. When they pass through rooms and climb the stairs, he is aware of opulence. The cornucopia wrought from misery.

"Knock gently on his door, and step in when he calls."

It takes only one rap upon the door to elicit a response. A man consumed with the weight of sin does not sleep heavily. Bhaskar enters.

"Yes?"

"A visitor."

"At this hour. Tell him to come back at eleven." An afterthought. "Who is it?"

The servant feels the muzzle of the gun press against his flesh. He retreats to a corner of the bedroom. Adam occupies the doorway.

"Forgive my intrusion. I know how 'superstars' need their beauty sleep."

Setting aside his cold sarcasm, Adam closes the door. Rage boils inside him at the sight of this creature, bolt upright in his silk pyjamas.

"What did you do? What did you do, Ilaiyaraja Khan? Why? Why do you destroy innocents? Why do you consume the lives of others for meaningless profit? Why? Why? Why?"

Adam advances upon the bed. To his surprise, his enemy sits unperturbed.

"Good morning, Adam. May I put my dressing gown on? This is such an undignified position from which to talk philosophy."

The revolver is held high. "You may not."

Khan smooths the ruffled bed clothes around him.

"Your question, my dear Adam, is most interesting. Why?"

This man of plenty preens himself from his semi-recumbent position. He is the sort of man who can strut whilst sitting down.

"Oh you simple men of faith. Do you not see what is before your very eyes? The world is a pit, and if you wish to escape its suffocating filth you must clamber over the millions of others who are also seeking the mountain top of decency. Life is a hill to be climbed, and a damned difficult one at that, without encumbering yourself with the weight and weakness of charity."

Khan's passionate declaration shocks Adam. He realises that they are scaling the same slopes, but by different routes and to a different end. For a fraction of a second he loses his grip. He feels the piton loosen in the rock face of his faith.

"No! No, you are wrong."

Khan is imperious. "What am I wrong about?"

Adam is silent. He cannot quite marshal the thought.

"See, you cannot even answer my simple question."

"Decency...decency..." Adam lifts his head. He sees sunlight emerging from the East. It filters through the gossamer curtains swaying in the window. The light of day. He turns to Khan. The barrel of the gun points at the floor.

"Decency is taking people with you, hand in hand, not stamping them into the earth. God…"

"God!" Khan's laughter is the same as the telephone ringtone. *'The Laughing Uncle'*, enjoying himself at everyone else's expense. "People don't want God. Food in their bellies, clothes on their backs, and a roof over their head, and all the other good things of life. People don't want *your* God."

"Ping!" A piton has come free. Adam prepares to fall.

A quiet voice speaks from a corner of the room.

"They don't want Him, but they need Him."

Khan looks at his old servant with disdain.

Adam secures a fresh grip on the mountain. He looks at Bhaskar in grateful thanks. He turns, and a fresh look of adamantine confidence falls upon his tormentor.

"People *can* have it all."

For the first time since Adam entered his bedroom, Khan looks uncertain.

"They can enjoy the riches of the earth in their entirety..." Khan tries to speak, but Adam raises a hand, "...but they must hold their wealth with gratitude, as a gift from their Creator." An ice field warms as the heat of the day builds. "They must stand in awe of such a One who can create unceasing bounty..." A splintering reverberates like a pistol shot inside Adam's head. "Only then will they enjoy the fruits of the earth; unafraid and free from the miserable burden of always watching out for those who will steal from their grasp, and destroy them in the process..." Flood waters are released, and shards of ice sweep through his brain. "In loving their God, they will love their neighbour. We will all know peace."

His eyes look with compassion upon Khan. Softly, he places the gun on the end of the bed.

"Stand before me, brother. There is one final word I would say to you."

Khan slides from his bed, warily. Adam extends an arm, as if to say, "Come close to me."

They stand face to face. Adam sees the mountaintop, a mere pace before him. He must tarry awhile before he takes the final stride. A strange lightness encompasses him. He is beyond himself. Looking from the doorway, he must soon step through, he sees brothers separated.

He is unafraid. Around his living body there is the shield of a Praetorian Guard. From each one of them shafts of brilliant light emanate. They fire his courage, encompassing him in the flaming heat of love. He sees his Mother, and beside her Hazel and Rose; Lucy and Ashley are as one in communion; Holly stands resplendent. Before him, with her arms outstretched is his beloved Mishka.

A seismic tremor grips his entire being. Now he has the key that opens his eyes. The door is finally open. Adam knows he is loved, and he accepts it with humility. Pity and mercy reach out.

"Ilaiyaraja Khan. You are not loved. I..."

Adam slumps to the ground. Khan waits. He summons his servant from the corner. Bhaskar examines the prone figure, and indicates that he is still alive. Khan opens a cupboard door, and selects one from an array of dressing gowns. He pours a small whiskey, from a decanter on a table in the window. Whilst he drinks, he looks at his flourishing garden below. The storm that was forecast did not come. He hears a distant rumble, far away over the hills. It will be a beautiful day. He moves from the window, and looks down at his adversary. Bhaskar retreats to a corner in fear. Khan kneels by the body. He puts his mouth to Adam's ear.

"Tell me what were you going to say?"

The stroke has been severe, but his speech is not entirely impaired. He mumbles. Khan is almost feverish.

"Come Adam. I will hold you. What is it you wish to say?"

The words ring out a peal of hope.

"I forgive you."

*

The sun is setting, and Madan labours with his brothers and cousins. His Uncle Billy watches from the verandah, beside Mum and myself. The task in the rose garden is almost complete. We are comforted as we watch the young men, and hear their sweet singing. I recognise the familiar hymn before they can even reach the third word.

"*Adbhut Anugrah...Amazing Grace...*"

Reaching for mother's hand.

"It travels well."

Days of sorrow are to be endured. Part of the natural order in the cycle of life. Gramps death teaches me something new about the life he has passed down through the generations. I can be a strong woman. Not only for self, but for others in need.

Billy is struggling to get his head around events.

"Getting bloody old. Please to tell me again."

"Shall *I*, Mum?"

Alex nods.

"Khan summoned Inspector Sharma. It was he who took Gramps to the hospital. He didn't survive the second stroke. He passed away just before we arrived."

"And that's it? Sharma does not go back and arrest that criminal?"

"He had done nothing wrong, Billy. Grandad broke into his house."

"Did the bugger have nothing to say for himself?"

"Very little, apparently. Rasool Sharma recalls only one sentence."

Billy leans forward expectantly, supporting his broken arm in its sling.

"He would do no evil."

"What?"

"That's what Khan said, 'He would do no evil.'
"

Billy waits a long time. We relish the ongoing beauty of *'Amazing Grace'*. Madan and his fellows have switched with equal facility to English. The job is done. Walking towards us they sing.

"Through many dangers, toils and snares

I have already come

'Tis grace that brought me safe thus far

And grace will lead me home."

"Did Adam not speak again?"

Alex replies to Billy with eyes glistening with pride and tears.

"My name is now Christian, but my name used to be Graceless."

"My apologies ladies. I appear to be number one top-hole dozy fellow. I do not understand?"

I reach under my chair.

"It is from this, Billy. His favourite book." A look to Mother. She approves. "Here Billy, we would like you to have it…Adam would like you to have it."

He stares at the cover of Bunyan's *'Pilgrim's Progress'*, and rubs his eyes. A hand on his good arm.

"Even an old soldier is allowed to grieve, Billy."

"We are finished Uncle. Madam…" he addresses Alex, "is there somewhere we can wash?"

"I'll show you. We must prepare too, Anna."

Full darkness has descended. Madan stands sentinel at the gate. He steps aside to allow the two vehicles to ascend the drive. Rasool Sharma's official vehicle precedes the ambulance.

We assemble on the verandah. I communicate our wishes to Rasool, who informs the ambulance staff. One by one the two stretchers are disembarked. Madan and his companions divide. The numbers are uneven. Billy dashes forwards. Despite his arm he is able to be a bearer. Rasool Sharma turns to Mum.

"With your permission?"

He descends from the verandah, and the bearer party is complete. It is but a short distance. The lifting on high is tricky.

The ambulance drives away. We are left together. Rasool, Billy, me and Mum. Stock still at the foot of the verandah. Six nephews form a guard of honour around the funeral pyre, lit only by the stars.

Our wait is short. We see the lights before we hear the singing. A crocodile descends the hill. It is ablaze with flaming brands. Pure voices are raised in song. The hymn is Adam's choice.

"Come, ye thankful people, come

Raise the song of harvest home

All is safely gathered in..."

The children snake along the drive. Jitendra Devi at their head. Lyrics that Adam sang as child sustain the journey, whilst the children circle the rose garden.

"Even so, Lord, quickly come

Bring thy final harvest home

Gather thou thy people in

Free from sorrow, free from sin

There, forever purified,

In thy presence to abide

Come, with all Thine angels, come

Raise the glorious harvest home."

Strength is within me in abundance. My words address the company, and the Earth beyond.

"We meet in the name of Jesus Christ,

Who died and was raised to the glory of God the Father.

Grace and mercy be with you..."

His wishes are respected, and the service is short. Reyansh is led forwards. His piping treble charms the night birds in the surrounding trees. This child, bright ray of light by name and nature, has mastered the King James version.

"I will lift up mine eyes unto the hills, from whence cometh my help.

My help cometh from the Lord, which made heaven and earth.

He will not suffer thy foot to be moved: he that keepeth thee will not slumber.

Behold, he that keepeth Israel shall neither slumber nor sleep.

The Lord is they keeper: the Lord is thy shade upon thy right hand.

The sun shall not smite thee by day, nor the moon by night.

The Lord shall preserve thee from all evil: he shall preserve thy soul.

The Lord shall preserve thy going out and thy coming in from this time forth, and even for evermore."

Stars and moon, aloft in the heavens, illuminate the bodies of Adam and Mishka. Their features stand out clearly; resting hand-in-hand. The lights of Ooty, far below, are dim by comparison. Two little girls, saved by the grace of God through his agent, pass their burning torches into the hands of mother and myself. Softly the children sing:

"Hills of the North, rejoice;

River and mountain spring,

Hark to the advent voice;

Valley and lowland sing;

Though absent long, your Lord is nigh;

He judgement brings and victory."

We plunge the fiery brands into the pyre. The tinder is dry and brittle. It flames immediately. We withdraw to the edge of the circle. The advent hymn continues; one by one the torches are added to the ever-blazing beacon of hope. Time to draw Mum away to the verandah. There we can look downwards, and catch one last sight of our beloveds.

The last verse is sung whilst the children are led down the driveway; conventional torches light their passage. Rasool Sharma's car goes slowly ahead to see them safely to the Orphanage.

"Shout, while ye journey home;

Songs be in every mouth;

Lo, from the North we come,

From East, and West, and South.

City of God, the bond are free,

We come to live and reign in thee!"

Mum links my arm, and rests her head on my shoulder. Slip the arm free and wrap it around her shoulders.

"Come on, Mum. Let's go home. I have work to do."

*

Printed in Great Britain
by Amazon